A Line Below the Skin

A Line Below the Skin

a novel by

Fran Muir

TURNSTONE PRESS

published by
Turnstone Press
607–100 Arthur Street
Artspace Building
Winnipeg, Manitoba
Canada R3B 1H3
www.TurnstonePress.com

Turnstone Press gratefully acknowledges the assistance of
The Canada Council for the Arts, the Manitoba Arts Council
and the Book Publishing Industry Development Program,
Government of Canada, for our publishing activities.

The Canada Council | Le Conseil des Arts
for the Arts | du Canada

Canadä

Author photograph: Andy Mons
Cover design: Manuela Dias
Text design: Sharon Caseburg

This book was printed and bound in Canada
by Friesens for Turnstone Press.

Canadian Cataloguing in Publication Data
Muir, Fran
A line below the skin
ISBN 0-88801-259-4
I. Title.
PS8576.U338L56 2001   C813'.54   C2001-910099-X
PR9199.3.M74L56 2001

for
Wes   Connie   Adrian

ACKNOWLEDGEMENTS

This is a work of fiction and does not represent actual people or events. Where it does intersect with an actual historical context I am indebted to archival and other published material as well as what is public record, and in this regard *Boadicea's Chariot: The Warrior Queens*, by Antonia Fraser, *Women of the Celts*, by Jean Markale, transl. A. Mygind, *The Witchcraft Collection at Cornell University* and *Enemies of God: the Witch Hunt in Scotland*, by Christina Lerner, were of particular help, as was *The Ghost-Dance Religion and the Sioux Outbreak of 1890*, by James Mooney, as well as various references to the flooding of Indian lands. Barbara Walker's *The Woman's Dictionary of Symbols and Sacred Objects* provided insights regarding the name "Lily."

My appreciation to Anne Geddes, Reference Librarian, The Dick Institute, Kilmarnock, Scotland; Mary Thomson, West Lothian District Library, Linlithgow, Scotland; M.S. Cavanaugh, Local Collection Librarian, West Lothian Librarian Services and to staff at the National Library of Scotland and to the Edinburgh Central Public Library for generous help in locating historical information. Also to the National Archives of Scotland and the Provincial Archives of Ontario, Manitoba and British Columbia. I am grateful to Margaret Whetter for her hospitality and assistance, along with Brad Coe and Irene Hill, in locating Manitoba family history.

An excerpt from "The Stolen Child," by W.B. Yeats, appears reprinted in the text by permission of Scribner, a Division of Simon & Schuster, from *The Collected Poems of W.B. Yeats*, Revised

Second Edition, edited by Richard J. Finneran (New York: Scribner, 1996).

Excerpts from song lyrics that appear in the text are from "Trees," written in 1922, "Buffalo Gals," a popular song written in 1846, and "Carrighfergus," a traditional folk song.

My thanks to the Canada Council for the Arts for their support in the research and writing of this work and to Connie Chisholm and Jeanne St. Pierre who read early drafts and provided such helpful insights. To Turnstone Press, to Manuela Dias, Managing Editor; Jeff Eyamie, Marketing Director and Pat Sanders, my editor, for taking the work on and for all their care and attention to bringing it to publication.

The Dig

Even where traffic passes
the ancient world has exposed
a root, large and impervious,
humped like a dragon
among the city's conduits.
Look, they say,
who would have thought
the thing so tough,
so secretive?

—Pat Lowther
Time Capsule, 1997

LILY RUNS FROM ROOM TO HALL RUNNING at a fast walk running on ahead of herself looking in each door, each bed-filled room. October light flooding in behind Lily from a red ball of sun slipping over the edge turns her black, blinds Dolores who almost bumps into her.

My mother's heart's gone wild, Lily tells her, breathless, her own heart hammering to get out of here. Dolores not wanting to stare into the sun, looks away. Pardon? she says to the wall which is easier to look at than Lily. It's my mother, her heart, something's the matter . . . Lily running out of breathing space; what is already in her lungs can't get out, leaves no room for more.

Is her tongue blue? What? Is her tongue blue, Dolores says more slowly, or her gums? I don't know. What about her fingernails? Dolores remains smooth as the clean bedding she's holding in her arms, Lily who can't control her lurching voice, something happening to her balance, she feels herself drifting sideways.

I'll take her vitals, Dolores says, without hurry. Lily apart watching this feels something urgent gone missing. Grossly irregular, Dolores says, looking up at Lily, waiting for her to say Lily doesn't know what. What do you want me to do? Dolores says it turned toward the window, away from Lily, who doesn't remember, not now in this moment, signing instructions. *NO HEROIC MEASURES.* Remembers everything else. Everything? before become now and what comes after here now as well, no longer beginnings middles ends, start and finish in that order. Is the navigation celestial? sonar? November, is it next? Day of the Dead in Mexico and monarch butterflies returning from Canada will fill the air with their light, moving as a river through sky to gather for the winter in the mountain forests of Mexico.

November in Canada the Pleiades will be visible out there in the eastern sky, bright enough to be seen by the naked eye, however the eye is when it is naked, *tight cluster of bluish-white stars the size of a full moon, directly above the bright orange star Aldebaran . . . they are also known as Seven Sisters, Seven Daughters of Atlas . . . Maya build streets and pyramids to line up with the point where the sisters would be seen to set on the western horizon.* Four hundred light years in what direction? Time-lapse photos expose a nebulosity, a mist rising, a vapour. It is predicted the sisters will drift apart with not enough mass to keep them together and may be gone in a few billion years.

Morphine to kill your bone pain. What for your heart swimming its own natal sea? Is this navigation sonar as for fish? Follow your heart, Lily wants to tell you, not knowing what that could mean. Whispers it in her head, and your heart goes wild. Is this the navigation celestial, as with birds? A memory fugue? memory of water, light, sound, labyrinth of silence, return and return to this minotaur Lily cannot, does not slay that hides deep in the gap; if not, then befriend her, minotaur and gap the same. Collect bones and feathers of sacrifices made to the minotaur from the winding tunnels of the labyrinth and from these fashion wings for you, herself? Don't go near the sun, Lily hears your mother voice over and over, or we will burn. But now your heart has gone wild, a mind of its own in this darkening transparency of skin, line of light a folded edge glimmering through; tiny lantern hanging by its own thread, spun out of itself, holding within a shape of wings. When does she first see it?

YOU SILENT UNDER WHITE SHEETS, in a white hospital room into which they've come in their surgical greens, with their wary eyes. They don't say they cut away your left breast—*we got it all,* what does this mean? Lily notices the opaque skin of their careful eyes watching her as they say this—not to you, but to her—waits for more. More spaces between words. They murmur about anaesthesia, your heart stopping, blame it on your heart, its irregularity. Digitalis essential now, like food and water, to keep your heart *normal.* The young surgical residents shuffle their feet. They must move on. Voices in Lily's head begin to clamour, a clockwork heart? what about instability, randomness, wild inarticulate impulse, pulse of life, how we got here? The butterfly appears, enigmatically gleaming just inside the door of Lily's memory, or her amnesia; light under milkweed.

Jan and Stephanie, three and five, want the Butterfly Book read to them, a nightly ritual to sleep and dreaming, their small bodies curled against Lily's, asking the same questions, wearing down corners and edges to a favourite shape they take with them on their nightly journeys to wherever it is they go Lily can't follow, leaving her their cast-off familiar shapes. They do not question the flight of the monarchs far, far away to Mexico and back to Canada, but how and why?

How'd they get here?

Their great great grandma came from the south that spring.

Why can't they stay?

Too cold.

Why can't they hibernate?

They do, but where it's warmer, or they'll die.

How do they know where to go?

I don't know. No one on the trip south has ever done it before, the wind helps, warm air carries them.

Do they all come back?

Only the females. They each have eggs to lay.

Why?

Why what?

Why do they have to lay eggs?
So there will be more butterflies.
Couldn't some of them just play, or go visiting?
I expect they do...

Jan who does most of the asking, being the oldest, their bodies, Lily's, her daughters curling each other, light curving petals of their abandoned flesh as they slip away through the trees and up into the sky. Following butterfly streams to their source, the river of light, they are butterflies riding waves, currents, hanging in trees, waiting for wind to carry them over the water to sunlight, water, nectar from their favourite flowers, yellow ones and purple, the butterflies can't see red, in the mountains of Mexico.

How do they know what to look for? How do they know when they find it?

I don't know. They taste things with their feet and climb trees to keep warm at night.

You do not read Lily stories. You send her to the public library. Books are important, you say. The book Lily reads over and over is how the Panama Canal was built connecting two oceans and moving huge ocean freighters up and down stairs of water.

MAMA? LILY HEARS YOU CALL, CLENCHED FIST in the cavity of your chest letting go, sinking under its weight of blood, flinging random clots of it into space between synapses. You do not stir under smoothed white sheets. Dolores stares from Lily to you. You should go home, she tells Lily, snaps the sheets around you. Home? Where is that? Jan planting trees up north and Stephie gone Lily doesn't know where. Your granddaughters. Lily here beside you waiting for what has never been to end. Is home these stories from the memory of water, fragments that stir and flow under the skin, between synapses, between you and Lily, in the gaps where everything is?

Where's home? I don't know where to go, you say to Lily, say it again and again before the morphine takes you down. Home the stories told, not told each other?

I'm going in for a lumpectomy, all you tell Lily back then, six years ago, before they took your left breast. Lily can detect nothing more, except that it is June and she has told you she is getting a divorce. Notices your hand is on your stomach. You, sitting in your pale chintz chair, tell her she's crazy.

I always liked Bruce, you say, I hope this doesn't mean I won't see him again. Are you crazy? what you yell at her when she marries him. On the wall above your shoulder a watercolour of a Scottish moor that has hung there for years draws Lily into rosy purple brown sedge and lifting crows lifting Lily to somewhere she doesn't know. She looks away, out the window overlooking the apartment next door. An old woman with bent back comes out onto her balcony to water flowers. Your back is very straight. How oddly you have hung the pastels Lily has done for you, crowding them almost behind lamps; one of the river, November trees, bare limbs silver lacework on threadbare sky light; the other of the lake, West Hawk, in its delirium of Indian summer bleeding colours seen, not seen. Are they true, not true, named vermilion, cobalt blue, indigo, crimson lake, permanent yellow, viridian, permanent green bleeding stories waiting to be told each other.

Your granddaughters Jan and Stephanie navigate as the butterflies frontiers of distance between you and Lily, a distance suddenly shrunk to now by this unexpected why? of yours. Why now this why? A gap in the wall of silence Lily looks through, startled by a sonar pulse, a beat, as in, missed. You warn Lily it's hard being alone. Don't be like you what you are saying? A little late. I'll be fine, Lily says.

A small lump come up in your breast, you tell Lily, west coast spring slipping benignly into summer undiscernible; back there everything racing to catch the window of opportunity between winters, Manitoba lilacs and roses bending the air with their weight, skin, hers and yours unfamiliar territory to each other, hiding spaces beneath where shapechanging shadows play with memory's fire, loss and joy too long in the birth canal is born still. Winter beginning or ending . . . ? The butterfly must leave before the cold comes or it will not be able to fly . . . a butterfly flapping its wings in a distant northern latitude becomes a hurricane in the gulf of Mexico . . . unbalance in a cancer cell becomes another story . . . Lily connecting her divorce with your lump, the way she links her father's sudden death when she is eleven to her singing her heart out at noon on a Friday four days after Thanksgiving. *i think that i shall never see a poem lovely as a tree*, singing her heart out to the tree, not God the song says made the tree, *a tree that lifts its leafy arms to pray* . . . her father drops where he stands thirty miles away, as she is singing, practising her singing lessons, which she almost never does.

Her tongue this muscle discovering mouth, teeth, throat, belly, eye, ear, a mutuality bringing into being heart breath, reading body cells of her forgotten memory, another's memory in her, mouth bent to shape of words, shaping words?

Shape of your breathing hidden under white hospital sheets smoothed and tucked around you. Of many possibilities Lily thinks of a straightjacket, which makes her want to get up from there and run down the six flights of hospital stairs and out into the street.

CONSIDER THE LILIES OF THE FIELD, *they neither toil nor spin* . . . Lily takes no notice, refuses any connection, because everyone else giggles, smirks, makes her feel odd whenever this passage is read at Sunday School, in the United church around the corner where you send her to keep the minister away from your door. That bible text read often, because the words are so suitably poetic for memorizing. The kind of remembering that knowing by heart isn't.

Lily hangs over the fence at Granny Hepworth's, not her granny, but someone's. Not Granny's front yard, which is sunny, neat, full of flowers, but behind her house, the back yard, an overgrown shadowy woodland of trees, bushes, scraggly ferns and wild-looking plants. Underneath it all, hidden away like violets where the sun doesn't shine, lily of the valley spreads, covering dirt and roots with a forest of tiny white drooping trumpets. Grows like a weed, poisonous, but the wise women, witches they used to call them, knew how to use it for heart medicine, Granny H. tells Lily. Lily develops a certain childlike empathy for both, feels no connection at all to the perfect cream, velvet Sunday trumpets on the altar, or behind glass in the florist's cooler, until her father dies suddenly when she is rounding the corner into adolescence, when their cloying claustrophobic presence around his coffin mixes with the goneness of him dressed in his best blue suit and no goodbyes. After that she cannot abide their smell.

Juno, Star of the Sea, fertilises herself with her own sacred lily and one of her daughters, the Virgin Mary, also goes by the name of Lily, also known as Fireflower. In a Slavonic tale, to seize the fireflower's midnight bloom from demons guarding it means forever after to understand the wisdom of trees. Also known as Lotus in the east, whose root is a myriad of resistant threads. How is Lily to know what you had in mind when you named her? Lily never asks. Your silence hers. Does she assume, daughter-like, yours, that you think nothing of these things because you never speak of them? But why Lily?

How Lily comes to name Jan and Stephanie, is there a clear why of it? In the moment of arrival, lips of passage, Jan and Janis Joplin arrive together. *I am here*, the blue blues woman sings, voice streaking out of a Texas fifties oil town, fretting sky until it bleeds; nemesis, nobody's, everybody's child. Jan born a Libra. When they first lay this new-born daughter between her thighs, Lily feels weighed, the weight of herself, something solid underneath her, then blood everywhere, something to do with the placenta, she is groggy, euphoric, can hear words from above, clinical words with no meaning for her pressing her down, on her belly hard, blood gushing, pouring from inside her.

Stephanie, a Sagittarian, like Lily, does not want to stay inside Lily, wants out before her time. Lily starts to bleed, calls her doctor. It is after midnight. Save what comes out and I'll look at it tomorrow, he says, hangs up. Executioner. Lily lies waiting through the night, refusing to grieve. Stephanie comes in the morning, quickly, and small. In the moment of first meeting this second-born daughter, Lily is disturbed by an image of the stoning of Stephen, one of those who refuse to believe Jesus is dead—one of those pictures from one of those Sunday School papers Lily carried home light years ago now, pictures that stay after words are gone, of the light shining around the young Stephen kneeling under the blows of stones, light protecting innocence betrayed. The picture says the young boy doesn't really feel those stones, he is somewhere else. Is it the inevitability of innocence betrayed and that inevitability's connection to light, to some kind of saving grace that arrests Lily at this second coming she calls Stephanie? Jan proves the intrepid one, Stephanie fearful, both Lily feels, wiser than she.

WHEN STEPHANIE IS BORN Petra in Paris is taking her studies in physical anthropology, what lies under skin, bearing the surface of sense, telling the story. Petra's memory of dreaming begins here. She choses physical anthropology because of her endless curiosity about the human form, what holds it in place, makes each one unique. And because of her need to make a living. Her adoptive father a minor French official, her adoptive mother a teacher, Petra has been given all the opportunities they could afford, dance classes, art school, singing, a succession of cats and a modest inheritance when they pass on, as the nuns call it, and tell Petra she must go to the university, as her parents wished. Petra the name her birth mother gives her, the adopting couple make no attempt to change it, and are willing to let the child have her mother's picture, the name Elena printed on the back. Circled in the picture a tall, intense young woman looking out at her, a student standing with a group of other students, or perhaps guerillas, with their arms around one another, smiling, but the eyes are not, the smiles almost a grimace, or so it seems to Petra, perhaps the strong light the day the picture is taken.

Slender to almost bony, pubic bone noticeable under her long rolled-up cotton pants, long dark hair to her shoulders, falling on either side of her face, parted on the left. A narrow face, level dark eyes and eyebrows, high cheek bones. Not unlike Petra. Transparency what Petra now feels from the woman in the picture, absence of skin. She is fifteen when word comes of her mother's disappearance, before anyone has heard of Argentina's *dirty war*. There is no more to know. Maman suggests it would be wise to have something secure at which Petra could make her living.

9

GRANNY H. PUTS ON HER SILVER GREY HAT over her white hair, and her grey coat with the fur collar over her long black dress and walks to the Osborne Street movie house every Friday night and the Anglican church every Sunday morning and evening, before and after breast surgery at eighty-five. When Lily is in high school she hears Granny H. has died, leaving a son with no legs, another with a wife and daughter. Lily has no brothers or sisters, no aunts, uncles, no granny or grampa, or this is how it seems. Later she will find the photo in your drawer, *Rachel and Jean, 1910,* written in a firm neat hand across the back of it. A woman and child, the woman looking old enough to be the child's grandmother. They are not smiling, Lily looking at her own grandmother for the first time. The face looking out at Lily, the presence, familiar, cuts; Jan's face, Lily thinks, Jan's face there, traces of Stephanie in the face of the child in the photo, who is you. Lily cannot find herself . . . lost where nothing said is the rainbow bleeding colour through sky until sky does not know itself.

Are these colours true, spilling and drifting, spinning and weaving, spiralling in ever larger circles, or to a point, a period. Ending or beginning? Is there one? Are you Lily's story, is she yours? Or are you both caught in the middle of a story that keeps changing its shape, its voice many voices? You had a mother. Lily had a grandmother and she had a mother and there are great-great-grandmothers, and great-great-granddaughters, here, looking back up at Lily from this photo in her hand, these voices from your silence.

I don't want you talking to them. Fear in your voice, shades of it in your eyes Lily's body cells know well. By *them* you mean the ones who took your left breast? You awake now. In the absence of words, breast is a cavity, a space full of questions, what is gone? what remains? why is so much taken? what will the fallout be, the falling out of story, time, place? The words take on each other's meaning, slither, slide, slip across borders, stormy petrels, ancestor arrivants. Lily eating your shadow, a nameless felt weight of what is gone, has not been, what is left, form without spirit familiar,

familiar still to sight, but untouched, body still warm, heavy with absent presence. Can she resist plot, take the story somewhere else? Lily tells the nurse you seem confused—is anything the matter? The nurse intent on soothing anxiety suggests it will take some time for you to recover from the anesthetic. She does not mention the fibrillation. How long? Hard to say. A little confusion normal at that age, she suggests. You look up at Lily out of very clear, resentful eyes, more awake than Lily thought. A crow lands on the windowsill, something black on a white field—sheets, walls, your silent breathing. It caws urgently, hooded eyes intent on engaging Lily's. *Dirty things bring disease*, the nurse warns, *you're not allowed to feed them*. Some must. Gulls swoop and scream for space on windowsills. Their crying and the crow's cawing mingles with the chattering and yelping of school children passing in the street below, out on a day trip with their teachers, in amongst them the ungainly voice of an older, boy-man yelling with and above them, *I love you*, his voice breaking, *I love you*, he cries out up the street, until they all turn the corner and are gone. The crow remains where it is, watching Lily out of an insistent eye.

COULD LILY IMAGINE TO ESCAPE THIS NOISE OF SILENCE . . . what happens when time collapses the heart goes wild and only this space where everything is? Dolores injects more morphine through the small IV patched to your shoulder. She does not look at Lily. How much should she have the question always waiting for Lily. As often as needed, if there's breakthrough pain what she is told. How would they tell, so seldom in here; they leave it up to Lily. Lily stares at Dolores already turning on her heel. How can you afford to spend so much time with her? Dolores says it heading out the door, leaving Lily openmouthed, staring down at you wondering what you have heard. Morphine takes you down somewhere swimming that deeper sea. Lily follows the waves of your breathing until they become hers, to the image of a tree breathing; trachea, lungs, feathered bronchi gathering water around an overworked heart . . .

up island, island in the sound, a deep blue curved shadow of space, trees breached by revelations of ocean and distant mountain inlets merging to ethereal pacific haze, high azure; sometimes from heights, at other places close enough to smell rank glimpses of tide flats disappearing into sky. To Port Hardy and the ferry north, home to Jan and Stephanie. Lily and you and the car running low on gas on an impassive highway cutting a swath through golden green trees, velvet how they touch her mind in the light of this expanding afternoon. Dew worms for sale, ice, running close to empty, on reserves now, not shown on the gas gauge. You doze, swimming, head drifting toward the red seam carved and stitched across an irregular heart no longer covered by your breast and silently flinging a rain of tiny meteorites on a collision course with today, yesterday and forever. Lily watches the road ahead for signs of a gas station; and the trees.

i think that i shall never see a poem lovely as a tree . . . a tree that looks at God all day, and lifts its leafy arms to pray . . . dance, yes, reach up to touch the sky, curious, exploring, but pray? Will she ever be able to look at a tree without that fragment, wisp of those long-lost singing lessons running amok in her head, the dreaded practising she never did, except that day, why that day, home from school for lunch, she suddenly sings her heart out. The same time her father is rising from lunch to return to his classroom in a small town called Selkirk, on the banks of the Red River. He would be coming home tonight, but for one small clot that nestles in his heart and he falls to somewhere else. Was there pain? Did he know he was leaving? Lily, your child, and his, sings her heart out on a sunny day in October and she doesn't know why, hides her guilty secret from you—they give you his time of death, noon, when she is singing—did her father die because she felt nothing for God, God the father, when she sang her song to the tree?

LILY SITS IN A TREE, a tree she knows in a vacant lot. Not an apple tree. There are no birds. The tree has many branches, fills its corner. There is a fence made of spiked iron posts around the lot, covered by an overgrown caragana hedge. Whose fence is it? How did she get in? How will she get out? Perhaps it is not a vacant lot, belongs to someone. Lily plays football here with boys, her friends until they kick her, tell her to go away. Did she play too hard, not hard enough? Left, without an answer.

The caragana blossoms are very yellow, very sweet to suck. The tree wraps her in its own greenness. Is she tree, sunburned sky, grass, rabbit hiding there, butterfly, bee in caragana, blossoms so yellow blossoming sweetness in the tree rocking Lily carving the tree's heart with her hands, lying in the space where the heart was, feeling tree's skin where it is peeled soft, smooth, new skin, her skin, rocking herself in the heart of the tree, in the whole hole in its heart, in hers.

Lily in her tree, you in yours, a slender elm, watching for their coming. Father and Mother small figures drawing closer, in your eye coming closer in spirals of dust through the grassy sea every shade of green gold and blue and never still, the colours of the sea, the tall shadow of the man driving the buggy. Where is Mother? Voices cry on the wind. You cover your ears. The cries are from inside you.

Suddenly quite still, you are standing in long grass, shuddering for fear of seeing snakes lift their heads and peer around. Father, your brothers laugh at your fear of them, hang dead ones over the fence. This is not what keeps you so still. The voices do, sighing and weeping through the big bluestem, Indian and switch grass and the buffalo grass, through your father's fields of wheat and timothy and green oats and rising crow calls and grasshoppers' brittle whir, calling to you now from a hole opening up inside you you feel yourself falling into. The child can no longer run back to her mother's garden, to the dark sweet whelming of earth-rooted things where she can hide and watch.

Mother comes from somewhere else. How can that be? What can it mean that a child and her mother are from different places? You are given your grandmother's name, Jane, but called Jean. But you want to be like your oldest brother, already a man, who is called Robert, after father. You want to be called Rachel like Mother. You hear it said Robert has his mother's music. You call your brother Bert.

Bert and Mother come from somewhere else. From your bed you can hear them—Rachel your mother singing, laughing, Bert playing his violin, songs from back *there*. Their faces lit by a smoky coal oil lamp, night shadows hanging sooty webs over them. No, it's not a game, you are told, sorting seeds for Paris, an international prize. Father's wheat, why isn't he here?

Sleeping, Bert always says, don't go in there. Stay away, Mother says. This child who waits in the tree learns to search the sky for signs and when she sleeps father's seeds for Paris pour down and down on her and will not stop. She must wake up to breathe. When she is alone and the sky is blue she calls herself Rachel. When it is not, she doesn't know what to call herself.

The Indians always come when the men are away. They come for tea, bring things that grow wild in the fields. They are starving, Mother says, gives them whatever is on hand. You watch from behind Mother, sniffing out what is there, caught skinless in the smell and strangeness of their coverings, burnt skin, their silence. Whenever they smile at you you look away and they laugh among themselves, which you don't like. Do not like the confusion of weak and strong you feel from them. Or the fear rising in you they will see the horse and take it with them when they go, the horse from out there beyond Father's trees you watch from between the garden rows, your hands covered in broken smells from pulling at what Mother says will choke the vegetables. Like the other horses Father finds, brings back, tells you to stay away from.

In the watching is a tightness growing inside you into something trying to move, to take you somewhere you don't know, or maybe do, lifting hair on your skin into searching antennae for what is out there. Quivering, flashing, beaming light, alien familiar world of horse, you and sky, blue eye you are born under.

The Indians will get you out here, Father says when he finds you sitting under the chokecherry bushes beyond the shelter belt of trees he plants. Is that what you want? You sit in the too tall shadow of him and try to find the n-o-o shape inside you and let it out, but you can't. Don't you have a tongue, Father says, laughs, not the way Mother laughs. Father's laugh, like the chokecherries, sharp and bitter on your tongue, makes all the shapes inside you go away and you can't hear anything inside you or out but his laugh making your skin disappear. You need to pee. By the time you look up the too tall shadow has gone and you don't need to pee anymore.

Too much sky, Mother will say, hitch the buggy, take you across a flat sea of forever distance to town, to neighbours. Waiting for Mother in gardens, theirs. In Mother's garden sky is mottled purple, yellow, green, black, Mother's back stooped, leg bent, arms stretched against garden rows, sun hot, bugs whir, buzz, click, sun hot, Mother's heavy dark skirt spread across snap beans, covering mottled skin of sky. Snap beans, carrots, potatoes, chard, dirt, fill up the big enamel basin, a hollowed stone. Father, brothers, men who come to help eat everything every day. Always watching Mother filling the hollowed stone.

You poke at what the Indians bring, wild plants, roots, bark, berries, finger the hairy featheriness, rough stems, burrs, scales, their purpleblue, green, white tinged pink heads, brown and yellow faces. You feel the wild stink of them down in what your brothers tell you is your gut and below that, they say, grinning at each other, is your hungry hole; sky mouthing your shoulder. The plants are medicines, Mother says, hangs them to dry, cooks them, plants their seeds. How does Mother know what the Indians say? I don't like them, you tell Mother. They have been my friends since long before you were born, Mother tells you, and the child knows why she hates them. *Black root, yellow root, pucoon, gayfeather, black susans, wound medicine, Mother says is yarrow, bitter medicine, Mother says is ragweed . . . bark of willow, chokecherry, root of sumach* . . . teas, poultices, salves, you learn these later, when the Indians don't come any more.

The shelter belt Father plants to stop the wind, elm, cottonwood, white poplar dance shadows across your skin; leaves and horse never still, caught in evening light coming low and straight from behind, hot against your back, neck, where the thickness of your hair parts, goes in different directions. Your body, breath, held so tight, lets go in spasms of shivers. The horse pauses, eyelashes gleaming, staring at you, before you both shy, horse along the fence, Jean who wants to be called Rachel running for house, a corner of her bed where no one will see her huddling there hugging herself, someone clear as glass, falling like water into her recurring dream of whiteness ... Mother, her, horse and buggy, following a line of fence poles, dark shadows, horse galloping faster, faster against wind, faster now with it, streaming, running like water, like fire, fire in her lungs, moving through air, light as air across what she knows, doesn't know. Deeper is lighter, spacious galloping pounding joy, hooves drumming earth not earth, sky a blue-skinned woman, flaming hair, flinging her arrows from her bow, turning earth orange, purple, red where they strike, heartbreath in deepness of lost speech beating on time and silence, horse snorting, heaving, no more lungs, or pain. Inside Jean who wants to be called Rachel is a memory she forgets is there, of someone she has met.

Next morning the horse is gone. You don't want to go where the fence is pounded down, cannot stay away, look, but do not touch. Stay out of his way, Mother says when you are in the garden, sky high, empty, hot. Trees do not shade this garden, their leaf talk sharp, rattling in the dry wind.

They find the woman two days after she's gone, early in the morning, in scrub willow at a point on the grid where one section ends and another begins. She slips between them into the grassy sea. Running the whole time, she surprises everyone, getting so far, the river seems more likely. Had she followed the river part-way, wandered around in the bush down there? did she swim? cross further down? A horse could do it, or a cow. She must have gone late afternoon, supper left ready on the stove. The words tumble down on Jean from above where she stands near her mother and her mother's long black skirt that holds, somewhere within its folds, the garden of her mother's hollyhocks, delphinium, sunflowers, its circling horizon, mottled sky, what she can't name. Her forehead pressed against counter glass, staring in at neat rows of beads and lace, thread, buttons, thimbles, crochet hooks, knitting needles, the words with their questions falling into her. What is it they keep saying they don't know gets into them, *the*

*craziness of women that makes them up and run like that until their
lungs explode like it was the devil comes and takes them away.*

Mother says nothing, drives the buggy out of there across frozen
earth before winter skies overtake them, let down their whirling
blinding whiteness. Why does Mother say nothing? What is not to
be spoken about? The unknowing that becomes knowing Mother
cannot be let out of your sight slips into your bones, forgotten, it
would seem, along with the sky of her garden, its circling lip. With
Father's axe you cut the slender elm, for the nest at the very top,
where you are afraid to go. Take the nest to school and get first
prize.

GEESE HAVE ALREADY LEFT, wings hoofbeats across the sky in your
ear, at your shoulder. Supper sun behind you too hot on the skin of
you where light comes low and straight from an ocean's lip. Fed by
your own daughter Lily what you don't want to eat, can't swallow,
but try for her sake, for the sake of the child who does not want to
be left. Leaf shadows dancing. Mama, you say to Lily, I'm still here.

HELLO? YOU SUDDENLY START UP, EYES WIDE. Hello, Lily says, half-rising from her chair. The morphine pulls you back in slow judders against your struggle to rise beyond a weight of lungs and confused eyelids enclosing you from Lily, this room of smoothed white sheets, traffic in the hall and street, from that hungry yearling gull out there crying into your dreams. What's that? Who's there? you call out from the labyrinth, some complex cavity of inner ear, ancient tracking, drift, blur, ear seeing eye hearing voices where there are no words and the compass is spinning.

Lily's eyes close, behind them the two trees, cortex branching, fallopian root uprooted, split, seeking earth. Anna's voice ghosting through a pool with no bottom, dreaming the dreaming. We'll begin now, Anna's hands touch Lily's feet, they're cold, she says. Lily notices it then. Anna wraps her in a blue blanket. Her fingers press, not hard, firmly, on Lily's left leg, on two energy points, as Anna calls them, on the map of senses, meridians, galactic longitudes.

There is a house, darkness, lots of it around this house, Anna's voice beyond Lily's closed eyelids pauses, moves through her dissolving skin like feeling eyes of the blind into the breathing, listening, receiving places, underwater creature curled in your second heart; a belly glows ochre, fish flesh, water the colour of tea, of ditchwater, ponds, burnt sienna, filling cavities, strands of grass, a siren wails up Anna's street. Glass breaking somewhere near, at her ear, Lily strains for what slips out.

I keep watching a little baby, Anna's voice, her fingers press against Lily's solar plexus, a baby that seems to die at birth, in the house, buried in the basement, under the house or very close to it, a ball of light, crosses . . . I'm getting a sense of shame, a lot of shame. I'm puzzled, does this make any sense to you? Lily somewhere else watching, no, feeling she can't see herself, gone observant blind, not up on the ceiling watching, not split from, but gone somewhere not comfortable, heavy, womb, cocoon, thought-less, weight on her solar plexus moving to her breastbone, bearing down between her shoulders, pressing her to Anna's table, to melancholy, the heart point, Anna says, a yearning, the yearning for love . . . imagine the melancholy as gentleness, move gentleness into it, see if you can, a little, see what happens, Anna's voice insistently gentle.

By now the presence of a gnawing hollow in Lily has gone from hunger to nausea, the beginning of a migraine. Lily tries to gentle the melancholy, as Anna suggests, in spite of a pressing need to be ill. What can you feel? Grief, Lily says. Melancholy another name for grief, mourning, another name for yearning, another name for love? I can feel the back of your heart soften, just a little, a missing woman, running from her gift. Gift? Lily murmurs. Compassion, Anna says, compassion for herself knowing who she is, what she sees. Lily floats in pursuit of the notion of her heart having a back, a front, backbone, lungs, a mind, heart of its own, arrives at an unwelcome gravity of continuance, carrying the past with her, bones and blood of it that settles onto Lily's chest. She doesn't want, can't bear the weight of choosing or not to be thrust again from the narrow neck, water to air, relearning where she's been by the fear of it, a sea anchor she drags around, afraid if she cuts off the anchor, she'll float away, if she doesn't she'll drown.

Her last image, before Anna's white ceiling tiles, coal black eyes, are white trees on a white field, her hand pressed into a frost jungle, melting an eye hole she cannot look through, not wanting to see the abandoned house, high grass, afraid to walk through April, month of trains. Lily looks up into Anna's face, feeling there is much Anna is not saying.

FURTHER UP ISLAND, where Lily stops the car for gas, in a small shop window filled with old jewellery and people's discarded dishes, is an openwork brooch of amber set in silver, Celtic in its knotted design, so Lily is told by the proprietor. You do not understand why Lily buys an old piece of junk someone has got rid of. Lily doesn't either. The proprietor presses on her one of what he calls his gently used books for an extra couple of dollars, worth much more he murmurs, some Celtic history, to go with the brooch. The amber catches light like frostbitten trees shedding their chlorophyll greens. You want to be on the other side of the street, out of the sun, afraid of its cancerous effects on your skin.

Amber, the Celts work it, Lily reads later, when they find Miranda's Bed & Breakfast, *amber, stone that burns, releasing its resinous scent of ancient pine; said by the ancients to cure fever, blindness, deafness.* In a Greek myth amber are the tears of the daughters of the sun who by their tears are turned into poplar leaves by the stream of forever mourning a fallen hero. Romans moving north through Gaul and into Britain find a race of Celts working the amber called the Iceni who dye themselves blue with woad and neither read nor write, sing instead and dance, speak their stories, weave their past and future in the telling of it with their bodies; a race of people it is said who can make the Romans laugh, cry, or put them to sleep.

But when Boadicea their widow Queen says no to Imperial Rome's plunder of her nation, her daughters' inheritance, and refuses protection of Roman patriarchs in exchange for cheating on her people, Rome, wanting everything—lands, amber, precious metals, slave labour—calls her *barbarous, we talk peace, she talks war.*

Lily searching for Boadicea in spaces between, what is not said, not written down in Roman hand for the Record, as ice water, cutlery tinkles discreetly and a grey whale spumes in the bay beyond the restaurant's french windows. Lily mentions the view, forgetting the glaucoma in your eyes will flare light to haloed suns; you say nothing, Lily feeling something . . . wail, grey whale in a grey sea lodged tightly where she is trying to breathe in, air. Back at Miranda's Bed & Breakfast by the Sea, you want the heat turned up, cannot get warm, don't want Lily to go out for air, not to the beach, not after dark, I never go out after dark, you tell her.

Boadicea beaten naked before her people, her young daughters gang raped. Romans force words into her mouth to speak for her, write her out of the story, annihilate; call her *an uncivilised woman running amok, dishevelled fury* when she fights back, almost drives the Romans out of Britain. *All this ruin brought upon the Romans by a woman,* Dio Cassius will say later, perhaps because he is Greek; also, that she had *a mass of tawniest hair hanging to her waist and was very tall with a fierce expression, almost terrifying, and a notably harsh voice.* He has never seen her, makes of her what he will, a freak of nature going against the nature of her kind, her sex; amazon as wild animal surrounded, brought down with a well-aimed thrust, twist of a lance. In the story she takes her own life rather than fall into the hands of the Romans a second time, what remains of her people slaves of the Romans for another four hundred years. If she took her daughters with her no one knows. They disappear with her into the red layer of burned earth deep under Colchester and London excavated a thousand years later, laying bare the fiery root.

You have gone to bed with the heat turned up. Lily strains for the goneness of your breathing in the roar and hiss, tide sucking back, slipped loose, wailing into Lily's pores, keening in long slow swells ebbing and rising over black shining rock, stumps, roots, sand, and driftwood peeled skinless. Hungry ghosts waiting to come home in the waves out there breathing down on shore, where Lily would rather be right now. Miranda's kitchen downstairs full of people who do not appear to be guests of her Bed & Breakfast.

Liquor bottles lined up next to her battered bread box shine in their various states of emptiness.

Someone called Malcom offers Lily a butter tart from a biscuit tin. A woman named Charlotte is laying a Ouija board in its soft flannel wrapper back into it's bag, Miranda lighting candles as Hazel begins turning off lights. Miranda frowns at her kitchen table, square arborite, candles clustered at its centre. Not round, too bad, she murmurs, circles are best . . . alright, Hazel breaks in, brusque. Oh good, time to hold hands, Malcom says at Lily's ear, his hand, voice, a shadow on her left hip, sliding down her thigh. She steps away, knocks her groin against the edge of a chair, wraps her teeth around the pain to swallow it. Ouch, Malcom says at her back.

Why don't you join us, then we'd have an even six, Miranda's voice from eyeless shadows merging at the table. Lily excuses herself through clenched teeth, too embarrassed to acknowledge she can barely walk, aware of an urgent need to remain hidden and the possibility her body might suddenly scream.

Suit yourself. There's tea in the cupboard and the kettle's on the stove. You're welcome to sit by the fire. Lily walks stiffly over to a counter and sink full of dishes from supper. There's a teapot somewhere, Miranda continues so evenly she makes it clear Lily has breached some expectation, but what, a game they play with strangers, raising spirits? is it the dead or living they want? What angry spirits would be raised here, between ocean and clearcut?

In the scented glow of tea Miranda's living-room clutter slips into images, patterns, debris, the huge rock fireplace a large mouth ready to consume, burn everything to an offering for whatever spirits gather. You upstairs with the heat turned up, not snoring, so still, as though you are gone into the silence in that deep blue roaring out there, surf beat, sea spittle everywhere that keeps getting lost among rocks, ill at ease, eddying, snatching at driftwood, slapping at margins like a doused fire; a truce within terms of existence, yours and Lily's. Lily unnerved, driven downstairs to these voices, behind her now, coming from Miranda's

kitchen, cards shuffling, something between Scrabble and strip
poker . . . their voices slip beyond her ear's drum, become silence,
deletion, bark peeled from, skinned willow wand, dousing . . .
what is it they want from each other?

Soon time to join you upstairs, but not yet, still drifting here in
tides of radiant heat. Between sleep, not sleep Lily hunts, slipping
into spaces where nothing happens, nothing is remembered,
embers flare, fall apart, shapechanging, walking the deep curve a
balancing act. Do Lily's feet know the way? If she falls, where will
she fall to? *Descansos*, resting places, small crosses along the way,
wayside markers where death comes suddenly, by accident, not
expected, little deaths and large. Could she fall into a different
story? A bird alone, riding high, mewing and laughing between
moon and sand shining silver, black where waves slide back leaving
tracks of trees, rivers, cut in sand, branching stems etched in sand
by the memory of water. She rears up from surf, this gleaming sea
animal, black body, white moonish face. Bird wings alter course,
breathbeat tracking space, Lily falling through darkness into the
lull of surf, soft laugh, hard black sand, tree tracks.

Running from forest burning to water, landed sea animal
swimming to where she sits with the animals to watch. You'll be
alright now, they tell her, press their fur against her, comfort, take
her deep into trees, lie down around her and sleep. She is very
tired, sleeps a long time. The animals bring berries, roots. When
she is well they all come to show her their voices, because she has
no voice. Each bird and beast, each insect has its own, makes its
own language. What is it sticks in her throat? Her hands gripping
the mug of tea, trembling coming from somewhere under her
shoulders, lungs trying to breathe, small fist pounding in her
throat. Roused by a woman's wail lifting hair on the back of her
neck and then abrupt silence, a scrape of chairs from the kitchen,
someone up washing dishes and one of the men saying something
about turning in; back door opens, shuts. Malcom is reaching over
her to snuff candles on the table beside her, leans with his other
hand on her back between her shoulder blades, the heart point,

Anna tells her, backside of her heart, on light years of acupuncture and massage therapy. Familiar dull ache of breathing, breastbone, words she swallows down. You still here? he says. She watches small flaming wicks extinguish, one by one between his thumb and finger, feels the stone weight on her back, the wail that woke her trapped in her gut. He leans, pinning her there to the sofa until Miranda's *you can find your way upstairs?* releases her. Yes, of course, Lily navigating around the sofa and toward the stairs, away as quickly as she can by the outdoor light coming in through the kitchen window, left on for these people to get from the house to their campers at the end of the sea path. See you and Charlotte in the morning, Miranda says behind her to Malcom, as though warning a child. Lily hurrying up the stairs, trips on his laugh coming from the kitchen.

Mist in off the ocean this morning. From upstairs she can make them out cleaning their camper trucks. Downstairs she finds Miranda baking muffins. She doesn't look at Lily, indicates the table set for one. Lily spreads Miranda's homemade jam on homemade toast, asks if these are local berries. Your mother not coming down . . . she's well? all Miranda says, Lily not knowing what to say, says nothing, watches Miranda stoop, pull tins of muffins from the oven, tap them loose from their tins onto racks she's laid on the counters; so effortlessly the muffins drop. Remembers your cakes, banana bread, your jam pies, can smell them, whiff of vanilla. There's too much memory, too much family, don't you think? Miranda, ignoring Lily's silence, serves this with the tea, rattles the empty muffin tins into the sink and the ginger cat asleep on the windowsill leaps down and across the room, sits blinking its dilated green eyes back to inscrutable. On your own are you, apart from your mother? Lily instinctively moves her ringless hands to her lap. Two daughters. Widow? Divorced. A long silence before Miranda says, mine's out there. Lily wonders does she mean fishing? They never found him, or his boat . . . all that water . . . Miranda sighs, lip of a distant ocean touching shore. The cat stalks out.

This collapse of time, this unwelcome chance intersection of disappearances troubles Lily's breathing. So unexpected now, this smell of broken trees and frightened animals, density of rock, cloud, this rainforest mouth that swallows all visible signs of Jan and Stephanie's father, his metal wings. No, she is not a widow, divorce comes first, losses carried forward. She imagines Miranda wanting her to stay, have a seance, just the two of them. Then what would she say, *the only answers I want are mine, the ones I don't seem to have?* Miranda offers fresh muffins for Lily to take upstairs for your breakfast. We probably all had too much to drink last night, except you, she says ... an observation, not an apology, keeping it open. Charlotte keeps Malcom on a long leash, Miranda adds, her tone as inscrutable as her cat's eyes. Leaving Lily the multiple choices of something to be expected, accepted, ignored, or denied.

You want to leave. Lily leaves you waiting in the car, scrambles out onto rocks, bluegreen tide pools, orange and wine kelp stranding, winding her deep into desert sage, ochre, mauve, in a rocky basin she dips her hands into, stirring up fine sand from the bottom, disturbing this moving slipping shape of no one she knows looking at her from a desert under water. She keeps her back turned from the others, not wanting to see or be seen, not wanting them to know this, so it's out there between them, a drawn line. Finds you fretting in the car.

WHEN YOU FIRST COME NORTH, you still have your breast. You come to visit Bruce and Lily and your grandchildren here in this town cut from surrounding wildness at the end of a long finger of ocean. You sit with your back to the ship's engines, moving solo through October into rainforest, Lily waiting on a dock with Jan, Stephanie, waiting for a freighter carrying you up the inside passage, you who never could put your face into water, who cannot swim. Something shifts, this move of yours a warning note of something not accounted for at this edge you and Lily stand beside, its dense green vertical poised over, flowing down to kelped

rock, benchmark tidelines etched in stone on this wide valley a
river runs through, south from the bigger one heading west, both
toward estuary margins of a shifting salt line, moon rhythm edging
high cedar, Douglas fir in air moist, scented. Here among wild
crabapple and high bush cranberry errant descendants survive,
escapees from abandoned improbable colonial gardens long slipped
to salt pasture, as an ocean reaches in its long arm, spread hand to
this point on a power grid from dam to smelter to clearcut
townsite to Indian reserve.

AT THE CENTRE OF A TOWN built on clearcut by Trans Oceanic,
the employer of most who live here, including Lily's husband
Bruce, whom they hire out of Toronto and bring here with Lily
and the girls still babies; here Lily listens to your sudden
unexpected laughter of recognition, and its slip into derision—the
museum's windup telephone, old Victrola and farm tools. Your
hand reaching for, pulls back from the black wool dress with a
small horsehair bustle built into it, darned and mended, puffy
sleeves added as the styles change. A colonial farm woman's good
dress, worn for years, a lifetime, holding everything in its folds. You
don't expect it preserved here in a small concrete bunker,
surrounded by strip mall in the midst of rainforest. And then you
are quickly bored, weary, do not want to hear about oolichan,
candle fish the children catch in plastic pails along estuary streams,
once harvested by the Indian nations for oil; heat, light, wealth. Or
the grease trails, trade routes through these mountain passes, of
nations who were here, are still. And you are irritated with Jan and
Stephanie running around peering through glass at fossils arranged
neatly in their geological periods, shells in their grid of intertidal
life, and asking Lily questions she can't answer about archival
photos of Indian women in red cedar bark hats, capes, skirts,
harvesting their rainforest gardens. Let's go, Lily says, overcome
with sudden lassitude at the weight of your unspoken anger, your
resistance to these stories. Why? Because your own have gone

missing along with you? Is Lily responsible for what you never told?

We just got here, Jan says. An unfamiliar belligerent tone from her older daughter as Jan takes Stephanie's hand and runs with her up the stairs past colour photos of spawning salmon, wildflowers, edible berries, the brilliant red, speckled white destroying angel toadstool, which its label warns on no account to be thought edible, or touched; in that other body in her head, Lily runs with them. There's pictures up here, little Stephanie excited by rebellion squeals down from a windowless concrete space, the art gallery and meeting room. Another time, Lily's voice flat, thin, without resonance as she says it, not looking at you. We just got here, Stephanie's voice whines down the stairs, bruising Lily's nerves. *Let's go* Lily says, some warning in her voice that brings them down, silent, looking at her sideways.

YOU RELAXED NOW, away from the museum, standing with Bruce surveying this small parcel of forest Lily and Bruce clear by hand, the dog a golden shaft between trunks of cedar, hemlock balsam, fir. You plant yourself in Lily's rubber boots, the dog following her nose through huckleberry, sumach, ferns, over soft silent moss, lichen, needles, rotting limbs and trunks, searching for the underneath, some scuttle or silent breathing only her nose, ears pick up.

Lily stands apart, watching you, Bruce; caught outside anger by you naming dry and dusty plants by the road down to the lake, Thanksgiving weekend . . . *milkweed, Queen Anne's lace, burdock, foxtails, lambsquarters, goldenrod, nettle, red clover, scottish* (you would never say scotch) *thistle, wild oats* . . . the child Lily does not expect the possibility of this knowledge of yours, or this companionship, or such an existence beyond Osborne Street with its streetcar tracks over the bridge you cross to work downtown. For the air force, you tell her, the war still on. Lily, eleven, forgets the other journey six years and a whole war earlier, when you take her and run from saws ringing on melting air and returning crows crowding bare poplar branches, train moving it to memory and you and Lily to boarding houses and rooms with no running water on a street of hard innocence, where streetcars grind double curves onto, across and beyond, round the bend. Drunk women on the stairs tell Lily their lives, men in trucks take her for rides, make her promise not to tell her mother. *I didn't know*, you whisper cry, Jan and Stephanie, still sleeping babies. *I didn't know, I grew up on a farm, I didn't know, don't shout so, everyone will hear.* Lily doesn't tell you nothing happened. You don't ask. Nothing happened, everything. Why don't you ask?

Alongside what she knows, Osborne Street, coal and railway yards, abattoirs, is this other existence containing market gardens black as far as her eye can see, then pastures strewn with rocks, cows resting on folded legs, horses standing in morning light, heads bent. And then rock, pushing up everywhere, cattails in ditches, marsh, the boreal forest, her father says, the Brokenhead River, Water Lily Bay, almost there. Lily doesn't know why her father shouldn't wear his best clothes for this remarkable Thanksgiving weekend together here in this paradise she did not know existed, you angry, his best suit, white shirt, tie, angrier still when he has to change a flat tire. Do you suspect he is waiting to go, anger your only defence?

You and Lily walking together, the strangeness of it, Lily in a dream, trance, another language here, this lake you walk beside, circular and very deep, you naming dry and dusty plants, Lily gathering their seeds and pods for a school science project, her eyes, skin feeling the texture, smells of earth and winter coming, sage and silver and the deep deep blue of lake and sky. Back along the curve where water lilies grow, minnows, tadpoles, stones catch fire, dragonflies fill the air with sparks, you find watercress still growing in a mossy pool. Thanksgiving. Indian summer. This lake, shocked into being by collision with an interplanetary body a hundred million years ago, Lily's father tells her. Tells her he doesn't know what's out there, out there where collisions come from, fiery births, holds Lily's hand in the darkness by the highway's side, cars gearing down, then up, chasing beams of light around the curve. Did you ever? hold Lily's hand?

The district was shocked on Friday afternoon when word was passed along of the sudden death of our school principal . . . our sympathy goes out to his wife and daughter in Winnipeg . . . the bus takes you and Lily to Selkirk. His body must be brought home, papers to sign, questions to ask. Lily has her first migraine, shivers and sweats beside you, clammy and nauseated, head throbbing with every jerk of the bus. She cannot look at the hot light out there doing strange things in the dry fields, or stop the rain of bursting lights deep in her eyes filling her head. She sits erect beside you, her body tensed to hold her head in place against the back of the seat, so you will not know; matching your silence. Gas fumes at the back of the bus and the memory of the chocolate milkshake she gulped down before leaving keeps her belly climbing into her throat until the coroner's office in a red brick building with dim halls and dark brown linoleum that is too shiny, where Lily can throw up in a public toilet, while you are given the cause of death.

Is Lily to blame for his leaving, singing her heart out to a tree and not to God? She holds brown paper towels under the cold water and against her face, her banging head. The straw flowers feel like paper. His landlady tells her they are also called everlastings, keeps patting her head. Those nosebleeds that wouldn't stop last summer, a blood clot on his heart, he wouldn't feel anything. You repeat for Lily what you are told, *coronary thrombosis*. Lily listens. Blood clot, tiny meteorite on a collision course. Nothing? did he feel nothing? But then Lily doesn't feel anything either, not yet, except her blood drumming her head. Cannot tell what you feel except Lily the child is sure you hate his mother Isabella, deserted by his father and left to raise her three surviving children on her own. She's an old woman, with a son and daughter to look after her, you shout at Lily, because he has left most of his life insurance to her, seventeen hundred dollars to Isabella, thirteen hundred to you. Lily surprised the numbers remain in her head.

After this, money comes from Isabella for music lessons, piano this time, as Lily no longer wants to sing. She must now take the streetcar after school, through long frozen winter darkness to a square bare cubicle at the conservatory, no window, large brown piano, stool, and her music book, which she often forgets. Five days a week and Saturdays, the cold dark tunnel of winter at Portage and Memorial, crossing the streetcar tracks between safety islands to change cars, everyone coming home from work, you among them somewhere, crowding onto streetcars, winter animals looming in whiteness whirling out of darkness, icy breath hanging in clouds. She crosses, cannot look down the dark slot between, the open mouth waiting to catch someone there between cars going east, west, grinding the curve south to Osborne Street, you somewhere on one of those cars. But Lily sees you slipping on the ice, sliding beneath metal wheels, unable to stop the pictures, crushed and bloody bones and skin and pulpy mass. Is it Lily or you? Is there a difference?

Piano lessons end because Lily will not practise. They tell her at the conservatory they could have made a concert pianist out of her, that she plays with *great feeling*. Lily does not believe this, part of her detached, curious why they would say it, another Lily not wanting to know, or be known as someone with *great feeling*. She doesn't know what that means. Perhaps they are mocking her. When Isabella dies she leaves Lily three hundred dollars, enough with her summer's work at the abattoir for tuition for her third year of pre-med. Lily uses the money to get to Toronto, finds a job as a lab assistant. Leaving you leaving Rachel.

Lily's father is buried overlooking the coils of the Red, the river he fell beside, fell to where? where is he? Lily asks you, watching the ice-clogged river rising, cow floating past on a barn door, not bawling but silent in her terror. Midnight sirens, drowned streets caked in river gumbo drying to hardpan. Lily wanders cracked clay paths, looking for willow, lilacs, tall dark trees bridging flanks of a thick brown river coiling east, north to Franklin gulls, polar bear. Is this how it was for those homeless Celts on the move again, driven here from their own land by men like Selkirk—Scottish chiefs, lairds, landowners to whom sheep mean more income than the crofters they drive from their highland clans and homes down to water's edge? With no choice but onto boats, on to here, river and wild grass plains, forty million buffalo, tribes of people inhabiting a land that inhabits them. Now they are Red River settlers clinging to the sides of a river in a land called empty, flattened by comings and goings of polar ice, where two rivers meet, Assiniboine and Red, move north together past the rapids, past Selkirk to the delta, into remains of an ancient inland sea, Lake Winnipeg and beyond, to Hudson Bay, the route the immigrant wanderers came by, south to here where these two rivers meet and disappear into returning ancient seas when flood tides come spreading unimpeded over land at one with its horizon. Louis Riel's grandmother, Marie-Ann, the first white woman on this land, is near her time to give birth. It is the middle of the buffalo hunt. What does her horse know, the horse they say spooks and runs wild? When they finally catch the mare she has carried Marie-Ann safely out of the hunt and Louis's uncle, born not long after without further incident, lies with his mother on prairie grass. When her grandson births Manitoba twenty million buffalo are gone. Five hundred wild buffalo left by 1885 when your mother Rachel arrives. Are there any when you come out of Rachel? *Natal* . . . nativity . . . who is Rachel, the lady from Edinburgh you call her, but never speak of her to Lily or name her as mother?

The dog emerges from the trees, waggles her behind in pleased circles around Bruce, you, Lily. Further in, derelict houses ghost Lily with their silent emptiness, abandonment, their signs of an anonymous someone's recent presence. Jan and Stephanie who bridge the gap. Lily wants too much. They don't want anything, not from you, are safe. A wild explosion of yellow warblers from the trees, hot stroke of sun in her eyes following their sudden flight.

YOUR EYES OPEN WIDE, staring at Lily . . . they have propped you up in your recliner chair with pillows against the weight of your lungs and pushed your recliner against the wall because you fall over, always it seems to the left . . . *the wall is the mother, the wall is the female, the wall is the timeless child* slips through Lily, from you? or Lily, this language crying pain the shape of breath slipping from amnesia?

You still here? why don't you go home, your mother will be fine, a greeting Dolores always flings at Lily when she comes on afternoon shift, as though Lily's presence here with you is gratuitous, superfluous, Lily herself redundant, an inappropriate child with a grip that won't let go. She has no answer for Dolores and it's plain to her Dolores doesn't want one, has said her piece. Lily's eyes, ears already dropping away to follow your breathing, a crow's wings spreading night rising, shape of before forgotten memory.

HE EXPECTED THERE WOULD BE someone from the local Indian band. A tweedy professorial bureaucrat with moustache and a pipe which he places in the pocket of his suit coat. We invited them, he adds, letting his disappointment, annoyance show. The woman with him smiles energetically at everyone in the room, all women, airless space of the museum's art gallery and meeting room closing in on Lily. Paintings on the concrete walls struggling for light take her to the shore of smooth round stones below a darkening valley wall, back-lit jewel green, she can't call it tender, and a moon rising in a violet sky behind her pulling saltwater south, drawing her eye to where saltwater turns, elbows westerly, light flooding in there, turning rainforest walls to desert canyons, magenta, wine, purple, snow turns gold, ochre, orange, gone before she can translate to sketch pad the delicate intensity of elusive visions of light. She discovers a row of children, several pairs of watching eyes from behind her and a woman coming down onto the beach, no nearer than the children. Aloof, present, open, guarded, the woman acknowledges Lily's smile by calling the children away.

Sorry, we overlooked you, the woman with the energetic smile who calls herself Margot catches Lily at the bottom of the stairs, Lily slipping out before the usual post-meeting coffee chat. Overlooked? Lily's eyes query. A brief flick in the other's eyes, embarrassment quickly covered, Lily taken for those women she sees down at the mall waiting for their rides out of town back to their village, the reserve, who will not look at her when she tries to smile hello. A way of claiming space, Lily wonders in this moment, of being without Lily's white woman's eyes demanding a friendly greeting in return. This woman's eyes now, demanding attention, acknowledgement from Lily. She finds Margot's card in her pocket later, Margot Ryan, an advocacy lawyer, from Toronto. I don't have any connection to them, Lily tells her, looking away from the woman's intrusive, too energetic eyes. None at all. And thinking of how the woman was embarrassed mistaking her for Indian.

SUMMER SOLSTICE, AND LILY EDGY from too little sleep, struggling with what isn't there on her sketch pad, what won't come. The children who always appear when she comes to sketch have grown bored with Lily's chalk smudges and play over boats pulled up onto a shore of stones. Lily sketches the stones, their smooth stone skin, roundness, shadows between them. The woman comes again to retrieve the children, Lily filling the page with stones light as paper, watching the woman from the corner of her eye while whoever it is has been watching Lily from further up, toward the village, threads her way through beached drift logs, boulders lit to luminance of skin; closer now, hair braided, wrapped too tightly around her skull, uncut, Lily imagines, sensing severity in her approach. Eyes flat, dark, not meek, the white woman asks Lily if she has permission to be here. This is reserve land, she adds, Lily feeling the proprietary edge in her voice. People drive out here, they shouldn't but they do, drive through the village just to have a look around. They don't even stop for a Coke at the store.

Lily, embarrassed, looks down, unable to think of anything to say, remembering a drowned village, rain, low cloud, abandoned, it had seemed. Lily, Jan and Stephanie getting out of the car, walking down to the dock to look for dugouts, boats carved from tree stems, Jan calls them. Lily takes pictures, still in a drawer somewhere, of hollowed trees, ageing grey cedar, floating on water reflections, cloud-neutered shadow. Jan wants in one of the dugouts. No, little Stephanie yelps, pushing her away, they might still be here. They? What? ghosts? Jan snorts, don't be so silly. Lily looks down at Stephanie's impassive face staring sturdily into the dugout.

Sarah the woman's name, teacher at the village school, missionary from a group known as the Brethren, strict, Lily surmises by the severity of how their women dress and behave. The school no longer residential and soon to be phased in with white schools in town, Sarah tells her, elementary classes the last to go— she has stayed late, tidying up loose ends, lingering. The metalworks across the estuary is dwarfed by its spume cloud rising from lines of furnaces filled with molten ore into ragged low sky, its own acidic microclimate. Lily's eye follows the spume's drift north along a path of defoliated valley wall, then slides along its main power artery pyloned over the estuary, over where she and Sarah are standing and up into the mountains behind and beyond, out of sight, back to the source, the damming, lost river, drowned land, no ark. You'll miss the children, Lily says. Sarah steps away as though dismissed, moves back along the beach with her arms folded across where she breathes, stomach, diaphragm, lung cage, warding off, holding in. Overly long skirt, cardigan sweater over a white blouse, sensible shoes, no stumbles, she floats on stones.

Sarah's figure an afterimage still with Lily when the irritated, suspicious, chronically anxious voice of Margaret's husband comes at her over the phone, a senior manager at the Trans Oceanic's metalworks taking it as his right to call, cross-examine a former company wife, demanding to know what that meeting was all about at the museum last night. Margaret was there, didn't you ask her? she knows as much as I do . . . it was a public meeting, Lily adds, testily. You involved with this coalition group? Lily ignores this suggestion of subversion as she ignores the avoidance in his wife's too ready smile and nervous laughter each time they cross paths at the supermarket. We've made every effort to be supportive, Colin is saying; coming from his mouth now it sounds like an accusation. Keeping her, Jan and Stephanie on their medical, dental plans once they are divorced, the company has always made abundantly clear, is out of respect for Bruce. When he flies his Cessna into cloud or fog, whichever was floating between those thrusting rock shoulders out there, sky becoming ground, they've already been divorced a year. Lily, still the beneficiary on his life insurance, becomes the improvident, improbable former rogue wife of one of theirs. They cut off her health benefits and her daughter's. *They, we* . . . to Lily, always they, them, never we, Lily never a member of the team, a team player, like Bruce. A dislocation in her when she hangs up, resonating emptiness.

I NEED TO EAT. HAVE YOU EATEN? Margot doesn't wait for Lily to answer, nor does she look happy to be here. Margot's hair, light brown, showing streaks of silver under the café's fluorescent light, is wound loosely on top of her head, looking ready to fall into some

kind of disorder around her very neat shoulders. Lily distracted by
the possibility, whether Margot would care if it did, why she is
thinking about this, feeling this anxiety of disorder. Margot in a
rumpled grey suit, white blouse, no jewellery, her smile and voice
returning halfway through a hamburger and chips to the liveliness
Lily remembers about her. She feels herself shrink as Margot
expands.

Is it always like this here? Margot pulls pen and pad from her
briefcase, moves what's left of her lunch to one side. The café
windows run with condensation; in the mall parking lot beyond
them rows of wet cars float on their own reflections. Early
afternoon and low-hanging sky that hides margins, detritus of
rainforest, marooned remnants. Pretty much, Lily says, her voice
muting. I guess people come to a place like this for work, or they're
married to someone who does? Margot asks, folding her hands in
her lap when Lily eyes her pen and notebook. Her voice feels loud,
too loud for Lily's comfort. Dark pouches under the other's eyes, a
six a.m. flight from Vancouver diverted to the coast as it often is
when visibility is less than two hundred feet.

Margot's been on a bus following the river back in, rain sluicing
down unnerving amounts of mud and debris from unseen scree
slopes above, following rivers to here, an ocean's edge she passed
over hours before. Lily can see them both in the cafe mirror,
Margot leaning forward, straining for missing words as Lily nods
without speaking and keeps looking away, uncomfortable with
Margot's, even her own presence.

I got your name from someone at the meeting we had up here
back in the summer, Margot says. I'm seeing a number of people
not just here, but all along the river. You don't have to have a
particular point of view about the power project. Lily still
uncertain why she's agreed to meet with Margot, annoyed with
herself for feeling talked into it, resenting the notion of appearing
in Margot's notes, which she will no doubt make after this
interview; of being raw material for her next published book.
Margot an advocacy lawyer, working on behalf of a coalition

against Trans Oceanic's continued ability to drown land and drain rivers, to break the law with government permission, the company which, to use its own words, puts food on table for the citizens of this valley, citizens who vary in their interest in what has been going on behind these valley walls.

Located by trees, water, sky, the trap lines run through the forest, arterial, webs within webs from centre to edge, ancestral territory, following his line from edge to centre, coming home now, to ravens calling from trees, calling out across rising water. Fire and flood, the devastation from his dream comes to greet him home . . . away on his trap lines when the Indian agent tells his people to take what can be carried, leave, before water released from a dam they know nothing about drowns their land and their ancestors' remains. He lives for two years in a wooden crate under a tree, believing the waters took his people, left him. She's seen the films, heard the stories—circumspect Trans Oceanic leaves Indian agents to burn homes, forge signatures that sign over absent Indians' lands to white nomads who have lost their hearing and speak this strange absent language of forgetfulness, of refugees in symbiotic relationship to private capital, anything possible, reverse rivers . . . dam, flood, take ancient habitat of a people inhabited by their land, by their ancestors, other creaturely spirits, leaving them no ark, no rainbow, no dove. I have no connection to them, Lily hears herself say, not clear who she means, but feeling cornered, a thumb press from inside her ribs, glancing at Margot in the mirrored wall lean back against her chair.

Releasing it all again when she spreads the blue binders, normally lined up neatly in alphabetical order, out over the museum's reading table, reads old photos of unsmiling Indian women looking beyond the camera lens, away, or down. Absent eyes of Indian women, graduates of the residential school, in pictures taken by English missionaries, ghost eyes dressed identically, Victorian uniform, the white, high-necked blouse and long dark skirt with hair plaited and rolled into thick bustles on the backs of their heads . . . *circa 1906*. Later the school burns, is replaced by the Women's Missionary Society . . . the women's children have always gone with their parents to the winter trap lines, the spring and summer fishing. Now they are kept behind to learn English ways, another language brought to them by British naval officers who sail their ships close enough to remind them of what happened to their neighbours further south who resisted dealing with the Hudson Bay Company . . . a white historian writes in his version that the British Navy is sent in to put an end to native savagery—secret societies, ritual practices.

Under protection of the Hudson Bay Company the first Christian missionaries sent in, agents of the mercantile, all working for the same God. Jasper Currie keeps turning up on the page. In the name of God he sails his missionary boat up and down the coast, convicted of their witchcraft, as he calls it, the dangerous violence of their heathen ways. His young assistant falls in love with an Indian woman, leaves the missionary enterprise to marry her and incurs the lifelong hatred of his former mentor. The young man's Indian wife is drowned, punishment for his sin, the missionaries don't say it to him, but he knows this is what they think. He leaves their baby with its Indian grandmother, returns to Scotland.

LILY LOOKS DOWN to where the water turns and heads west, out where space, light is, light that departs over the valley wall earlier each day, the long slide to darkness that cannot be stopped. Unable to focus on anything. A few tenuous charcoal lines on her board. The children don't come any more, play further down the beach, popping bulbous kelp under the heels of their sneakers and swinging the long strips at each other; whack of kelp, small grunts, laughter.

Light fading, Lily walking to where her car is parked, towards the figure crossing the road down to the beach, the woman who comes for the children. An artist, a painter, with your name, Jean, who paints thin women, all edges, hungry, with eyes, ears, hearts, feet and hands growing, glowing from their skin, skin that is stitched and scarred, drum, shield; delicate stick figures stepped down from a rock wall.

The painting no good from town? Jean's first words to her, mouth at her ear, warm breath that travels the labyrinth, her inner ear, melting her bones. Light flickering, drawing shadows on rafters open to roof boards running up to where she can't see, a chimney, rough stone opening onto sky. You painted me, Lily, not Lily says, before, or after or maybe during the fire, when her bones melt into Jean's for the first time. You see what you want to, Jean says. Tide flats, pools, browning ditches of sedge and saltwater meadows, wild crabapple trees; Lily follows Jean, climbing now, crossing highway to follow the river north, deeper into hemlock, cedar, balsam, fir. Darker here, fungi living on tree trunks fans of delicate green fluted at their edges, lichen hangs tangled hair in branches, footfalls on soft layers of rainforest floor. Smell of skunk cabbage where it is low, wet, too close to the rotting cabbage smell of grizzly, river between them and highway now.

Wet in here, ferns to her thighs, other growth she has no names for, her denims soaked. Below, close to the ground, another garden, turbulent persistent overgrowth, moss flowering, fruiting, pulling her senses underneath, hungry. Suddenly sky again, open, berry bushes, stumps, deadfall, pea vines and fireweed. White-headed eagles motionless in cottonwoods, crows restless, the river noisy. A logging truck accelerates on a flat stretch out on the highway beyond the cottonwoods drowning momentarily all other sounds. Lily's body a child and the force of the trees on her back, graven image, imprinted language of the tree, women crying out in silent pain wakens her, how did she get here?

An intersection of invisible shadows curving across a road on her back speaking words with no sense, telling Jean nothing and everything hidden under her eyes and behind her tongue, written in her body's child awkwardness and those paintings of Jean's upstairs at the museum that stopped Jan and Stephanie in their tracks. Tree moving in her, heartwood rings, old growth streaming a long look of the river back to them, the grandmothers, great-grandmothers carried in her body the child.

Dappling flashes, warm cool light in the shadows, quantum leaps, light falling on air, on water rushing to a deeper fall, on rock face; random collision, light with rock, trees, moss, turning it deepest emerald, deepest purple lichen, silver witches' hair hung from branches and sere, ochre, sienna, alizarin leaves, no longer permanent green, slipping into the silence, heavy, present, the hearing of it, coming to it again, but this time with the lost feel of an altered state. She scrapes canvasses, removes thick daubs, smacks of paint, everything spilling bleeding into out from else same, same other, colour a running river where it goes; but where? A becoming of relief to parcel up paint tubes, canvasses, the painting litter accumulated over years, take it to the dump and leave it there with foraging gulls and slack-skinned bears. Downtown, Indian women still avoid her eyes, won't look at her, turn away and survey the ground.

The ancient fishing camp, Jean tells her, before disappearing into the bush. Hungry, Lily drinks from her own water bottle to swallow the panic of being left here on her own in unfamiliar territory. What if a bear comes? lie down? play dead? Is a bear fooled? She tries whistling, throwing stones in water. Four logging trucks, one every seven minutes, still no Jean; bites hard into her apple, crunch in her mouth momentarily louder than the aloneness. Eagles don't stir. A crow lights on a log, eyes her, flies off when she tosses the apple core. Abandoned here to find her own way back. She eats the rest of her lunch, shoulders warm in sunlight, neck cool, prickly under her hair, the smell of food, what will it attract? Sliding gliding shadows, faces between trees losing shape, she's lost it, herself, someone else sitting here she doesn't know.

Jean hands her a plastic jar with berries in it. Acidic, earthy, sweet in her mouth. I ate lunch, didn't know how long you'd be, relief in Lily's voice sharp enough for an accusation.

Ready to go? Jean moving off, walking ahead through, into the trees, Lily reaching to touch them as she passes, assure herself they are there, shifting wine, purple grey, magenta shapes, solid under her hand. I wonder what I am to this forest, these trees. My smell, the feel of me. Does the brush of a branch read me as I pass by? Lily calls it out, to hear her own voice, Jean laughing—are you asking me, Lily? Jean's voice holds Lily like a mother, Lily between her thighs the way Jan and Stephanie lay on hers at birth, the way Lily cannot remember, or imagine lying on yours, melting into Jean, curled below her breasts, newborn moving blindly up, mouth open, searching. Lily's body a wakening child.

She feels them, the women in Jean's paintings, outsider, stranger within, sounds of breathing, hers, Jean's, moving through this forest's breath, breathbeat of wings above, beyond, behind, twit and click high in conifer tips, rustling underneath, her ears tuning to it now, waiting for the sound of frond unfurling, mushrooms breaking out of earth, Lily slipping out of amnesia. Who does know who they are? she murmurs at Jean's back. Didn't you ask your mother? What can Lily say, that you were not in the habit of speaking of a father who came from Scotland to buy Indian land from a white government, to homestead. Where and what is home? Is this how a child thinks, in the moment, no past, no connection to what, who, has been and gone? Why has she never asked? She's losing whatever it is she didn't tell me, the stories, Lily says. Gone, *gone away for to stay for a little while* . . . you hum, sing it in your tuneless voice, song from the old country, you say.

My great-grandmother, Jean says, married into this village, a daughter of carvers. Her daughter, my mum's mother, married a white man and drowned when my mother was a little girl. The white man went away, left my mother with her granny and then missionaries took her into their school, raised her there so she didn't speak her granny's language anymore.

What is your language? Hiroshima ends the war, you a widow soon after. Rental agency wait lists, two years of daily visits on your way home from work, find Lily and you this apartment beside a river, the escape from Osborne Street rooms with no running water, streetcars grinding nights to a double track rounding the curve, curve of the river here, this place, never lived in newness, raw plaster walls and out there, early prairie spring, trees bare, river rising. You surprise Lily with your song, *lilac, willow, cottonwood, basswood, box elder, ash, elm, oak, maple* . . . the shape, bark, you tell Lily, that's how you know trees when there are no leaves. And room for a garden, you say.

Ice jams, rivers flood, Assiniboine and Red, midnight sirens wail the city when sandbags don't hold. You and Lily go your separate ways. Lily floats from there to here. Sunlight tumbling down from rare blue brilliance, slanting through goldengreen hemlock running from road cut to meadows out of sight above, silence roaring in Lily's blood, bones. The new hemlock tips, Jean tells her, are o.k. to eat.

Auntie Jean, one of the children calls from the bedroom. My mother's name, Lily murmurs. That's why you're here, isn't it? Lily doesn't answer, does not know why she is here, where this is, where it has come from. Auntie Jean, the child calls again.

Go to sleep, Jean's voice calls back. When is she going? the small voice whines. In a little while. I should go, Lily says, bones coming together, bone again, supporting her crossing cold linoleum from couch to table an ocean away, sitting there, candle still burning, peanut butter crusts from the kid's bedtime snacks, a pot of cold tea floating on shining oilcloth, landfall beyond the couch, curve of Jean's shoulder, thigh river of light flowing into Lily river sounds entering the sea, remembering heat, fire, ember, ash.

Everything too fast, abrupt—how did she get here, why? Jean's voice floats across the gap as if she's in Lily's head. *Amputate* a word that comes to Lily, the way words can amputate feeling, construct a mind separate from body, body from heart, Lily from breathing. She could turn to drink now, has never been drunk or taken drugs, scared by the possibilities, her allergies to food, chemicals, plants, trees, air, where does she feel safe? Did she ever? Coming to the elemental state, moving beyond what she knows less and less, feeling it more, fearing what she feels, rage and hate perfectly formed, matched. Debris what Lily wants, to cling to, isn't that what reality is, debris? feeling the tree in her spine, shapes in the tree, Lily, you, Rachel, how many others does she carry? where are Jan, Stephanie? Where is she?

The museum's archival photos taken by white missionaries meant to tell one story, the unvoiced staring out at Lily tell another, what isn't here, what's been left out. Resist of silence, signal of great harm. A Day of the Dead, return of departed spirits feasting on Lily until she is bone and wind, bone and voice, Jean's voice wrapping hers, a double helix, a story for Lily to take with her to you. It slips into the cavity of her ear, warm breath, sweetgrass, opening Lily. Jean's mother not in the pictures, burned in a fire, she and the man who was Jean's father, drinking, Jean says, going crazy. Or taking life back, their spirits released by fire? Sarah there, in the row of white women standing, unsmiling as well, behind the Indian women they try to make like themselves. On our deathwalk, Jean says, unfinished business.

Flat black heart-shaped stones Lily finds by the ocean she stores in a box with crow feathers. Is Lily crazy, obsessed, hearing what she hears, seeing what she sees? Pasting feathers to the bones of you, the stone of you to bring you back, her, and her and her and her, the women you came out of, and Lily, voices from the labyrinth spiralling out of time and silence. Too much crowding in. Lily's eyes close, listening from a distance. Margot's voice louder than she remembers it, full of energy, calling from Vancouver this time. A parliamentary committee has reversed Trans Oceanic's exemption from environmental review, there's a good chance the project will be shut down. Why me? Lily wonders. Last week, clearing out things, she comes across Margot's card, drops it into the garbage. I'll be up there next week. What are you hearing around the town? I'm not in town all that much ... My house is up for sale, I'm leaving for Vancouver soon ... it's my mother, she can't seem to remember where and who she is ... I'm her only family. For some reason Lily finds herself not relating Jan and Stephanie to you, keeping them separate, needing to explain you.

The real estate agent not hopeful about the sale of her house—
just not a good time right now she tells Lily, maybe when the
power project goes through. Lily contemplates taking a loss. This
house they build, Bruce, Lily, Jan, Stephanie, on the fringes of
Trans Oceanic's clearcut, the dog buried here, her resting place. You
taken by ambulance to hospital, your silent bleed, hidden ulcer.
Nurses find you missing, two floors down, shopping for dresses at
Eaton's, you tell them.

I can barely hear you, Margot says. What will your daughters
do? Lily caught off guard by this intimidating woman with the
world on her shoulders who seems to feel free to just walk into her
life and ask questions Lily can't answer. Jan is involved in a tree
planting company . . . she'll stay here. Her choice, she says, feeling
defensive. Stephanie's still in her last year of high school. We'll have
to work something out. That must be hard—you said your
daughters were what kept you up there. Hard is when there is
choice . . . this urgency to find you before you are gone the prior
claim; bones melting to blood, Lily the river she is disappearing
into.

CAN I HAVE THIS DANCE, JEAN, HE ASKS, a tall, broad-shouldered man in white who lifts you against the weight of your gravity, from your recliner into his arms, holds you there while Dolores removes a disposable diaper and nightie, covers your body again with fresh ones as they discuss the hockey game playing that night, Canucks and Toronto, then, wordless, lay you back in your bed. I'll be staying the night, Lily says, watching from shadows your body clenching, restless, hair and pillow soaked with water draining from your skin, sea mist rising off you glistening the air. Dolores gives you another morphine injection. How much is too much? Who is to say if you can't? Your eyes stare at the light over your bed. Dolores turns it off. Leaves without speaking. Lily holds her breath when yours stops, waits, counting until your next wave sighs down her ear.

WHERE IS HOME, YOU ASK, I don't know where to go. Lily asking herself the same question, silenced by possibilities. Jan planting trees up north, Stephanie somewhere in the south of Mexico, where Chiapas Indians and the Mexican army are killing each other. Fear, the truth of it, sound of its note turning Lily to a child listening for your silence breathing. I want to go home, you tell Lily. I don't belong here. Angry, you sink down on the edge of an unfamiliar bed. I didn't think I would come to this, you cry, and Lily knows you blame her and there is nothing to say. Lily who gives away your furniture, what can't be brought here to Elizabeth Place, where they keep birds in cages, a fat black cat, fence the garden off the dining room so none will wander, everything blooming in its season you want to walk outside, beyond the fence, walk walk walk they have you now, require compliance decorum you are too difficult breaking out time no ends beginnings middles floating leaf landing where pain fear joy rage out of order their night your morning mourning night traveller you flit fly back to the tree watching for their coming, grassy voices whispering in your bones the moment to go?

PSYCHIATRIST #1 IS SMILELESS. Lily, dismayed by a funereal ambience, feels carefully watched, listens closely, watching her step, feeling for your escape. They won't let you, if they can't. *Possibly psychotic,* we can sign papers for you, the words roll like boulders from the psychiatrist's mouth toward Lily; like boulders. Papers? A Psychiatric Hospital, the Geriatric wing, a secure unit what they suggest, Lily breathing heavily linked to you fallopian, utopia, did we fall from it, grace? What did I do wrong you ask, I must be crazy. No, Lily tells you, tells the psychiatrist.

A warm July night Lily comes to see if you would like to go for a drive and you flatten against the door—*Where are you taking me? I need to know where it is you are taking me.* A drive, Lily says. Do you think she is one of them? Oh, you say, looking pleased, excited. This new power to please you cuts clean, sudden, unbearable. You sit together in the soft dusk up on Jericho Hill, watch myriad lights come on, galaxy of fires twinkling from those mountain flanks across English Bay, beyond lugged freighters. I can see it all, here, you tell Lily, pointing to your head, I just can't find the words, your face gleaming through dusk like a fish in water Lily tries to catch with her hands.

Tell me what you see, she says, Lily the child asking for a story,

the ones you never told, waiting in an overgrown garden wild
with what she has no names for and the pictures flow like music,
a song of the farm, your brothers, your mother Rachel from
Edinburgh, how hard she worked and nothing for herself, the
colours of the flowers around the house, the trees your father
plants, the garden, tears running down your cheeks. Lily has
never seen you cry. Long steady throb of a night heron's
wingbeat, flying low over where you and Lily sit with car
windows rolled down.

The psychiatrist's records note that Lily is uncooperative,
putting her mother and the community at risk, that the daughter
and mother appear to have a difficult relationship, since the
daughter seems to have no knowledge of the mother's history,
medical or otherwise, and could not or would not answer basic
questions about her mother's life; that the daughter is divorced
and, like her mother, lives alone.

SHE WAS REALLY GOOD TODAY. Renée the care aide corners Lily in
the hall. Had her bath and everything, no problem—go, look, she
says, grinning, triumphant. They tell her you won't bathe or
change your clothes, you who have been fastidious, elegant, wear
layers of skirts, blouses, hold them close to you, skin. Lily tells
them at least you aren't running naked in the halls, regrets it when
they don't smile, not even their eyes, realises she must be more
careful, for your sake. They've dressed you up in the pleated white
skirt you don't like and hide in the back of your cupboard. Lily
should have taken it away. It's not mine, you say. A white gauze
bandage bow tied in your hair, lipstick, rouge, strands of imitation
pearls around your neck. Doll. You look nice, Jean, all fixed up,
Renée tells you in a loud voice, tells Lily you like to be flattered,
as though you are absent, or deaf. Your eyes are somewhere else.
Someone you don't know is being talked about. Lily wants your
rage, resistance, you coming to you, coming to her. Waits in the
silence for Renée to leave.

You sleep in your clothes, this unfamiliar place not home you may need to get up at any moment when it is time to go. Whenever you waken is your morning, morning for dressing, another layer. Your morning their night shift. They lock your clothes away, suddenly, then tell Lily you bang on the closet doors with your fist and a hairbrush, tell her you are becoming unmanageable, aggressive, suggest you could become violent and begin charting your behaviour *incidents*. Lily notices your deep cough. Walks you past hydraulic baths, empty wheelchairs, waiting in a line, hampers of soiled laundry, past the air vent in the ceiling pumping cold in from outside, into the windowless smell of institutional antiseptic used to scour the green white and black surfaces of these bathing rooms to which everyone must come once a week. You refuse, unless Lily is with you, draws curtains close around your nakedness. Laid bare by your body, delicacy of your neck, shoulders, curve of spine, arcing thighs she wants unexpectedly to curl between, fist, heel in your belly, stroking the skin, walls of you with a soapy cloth. A sudden ache.

Infant, child woman, who is who? you sitting enthroned on your plastic bath chair, shower head, flexible, garden hose Lily places in your hands, yours the choice where, when, no more mixed-up words, it's too hot when you mean too cold, you both go by feel, testing it on her wrist, then on yours. The soft soapy flannel put into your hand you lift to your face, your neck and chest, one breast, hanging wing, your belly wrinkled, folded, desert geography, buried umbilical root, hairline, still red. You stand, hold the railing, take the cloth slowly between your legs, familiar cleansing strokes you repeat, until Lily tells you it is enough, washes your back, its gentle roundness strong, durable, figure eight, infinity your spine, its bony longitude, s-curve.

Not so hard, you say, sit again and begin washing your legs, pleased at the doing of it; surprising strength. When it comes to your feet, Lily bends to wash them, feels your distress, your hands flutter, reaching to push hers away. You don't need to do that, you tell her. I'll do it, Lily says, rough words broken loose, scraping her tongue; absent moorings. I'm cold, you exhale then; deflation in your voice moves in Lily.

Your hair wet, more light brown, red, than silver, surprises Lily. She combs it slowly, blow-dryer wavering in her hand. This time you spend together out of time, at the end of things or the beginning, hard soft afternoons. Neither mother nor child, everything changed, out of place, hair, skin, purple veins miniature trees knotting your temples and folded hands, deep cough, your laugh, grimace of pain, don't pull, you say. It's just a knot, Lily tells you—No, no-oo, my neck you cry, bare your teeth at her. Lily grits hers.

For you calls on the intercom are noisy neighbours, someone in the house who shouldn't be here. *Who's there* in your alarmed eyes listening, somewhere else, something in the forest looking out at Lily. Standing in your rooms on Osborne Street, a woman's moans and cries for help in her ears, curling around her heart and squeezing, Lily the alarmed child, silent, her eyes seeking yours. You listen to what is coming through the walls, say nothing, your face, embarrassment what Lily sees, your eyes turned away, look down, listening. Calls on the intercom today for someone to come and tell them what to do. Lydia, down the hall from you, is standing naked in the shower stall, with the flexible shower head turned on full and hot, aimed at anyone who tries to come near her. Come on, she taunts, strip, time for a shower, *come on.* Jubilant crossing the line; Lydia is medicated.

Maybe a little arthritis, a nurse says vaguely. They get these aches and pains, we'll keep an eye on it. What about that deep cough, Lily says. The nurse opens her book, says she'll make a note of it for when the doctor comes in next, which will be in a couple of weeks. Not soon enough, I think she's delirious. We'll wait for a few days, the nurse says coolly. The surface of Lily's body where these words hit feels clammy, ice cold, reverberates. Call the doctor now, she can hear herself say, the *now* a trembling leap, rage, coming from blood, throws everything off, crosses the line. You have bronchitis. Antibiotics don't touch the ghost cough. What they track is your behaviour, manageability, need for psychiatric reassessment. On their guard with Lily now she's become difficult, like her mother.

PSYCHIATRIST #2 CALLED IN to assess your state tells Lily you are wearing two skirts. You have been wearing at least two skirts for some time now. You don't undress at night, ready to leave, someone may come, and simply add another layer each morning until someone here notices, brings it to your attention and you look down, surprised, laugh. Oh, you say, I guess that's too many.

Very polite, pleasant, muses the psychiatrist, but then one sees the skirts and the memory problems. Your mother couldn't tell me the day, year, her age, or what city she's in. This psychiatrist's eyes are friendly, engaging. Lily asks if this is what is considered psychotic behaviour and the eyes grow distance. Your chart is opened. It is indicated there have been *incidents* . . . agitation, unprovoked aggression . . . My mother's been ill, no one noticed, they locked her clothes cupboard, she seems to be in pain, there is this unexplained cough, Lily says, receives no response. This psychiatrist knows what she needs to do, what she has been asked to do and how the means should appear respectful, considerate, and esoteric. She mentions the names of a couple of drugs she is thinking of *using . . . anti-psychotics to manage her behaviour . . .* Her letter thanks your doctor, one of three who make visits every few weeks or so to Elizabeth Place, for this most interesting referral.

OUT OF MY HANDS, your doctor tells Lily. She looks at his missing two fingers. What is it can be held in the hand, without slipping through, between fingers, or under skin into bone, blood? Out of our hands everyone says. Whose hands are you in? your own, it seems, yours the final responsibility to let them do what they will, or resist, and give them more reason to do what they will. Is this the time to go, Lily asks herself, to go back there, where Rachel came from to give you birth, you and me? *Gone away for to stay for a little while . . . but I'm coming back . . . though I roam ten thousand miles* . . . I'm going back, she tells you, to Scotland, to Manitoba. You clap your hands; this strange new ability to please you she cannot get used to.

In the doorway of your room you hold Lily now in bear hugs, and kiss her cheek, unfamiliar territory for you both, but you don't seem to notice, you, tall, erect. Take care of yourself, you tell her. Tomorrow will you wonder why she hasn't come? wait weeping by the front desk, telling them you don't know where to go? I'll send postcards, she tells you, turns away quickly, dismay a sudden flood of premonition. Why does she feel this urgency, that she must go now, abandoning you to those she does not trust, for the long look of the river?

JULY HEAT IN MANITOBA. THE WOMAN AT THE CAR RENTAL tells
Lily for a dollar more a day she can have air conditioning and a
Sunbird instead of a small four-cylinder hatchback. You don't want
to be driving out there without it, she says, meaning the air
conditioning. Says it with conviction, Lily remembering hot dry
wind that stops even a thought of tears, not this humidity. The
young man on the lot holds out the keys to her. It's brand new, he
says, indicates adjustable steering wheel, power steering, windows,
door locks. She longs for something small, simple, the unadorned,
aims the Sunbird south and west, over the Assiniboine, slipping by
her past, Winnipeg on her left, feeling for fault lines, skimming
surfaces, flatness, distance, emptiness, frightening space, the long
remove, crossing the inland sea she crossed, Rachel, both of you
and now Lily.

RAW JUNE WINDS IN SCOTLAND. Rachel's death certificate in
Canada out six years on her birth date. Lily finds this at the
Edinburgh archives, housed in stone. Rachel's son, Robert Jr. who
never marries, in his fifty-sixth year with Rachel, finally left behind,
gets it wrong, making her sixteen when he is born, instead of
twenty-two. The inattention of grief, or simple inattention to her
life? He writes in her birth place as No. 1 Wallace Rd., Edinburgh,

which does not appear here in the archives at Edinburgh. Lily stranded in microfilm, microfiche, eyes on the eye of the monitors staring back at her, glowing monitors circling, reading her. Facing one, back to centre, she traces, searching in the name of the father for your mother Rachel, you, searching herself, strands of story, how it moves through birth, marriage, birth, christening, occupation of the father, sons, death.

The records show Rachel, born to Arthur Forrester, ploughman, and his wife Jane, 1860, Edinburgh. Born to Arthur? Rachel the first daughter, fourth child. Sisters after her born in parishes outside Edinburgh. A lady from Edinburgh you once tell Lily, your mother, daughter of an itinerant farm labourer who moves his family to wherever the work is, bettering himself. By the 1866 census and the birth of the last child, he describes himself as Land Steward. Rachel, the unusual name. Rachel's mother Jane marries Arthur in 1841. Jane Fleming, born in sight of Crahill, where they burn witches as late as the 1700s, motherless it seems; the records show only Thomas Fleming present at her christening and Fiona, mother to Thomas.

SOFT YELLOW GREEN BLUE WAVES of ripening canola, alfalfa, wheat roll, rise, fall away to more and more and a circling lip of sky. Flat-bottomed clouds pass over with summer's speed. Wild grass, flowers, silken foxtails bent low in ditches, passionate sweet chorale too much for Lily. Ecstatic, wanting to cry, immensity closing in presses dense, the weight, you, her, islands in a gap. Late afternoon July sun still high, hot, driving into it, distant farm truck shimmering up ahead, mirage? When it is very cold, is it really possible that images from light bend, towns, islands, landfalls hundreds, thousands of miles away may appear in the eye? The mirage ahead turns, sends up scribbles of dust, signals of its existence, hers, in time, this place. Dirt concession roads, regular as telephone poles, click by, measuring the grid of sections, half sections. The land broken, claimed, occupied. Your beginning here where Rachel disappeared.

Past supper-time, Lily parks the Bird on the shoulder, navigates
its locking devices in claustrophobic moments until she's out of the
car standing by a dry ditch of dusty flowering weeds, itinerant
grains, relic wild grass. Rachel on her death certificate called a relict
of her husband, *relict, a person's widow, a geological or other object
surviving in a primitive form.* She recognizes daisies, brown-eyed
susans, red clover. White yellow purple pink faces go nameless. Is it
the mislaid smell of clover, hay, that raises her heart, smacks it
against the wall of her ribs?

Is this how Rachel comes, horizon in the eye of a wandering
queen? *Elissa-Dido, Phoenician Queen, plants her city Carthage, city
of fire, toward Africa and open to the sea* ... Cicero will say *their
inhabitants do not stay bound in their homes, but are always drawn
away by hopes and expectations which continually give wings to their
heels* ... 1885 the liner *Carthaginian* leaves Liverpool for Montreal,
on its passenger list, Rachel Forrester, *housewife, 25 yrs. & son
Robert, 3yrs., from Edinburgh.* Other women on board listed as
Lady. Slave ships have come and gone from Liverpool, come from
Africa, cargo holds full, heading for the New World, death on the
way a release. One hundred years after Rachel leaves Scotland
seeking this New World an African American woman returns from
there to Liverpool, sings out over the water, sings to herself the
memento of water, retrieval, celebration of who she was, is ... *seas
may burn, rocks melt* ... *come ye back* ...

Rachel and her child disembark at Montreal, head west by train
to a small station in Manitoba, where Rachel hires a driver with
horse and cart to take them south, into the warm light of Indian
summer, golden on this inland stubble sea, crows black ... cart
bumping hard against Rachel and the small son she holds close to
her. Wings beat up toward sky as they pass; crows, waterfowl, sink
back onto turned earth. Indians on horses move aside, watch in
silence this white woman and child in tight black coverings, this
woman with the face that cuts air, creaking past in her hired cart.
Big Crow and Little Crow, they laugh to themselves when the
woman and boy pass. Buffalo all but gone this Indian summer of

Rachel's arrival. Indians starving on reservations. Louis Riel waiting to be hung at Regina. The English will be satisfied with my head, he tells the ones who call him to their cause. An other story, inhabitation, native, natural, by birth belonging, a hole, whole in fragmentation.

BUFFALO GALS WON'T YOU come out tonight Come out tonight Come out tonight Buffalo Gals won't you come out tonight And dance by the light of the Moon, Lily on the s-curve over railway tracks, bearing to the right into what must be a main street, or was, into dense green surprise, tall elms standing so suddenly vertical, thick-leafed, and left, beyond them, where they open onto shoreline, an ocean of ripening cultivated fields taking her eye to distant undulations, to where her eye can't go, beyond its focal point to frozen plains, snowstorm smudging a horizon, white smoke, buffalo dark clouds within moving the storm one way then another. Wolves keeping them on the run, watching for the one on the edge, confused perhaps by the featureless snow, disoriented, tired. They leap at her with precise movements from the side and behind, draw her off from the rest, run her to nowhere leaping at her face, feinting back and forth between her horns, wary of them even now when the others hang on her hindquarters by their teeth, tearing chunks of her from bone, take her leg. She is still running.

Lily slows the Sunbird, she must find the right button to roll down the window . . . *caw caw caw,* they fly up, darkening sky, *caw caw caw,* from field to trees, imploding silence . . . asks a woman pulling a green hose behind her, watering her garden, how to get to the Bed and Breakfast. Heritage farmhouse, the *B&B's of Canada* lists it, in the town where you are born, where Lily wants to unearth you, the only one for miles as though it waits for her. Lily has to cross the river, the woman tells her, and turn south; if she passes the cemetery, she's gone the wrong way.

A LULL OF CREAKING CART wheels full of dust bumping in and out of ruts, Rachel's eye travelling taut leather reins to the reassuring rise and fall of the mare's gleaming rump and beyond, to a circling horizon with no line of distant hills, no landfall, not yet, on this inland grassy sea. Behind her, a summer trickle, brown stream echoes under stone arches, succulent green dock climbing from water to paths Rachel's feet know the way she knows her feet, that take her dipping and rising with the land to where the faint blue haze of Crahill, home of the women who came before her can be seen across a long remove of rolling fields, where the trap hills are. Land below her falling away to where the cows graze, land lying fallow, resting, renewing itself, but not the workers, not her mother. Rachel would have no memory of her mother resting, her motherless mother. No memory of a grandmother who dies in childbirth, only what her mother Jane tells her of her great-grandmother Fiona who became her mother's mother and Fiona's grandmother Lia, who comes from Flemish weavers making their way west, away from debt, unemployment, always leaving behind a look over the shoulder.

Away from secret police of the Holy Roman See. Celts on the move again, carrying with us, in us what cannot be left behind. Crossing water, from continent to island, heading north to these circling hills, where the crows gather. Limestone, coal, gorse bog, broom, water-loving trees. Fertile, if the land be drained. We must hire ourselves out to farmers who lease land from absentee owners. Women, wives and daughters working the fields in bondaged labour to have a fire pit with a shack over it for our families and a measure of peas, barley, oats. Splitting fingers spinning flax, weaving, selling, bartering, our labour goes cheap. Everything but work with the horses, skilled work the men say, only men do that, for more pay. Women who once rode into battle on horses, queens, poets, priestesses birthing, feeding, sheltering, clothing, the doctoring still women's work, but dangerous now even here to speak of what has always been, the dancing and singing to somewhere else, a healing touch, the seeing, knowing . . . the gift, handed on through blood. When the blood is called unclean we must go silent.

Cart rocking Rachel, her son fallen asleep again enclosed
between her arm and thigh. She holds him tight to her, says little
to the driver who says little to her. Rocked by cart, in and out of
grooves on a plate of earth under a bowl of sky, by train, water, by
the look in her mother's eyes *and if he won't have you?*

HALF A KILOMETRE off the highway, a solid farmhouse stares
squarely at Lily, willow and chokecherry bushes behind it hiding
the river. In every other direction ripening alfalfa fields run toward
sky, the town at Lily's back, elms, grain elevator lit by a lower,
softer sun, as though she's dreamed them.

But this is a bad dream, a stuck elevator that goes bump, no way
out. No hint there would be no one here, door open, no locks, no
other cars or guests, the note telling her which room is hers, that
Muriel will come by in the morning and that there are trails down
to the river. She should have been told, she should not be expected
to sleep here in this house alone, she should have been told. Lily
stares at the note written in chalk on a small blackboard, believes
this is your doing, this abandonment, this absence, this sudden
terrible vulnerability, not even blinds on the windows, but who is
to see? This aloneness.

WHEN LILY TELLS YOU, I'm going to Scotland, to Edinburgh,
where your mother Rachel was born, she can see you want to go
too, a heart's breath out of time thinking she can take you with her,
that expansion and contraction in her chest returning now in a
volley of gulls shooting up from her feet into sky over Haymarket
Station, snapping white wings and you lingering with her west and
south from Edinburgh to Glasgow and south almost to the Irish
Sea, from your motherland to fatherland.

The heart above everything else is desperate . . . exceedingly wicked
. . . this reading from Jeremiah is included with breakfast at the
women's hostel Lily chooses because it is cheap, centrally located in

Edinburgh, and everything else is booked. Gonged for breakfast at eight, reverberations climb curved walls, doors, spiralling stairs to vaulted and domed ceilings of this once-Georgian townhome, rattle ten-foot-high windows in Lily's room. The women here from all over, the Highlands, Border country, France, Germany, Italy, Texas, doing courses, linguistics, music, computer science, or in from the country on a holiday. They take breakfast in the dining room while Jeremiah is read a second time and a small sermon delivered by a woman whose smile has the hint of an apology in it as she tells them they might be tempted to think of God as a stern, cruel Father. She looks straight ahead, girl at a spelling bee, wanting to get it right, get it over. An evangelical message about sin and hell and punishment and God the Father's unwillingness to make us suffer and how precious we all are, especially if we confess to sinning and ask his forgiveness. The women don't look at each other, stare down into their bowls of cereal, stirring silent patterns with their spoons. Cheap, clean accommodation why Lily's here. She avoids the dining room, eats in her room or the parks to save money. *Know the truth and the truth will make you free.* Lily remembers that from Sunday School or was it Bruce's religion? What does free feel like? Is she free if she is not hungry, hungry to know, what truth, know in what sense, begetting, being both energy and matter, creating herself? Does being hungry make her a sinner? Is this the fear, of a great rage hiding under the fear there will be nothing to her, discontinuity, no voice, no story, no breath, Lily holding her breath, waiting.

BREATHE, SHE TELLS HERSELF, unloads her bag from the trunk of the Sunbird, eyes scanning uneasily the circling land, sky, for what can't be seen. Luminous evening, light coming in low from the horizon and when she follows trails through darkening bushes to a narrow brackish creek, a red afterlight of sunset turning trees above it, the water, black. Mosquitoes swarm Lily, covered in bites by the time she is back at the house thinking of sleeping sickness and your story of the baby called Lily asleep on the verandah, tiny naked body covered in bites where mosquitoes feast. Why, how does it happen? Lily doesn't ask. You don't say. The phone ringing. Lily runs, eager. A call from Vancouver, Elizabeth Place, she has given them the number here, to tell Lily they are putting you into a psychiatric unit. Her reasoned arguments become begging them to wait ten more days, until she is *home*, almost there, make no difference. Papers have been irrevocably signed in her absence, and yours. Would it make a difference had she been there, not here?

ROUND MOON FACE at the window flooding the upstairs bedroom, the "yellow room" the one the chalkboard assigns to Lily, lying in it now fully clothed and shivering on top of the bed waiting for moonlight to become morning. White fish in moonlight her hand pulling the quilt off the other bed, muscles rigid, eyes swimming for sun, seeing both ways, resisting sleep, fear listening to fear, listening for any alteration in the pattern of sounds in and outside this house urging her to go out, curl under a bush, tree, hide, learn darkness.

LILY'S GREAT-GRANDMOTHER Jane, a child in Fiona's garden, and by her firepit, where the old woman steeps her dyes, weaves her cloth. Always a job to be done as her grandmother spins and weaves her cloth. Fiona calling her, come child, help me with the wool, or stir up the fire, bring me this or that herb from the garden. It's so pretty, Gran, Jane tells the old woman as they pull the yarn from its dye baths and Fiona weaves.

It was your great-great-grandmother Lia who was the weaver, Fiona reminds Jane, silks such as you've never seen. She worked for a master and they were sold under his name but they were hers. Her grandmother's shoulders, her whole body rocks as she says it, the way old women do when they are on one of their journeys, or keening, and her grandmother's face lit by fire, staring into it, as she begins her story of Crahill and Jane's great-great-grandmother Lia being not yet ten. And Jane listens with eyes fastened on the changing shape of fire playing across the skin of her grandmother's face and hands, the fire's story reflected there in her grandmother's eyes become hers and soon she hears voices that seem to have always been, flowing like music lost, the rustle of silk or birdwings through air.

Lia's mother Rhian a widow, her aunt Brunis not yet married and Gertrede, the homeless woman they take in, a midwife who has lost her living in these burning times, keep themselves and Rhian's children by spinning flax, which they also dye and weave, and by hiring themselves out, Brunis as bondager to pay the rent, Rhian working the fields as well to keep them all and still barter for yarn from all the spinners around the kirk, to weave their cloth and sell it, sustain their fading dream to weave silk into fine garments and tapestries for the trade in Edinburgh.

Lia must tend the dye pots while Rhian is up in the trap hills, at the fens and into the glens for the clay and bark, the roots and plants for her medicines and to colour her yarn. Black pots steeping, smells familiar as breathing, colours in the light, soft pinks, browns, sometimes red like blood from the lichens; greens and yellows never the same twice from bracken and bog myrtle, broom and fanning leaves of the alchemilla. Brunis and Thomas away to the fields beyond their own little scrap of land in need of drainage that they work themselves. Lia's fingers, her whole body itch to use the backstrap loom hanging from the wall. Her mother and Brunis will soon move it outside for the summer. But not yet able to reach, throw the shuttle, she closes her eyes for the pictures to come again, their shapechanging swirl spiralling her down, swimming, drowning into light, shivering her into the dream, that elusive fish that comes just behind her eyes to take her following the flick of its tail through darker deeper waters until light and colour are gone and the waters press heavy on her, until a thrill of fear, not knowing where she is bursts her eyes open, waiting to slip from this dark shack to the garden, trees behind garden, up to the trap hills with Rhian, waiting arms of sky.

Open steady sky bringing Rhian high enough to see Edinburgh and the Crags and across to the Highlands, her chest tight, finding herself waiting on breath. Uneasy leaving the child alone so much, better when Lia is old enough for bondage in the fields, disquiet taking Rhian back down instead of further up, to the bridge where there is more red dock growing down to the river and roots ready in behind the stone ruins where crows are thick in the stand of ash, beech, poplar where she first sees Gertrede. The face tight over its bones, eyes darker than she has seen, clear voice halting Rhian along the hip of fringed gentian, maidenhair and heart's ease; against her instincts, she will remember later, in October, the harvest done and only turnips left to cut. Wind quiet, animals and fields steamy in golden light when the warrant is prepared under a general privy council commission issued back in 1591 for the trying of witches . . .

to search for, imprison and examine Rhian Fleming, sub-tenant, weaver, the child Lia Fleming, daughter, and Thomas Fleming, son, and as well Brunis Kell, bondager, and Gertrede Smail, vagabond midwife, who are vehemently suspect of witchcraft and whose names have been given up in a roll by the moderator of the Presbytery. Their dispositions are to be reported to the council who will thereupon give further orders, but the examination must take place within 15 days after the apprehension of any prisoners.

The pricker smooths, rubs, presses his fingers over a body they have already stripped and shaved, is it hers? his fingers searching for places to insert his needles where there will be no pain, a sign the devil is with her, places he knows well. Rhian feeling only an unfeeling his needles cannot penetrate, goes to a space where fright, terror, rage go silent. The pricker collects his fee for all of them. Thomas is safe, Lia examined all over again, to be sure. The men watch closely, remark how smooth and fine her skin is, without blemish and wonder when she'll bleed. The women are taken away, kept apart.

Rhian does not know where her children are, her body, bone, their faces, Lia, Thomas, the last look she stumbles toward, walking a half light, no way to tell, tell her gaolers what they want, anything, a story to rest, sleep, for food, something to cover the bones of her from the shadows, the hunger, weakness, *confess and save your soul, the others have . . . heart above everything else, desperate, exceedingly wicked . . .* words eyes tongues licking at her, rasping her skin, insides, inside her, in and out, *the devil's whore.*

Commissioners remain aloof from how the necessity of confessions is met, a private matter between the women and their gaolers. Gertrede Smail, 55 yrs., knows what's coming and hangs herself. Brunis Kell, 25 yrs., will not hold her tongue, confess or still her anger, which results in her gaolers torturing her to death. This also recorded as a suicide. Rhian Fleming, sleep-deprived, emaciated, hallucinates, believes maybe she is a witch, gives the names of those who came for medicine, thinking it will save her children. For this she is publicly strangled before her body is burnt.

Lia remembers only they took her mother away, and her Aunt Brunis and Gertrede, but not her, because her skin was smooth and fresh as an infant's, and not her little brother Thomas. And nothing is said, as though it never happens.

Lia too frail for the fields, Fiona tells Jane, stirs herself to set a dye pot over the fire, in the place where the flames reflect from Fiona's eyes to Jane's. What is it child, have I told you too much? What do you see? Fiona hands her the yarn. Keep your hands busy, Lia did. Quick fine hands flying over the yarn, they said. Bondaged to the Laird's house, his silk she wove, her work known all over, fine, fine work, her daughters bondaged to the fields, or in service.

What was she like? I'll tell you what I know, child, and you can make of it what you will. She hid from sunlight, fearing injury to her skin, any bruise, mole or wart, freckle. And from her body with its blood, wounds, nakedness. When it was cold her throat gasped, grasping at air. Jane can see herself in the fire in her grandmother's eyes looking beyond her. Fiona's eyes return to her cloth, her voice slips into Jane, Lily, finding all the hollow spaces, seeking them out, tuning her to Lia's song.

Lia old now, like I am now, Fiona sighs, and blind, calls me to come and hold her hand and walk with her in the garden. She lives with her oldest daughter Margaret, my mother. I am the youngest and have yet to go to the fields, but I will soon go. It is left to me to watch Lia. October when Lia begins wandering naked in the garden, digging in dirt, peeing and shitting among the plants. Who's there? she calls. There, at the end of the garden, she tells me. I can see them there. Who? I ask her. The ones who left . . . bad blood coming out in her, what others say. Her daughters, granddaughters, all of us keep our silence. Lia doesn't, shrieks when she is tied down. My mother weeps, sets her mother loose to grope for the fire, smell everything like a dog . . . stones, dirt, trees, water, her own body, air, the food in her bowl, afraid of what may be put there to numb, silence her.

There was a small pouch, Fiona says, Lia took it from around her neck and put it into my hand. Not rough, very fine woven silk of colours that bleed into each other. Inside, some hair tied with silk thread, some sweet-smelling dry grass, a stone holding a circle wanting to curl within itself my fingers wanted to trace. She wouldn't take it back. I put it around my neck. I was already out to bondage in the fields. When I came back one day she was gone. Gone? Where? Fiona looks at her. They never found her. That's all I know, she says, casting her eyes back down on her work. I see your great-great-grandmother Lia for the last time standing in the backstrap loom, the belt across her back. She tells me she is weaving earth and rock and moss and blood into a womb of light spiralling to embryo, black and blue the sea, her skin, wrapping, rocking a memory of water from the fear of what is gone, the weight of what remains. Jane watches her grandmother's hands move and knit together wings from firelight. When did you see her? Fiona doesn't answer. What happened to the little silk bag with the circle stone and red silk thread that Lia gave you? It was taken to the fields one day, by your father when he was a child like yourself, and lost.

Jane's chance to be a pupil teacher and go to high school stolen by the flax mill, the hated dust, noise, smell of it. Her father, stepmother can't survive as cottage weavers, their living stolen by the mills. Common land gone where they can put their few cows, grow their food, gather brushwood for heat, snare rabbits. She watches them become itinerant farm labourers, unused to the fields, their health broken. Jane is young, hardens to the labour, finds Arthur, born nearby, in the parish of St. Machan's, a hired ploughman; becomes his bondaged worker to tenant farmers who hire him. It is her work that pays for a cottage where they can live. Her daughters will do the same, including Rachel, now Arthur is a Land Steward. If he can hire out all his daughters, and Jane herself if there are no more infants, then he can do what they don't dare yet speak of, lease land of his own to farm, making Arthur and his sons tenant farmers instead of hired labour. Rachel must give back the scholarship to high school. There is nothing else to do, the land what they need. There will be time enough when she has daughters of her own.

Births, christenings, marriages, deaths, wills, ordinance maps, old names and new. *Wallace Rd.* gone, renamed at some point in the story, no longer on any map. Lily running out of time, moving in and out of it, across it, following whose mind, what silence to where the gaps are in the story, the women, mother of, daughter of, the female lineage, unspoken, not in the record. From archives to sunlight spilling down Princes Street, reverberations of bagpipes from Waverley station and trains dieselling west to Glasgow, east along the North Sea and south to York, west to Manchester, London, or north over the Tay River bridge. Black on white flanks of sightseeing buses stream her vision *PRIMALSCREAM. BJORK. DELAMITRI. THELEVELLERS. RAGEAGAINSTTHEMACHINE. CRASHTESTDUMMIES. DREAM* . . . archives to street to other frequencies spanning the girth of double-decker buses with blurry images of family violence, public service ads, *UNEMPLOYMENT, NOT THEIR*

FAULT, small words sliding by and clouds, clouds above in solstice wind and evenings full of light for walking.

The couple window gazing come toward her, down one of the side streets off Princes, the man taller, bigger than the woman, his arm hooked around her neck, collared she moves when he moves, watches what he watches, in and out of Lily's vision as she moves beyond them, feeling tired now, and hungry. In a cafeteria she argues with the short-order cook behind the counter. He tells her she can't pick and chose what she wants, she has to take the regular dinner. Lily tells him she's eaten here before and it wasn't a problem. He doesn't answer, fries eggs, puts vegetables, rice on the plate, hands it to her. Lily, frayed, annoyed, doesn't notice he holds the plate with a towel, takes the full weight of the plate into her hand, which is when he tells her it's hot. No, we don't have any ice, the manager, a woman says, smiling. My hand is burned rather badly, do you have *any* first aid? No, the woman says, smile now vague. Perhaps I will call the police, an ambulance? Lily goaded by that smile. The cook has his back to her, the woman bemused. Lily goes to the cold water dispenser, holds her hand under it, leaves her meal on the table without paying and walks out the door. No one reacts.

White-knuckled, clenched fist at her side at Marks and Spencers, she manages to collect a tomato, avocado and rolls, something she can eat between now and breakfast. Feels luck with her again when her eye catches packages of roasted chicken breast. Her burned hand reaches, claw-like to take one, wanting coldness for the pain. A woman next to her stares, turns away. The cashier calls her dear as she holds the one hand close, does everything with the other. Behind her a women blurts out—my purse, what did you do with my purse, an accusation. It's under your arm, the man with her says, laughing, you going to blame me for that too? Grins at Lily. She turns away from whatever it is his eyes want from her.

Avocado a challenge, braced with her forearm against the side of a plastic picnic plate, it finally splits under several slices with her pocket knife. Soft, messy. She scoops, eats, on impulse unclenches her hand and smears the rest of it onto the burn. The hand wants to clench again, squeezes slippery avocado flesh out between her fingers. Pain eases. Eased, Lily presses her knife into plastic wrap on the chicken breast, it doesn't look quite right. She reads the label more closely. Partly cooked, ready for microwave, what it says.

These are not housekeeping rooms, Miriam Legg, a kind of Protestant Mother Superior of the hostel, glares what feels like censure without mercy at Lily. She and Lily both gaze down at the half-cooked chicken breast. Yes, of course, I thought it was fully cooked when I bought it. Suitably apologetic, but skirting penitence. Even so, Miriam Legg says severely, we do not allow eating in our rooms. No, of course, Lily mumbles something about picnic and parks. Well, Miriam continues briskly, having made her point, we do have a microwave. I'm not entirely sure how to use it, but let's try. Here, give me this and we'll put it in and see what happens. She gives Lily another of her warning looks. Just this once you can eat it here in the dining-room, which is closed now, but you have to eat somewhere, don't you. You are aware you could have dinner here every night? Plain but nourishing. Yes, Lily says. Oh, I'd forgotten, you're the one with all the allergies. How are you managing with all that? Fine, managing.

Here you go, this looks ready now. Be careful, let it rest for a bit or it will burn your insides. She finds a plate and cutlery, sets a place. Lily waits for her to go away, but she hovers, busying herself behind her. What's the matter with your hand? she says finally, I didn't notice you had trouble with it when you came. Lily struggling to part chicken meat from bone.

Just a burn. Let's have a look, she turns Lily's hand over, clicks her tongue. That needs something, come to the kitchen.

It's all right, Lily protests. Nonsense, that needs looking after. Hold out your hand, she insists. *Hold out your hand* . . . the strap comes down, again, again . . . Mrs. Coxborough, otherwise know as *Miss Coocoobird*, grade five, divides her class into sheep and goats,

Lily the only girl in the goats, the thing is she doesn't know why,
because she's Lily?

Here, Miriam Legg bustles back from a tall window, this will
help. She splits pieces of spiny cactus open, spreads the insides, a
watery gel, onto Lily's open hand. Don't worry about the smarting,
that should stop it. Lily bites her lip. She drops the remaining
pieces into Lily's other hand for later. If it's still sore in the
morning, I'd be surprised, but it does look a nasty burn; come to
the kitchen and ask whoever is here, probably Gladys, to give you
some more. How is that now, better? Yes, you see, very good. Can
you manage now? Shall I cut your chicken up for you? It will be
stone cold by now. No, thank you, I can manage. Thank you, Lily
says, again. Not at all, dear. Would you be interested in joining our
Border Country Tour? A group of ladies will be leaving with me in
the morning. You're welcome to come with us. They're all in town
for the Highland Games this week. Lily tries to picture them, no
doubt why she has so much trouble finding a place to stay, thanks
Miriam Legg again, but no.

By morning her hand has come unclenched, is red, sore to
touch, otherwise alright. Lily splits the remaining cactus spear,
spreads the juice around where it is red and lays fresh layers of
Kleenex across it, tapes them there with Bandaids from her pack.
The garbage from last night she rolls into a plastic bag to drop in a
trash bin along the street. Bins along the street all sealed, the King
of Norway coming for a state visit on the weekend, the day Lily
leaves. She locates breakfast around the corner at the French Deli,
writes quick postcards, to Jan, Stephanie, General Delivery, last
known address, will they get them? Cards Lily brings with her,
written before she leaves Vancouver, to send to you twice a week,
she cannot send, throws away, begins writing you what she sees and
feels here, on large cards of Edinburgh turned salmon and gold in
solstice evening light. Will someone read them to you? Perhaps Lily
will, when she gets back. But you will see them, the light, Lily's
written words, someone will tell you where she is again and again
and perhaps . . . *tell me what you see*, Lily tells you, heron croaking,

undersong, how you both go on, missing melody, heart's mind, mind's heart finding you finding her, the possible within the impossible; voice, someone lives here; many.

MOON FACE A PALE GHOST riding the day in a sky changing colour above the window; train out there somewhere, melancholy wail. Still in her clothes from yesterday, when did she last spend a night with no sleep? Buzz in her head. Angry. How can she possibly do all she needs to do today on no sleep, how to focus, where to go, how, for evidence, footprints, threads of your existence, Rachel's. Why you run. Why Lily ran from you, from pre-med to Toronto, to a lab with its windowless cupboard where Lily must stay all night measuring blood levels of radioactive copper. The blood samples are brought to her at timed intervals. Lily wears a black badge that measures the amount of radioactivity she will absorb. The blood comes from a young girl of eleven, the same age as Lily when her father left. The girl is dying of a genetically inherited liver disease little is known about. There are green rings around the cornea of her eyes. The child stores copper in her liver and brain. It will, in a few years, kill her and there is nothing that can be done to stop this. She is studied, blood and body fluids scanned, and when she is dead her brain and liver tissues will be analyzed by Lily. She knows this when she goes up to visit the child. They play chess. The child wants someone to tell her she is dying. No one has. Lily does not want to be the one and begins to avoid her.

Levels of a copper-carrying enzyme in the child's blood, tagged with the radioactive copper—Lily cannot stop, the readings must go on through the night and the next day. The doctor for whom she works asks her if she would like her married name or her maiden name on the paper he will publish. She says it doesn't matter, married is fine, having just married Bruce. What if she had said Lily Jeansdaughter? out of Rachel, out of Jane out of whom? out from where? Rings in heartwood expanding or contracting?

She quits the lab soon after, tries art school. Jan and Stephanie are born. Janis Joplin sends her rocket into space. It doesn't return, as neither the dove to the ark.

IN PARIS, PETRA AT THIS MOMENT IN HER LIFE in her physical anthropology classes discovers the line below the skin, the curve light follows bending the story, darting here and there in all directions, running kinky spirals along uncluttered neural pathways, vortexes rattling this hollow the size of a question mark deep rooted, raising the possibility of existence without feeling it in her belly's involuntary breathing; voluntary suspended, how long can she hold this breath, her dream of absence.

Paris spirals out from centre to edge, Petra's arrondissement curling against the fifteenth, a small street there named after a man fascinated with the idea that no two people have the same combinations of ears, iris of the eyes, nose, mouth, chin; each with a singular landscape of their bones. In Buenos Aires, where Petra's grandmother and mother surface after the Second World War in Europe, another earlier émigré from Europe, a policeman, becomes equally fascinated with the unique and individual nature of skin that covers our bones and how it can be used to incriminate.

Before the outbreak of the Second World War, Petra's grandmother runs a pharmacy out of her home somewhere in Prague, a too-short journey now, from Nuremburg and Munich, through Bohemian, Bavarian forests, border slipping away. For this she has no medicine, no antidote but to marry a man whose father was adopted, a man in whose face are the unmistakable signs of a

Spanish Jew, one who fled the Inquisition. Petra's mother is conceived as the country is being invaded by Germany. Petra's grandfather goes into hiding and is not seen again. Petra's grandmother and mother surface in Buenos Aires in 1952, about the same time as a J. Mengele, who obtains an International Red Cross passport and sails from Genoa. Petra's grandmother never discusses with her daughter how she got them here. Argentina a mix of Europeans containing the absence of those who were here before the Spaniards came, the disappeared whose ears and breasts were hunted for bounty to their extinction from these southern grasslands become property, of white Europeans.

DID YOU SLEEP WELL? Muriel, cheerful, arrives in her white Chrysler. I didn't sleep at all, Lily says, surprising herself by coming out with it. Muriel boils her an egg, which is all Lily wants, says she guesses coming from a city, Lily wouldn't be used to being on her own out here, that Muriel will sleep here tonight, if Lily would like. Yes, Lily murmurs, wanting to say she thinks Muriel ought to warn people before they come, the house full of valuable heirlooms, antiques, a cd sound system, left on its own, unlocked, an idiosyncracy of its owner perhaps, but why should paying guests, Lily, be exposed to it. To what? Lily asks herself. Being left, abandoned like the house.

Muriel shows Lily where the keys are hidden, and the locks, the old-fashioned kind, buried in the sides of the doors, then nods, wordless, toward the dining-room window. A deer, her fawn, white tails flicking, browsing near the house startle when Lily moves to see them better, disappear between willows and river. A large farm garden between the trees Lily didn't see.

BROOM AND WILD LUPINES, blue heron poised among sedge and lily pads, horse lying in a field of yellow flowers, red poppies, train moving south from Glasgow, west toward the Irish Sea, your father born here, so the records tell Lily. No record of his mother Eliza's birth. She marries in the time of cholera, from low church to high, your father her eighth child, sixth son. The record at his birth states her occupation as housework.

Eliza's income from weaving, work of her hands her cottage business, disappears into flood tides of factories, mills, Irish running from famine, crossing water to this thriving industrial town to work machines that spin, weave filaments, silk, cotton, linen, wool, manufacture cutlery; still they are not paid enough to feed and clothe themselves. Someone making money, thriving. At this time in Kuangtung Province Chinese women are spinning and weaving silk, working fields, at many and all kinds of manual labour, resisting marriage as their mothers did foot binding, living in communities of women who support one another in sickness and old age, their highest deity a mother goddess. This independence accepted as their daughter's fate by birth families often dependent on them for support.

Lily waits for the train back to Glasgow and Edinburgh, her head still aching, not sure if from the trip here, the diesel fumes, or from this town, Eliza's and his, your father's. Below Lily soot-darkened stone buildings stretching out under hanging clouds in from the sea. Eliza's low kirk under repairs, new mall across from it now the town's centre with its taped music, U2 ethereal under domed glass, and a silent ugly eruption of violence in the middle of the day, thud of fist on skin, rolling eyes, blood, the woman's high heel shoe slithering through pop and broken glass, gliding across the mall's shiny terrazzo floor, lands at Lily's feet. Her eyes, an infant's, skinless, watching wordless cramped and toxic blows splitting skin from bone; something in her eating the fear. Going east from there to the high kirk the land rises, past Witch Road, to where Eliza marries, gives birth many times. Lily finds suburban malls, gas stations, car dealerships, a disappeared birthplace.

THE DEER HAVE GONE among trees along what Muriel calls the river behind the garden. Behind Lily's eye moonlight turning trees to glass, deer panicking in the reflection of their shadows, shattering trees, their flesh, moon white bone in their gaping wounds. Why did you come? Muriel asks Lily. What to tell her? For a story, a telling, to hear voices? Tell me what you see, the heron croaking its way through that dusky July night on Jericho Hill among the stars when you and Lily meet in Rachel's garden, Lily crossing to there, here. Sometimes you don't know who Lily is. Where is she, she never comes. Who? Lily asks you. Searching for a moment you frown, your face clears, eyes intent, Lily, you say. But that's me, Lily says, your daughter, I'm here. Oh, yes, you laugh, I wonder when she'll come. Lily here now, hot July Manitoba. I've already been to Scotland, Lily says, to the archives in Edinburgh.

Gallery of circling monitors eyeing her eyes straining for names, Rachel, Jane, Fiona, Lia, Rhian, back to Crahill and the burning of witches, this tracking on her innards, fingers pressing keys, searching the story's spine. I've just come back from there, she tells Muriel, following her out onto the verandah. I know my grandmother left there, and arrived here unmarried in 1885, with a three-year-old son. His father, my grandfather, had been homesteading in this area since 1882. I know she had another nine sons and then my mother, her eleventh child and last was born in 1904. I'm trying to fill in the gaps. Is the story to come this way, out of the gap, slot, mouth, whatever it is, when Lily is able to look straight on, if the skin over her eyes has not thickened too much or too little to see what she sees, a leap into the fear of knowing silence, what it holds, where it goes.

I've got a few hours, Muriel says, not entirely happily, Lily senses, but to make up for Lily's sleepless night. We can go into town, check the museum, what about relatives, any left here? Lily says she knows practically nothing, acute how the awareness is here of how much nothing is, what has been left unsaid, unasked, unrecorded.

Do you think we could find the old family farm? Muriel asks at

the museum. This is the granddaughter. Cam his name, face
neutral, he remains without apparent interest, recognition or
curiosity as he copies survey maps, puts a sheaf of black and white
Xeroxes into Lily's hand. Indian reserve land close to the town
shows on an old map on the wall. Who were they? Lily asks. He
doesn't know. Likely sold years ago, he tells her. The museum once
someone's home perhaps, with a store of some kind fronting it,
floors sloping toward edges, fall away. Cam offers to Xerox
anything Lily would like from what is here.

Fine, she says, fine, thank you. Stares down at the sheaf of black
and white copies in her hand, negatives, young men in army
uniform, your brothers, stare back at her, the town's main street,
circa 1906, buildings odd-shaped boxes leaning against one another,
is it the way the wind blows—dry, hot, cold, ceaseless. Your
brothers' names, war service, births, deaths, filed under the name of
your father, Lily's grandfather, his prize-winning strains of wheat, a
member of the Seed Growers' Association, Farmers' Institute,
Agricultural Society, Rachel not in the story, not named. Your birth
acknowledged, that you exist, somewhere. One of your brothers, the
youngest, dies accidentally in an explosion when he is nineteen,
another in his forties from injuries in the war, the first great one,
gassed in the trenches of France, the Great War, your brothers tell
you, happy to go, it seems, you wondering what that means.
Another brother, the youngest next to you, dies accidentally while
in the air force in the Second World War, when Lily is a little girl
and just before you become a widow, a relict. She didn't know that
either. Anything else? Cam asks. He can't Xerox what isn't here.

Later, in the archives in Winnipeg, Lily will search for the lost
reserve that must have been here when you were born. She will find
a letter from the new Indian agent to his superior in Indian Affairs
regarding a woman who hanged herself. The new Indian agent does
not know the Sioux woman who hangs herself, or how she came to
be here, this little reserve surrounded by white homesteads and soon
to be sold and disappear from maps. She may be one of those who
made their way north to here from South Dakota after trouble at

Pine Ridge . . . does not ask her name, writes a letter to Ottawa: *I have the honour to report that a woman, the wife of one . . . hanged herself recently. It is supposed she did it because . . . a jealous fit? her husband took other wives . . . I have the honour to be, Sir, your obedient servant . . .*

Did you see her, from behind Rachel's skirts when they came for tea, bringing their medicines from the fields, *black root, yellow root, pucoon, gayfeather, black susans, wound medicine her mother says is yarrow, bitter medicine her mother says is ragweed . . . bark of willow, chokecherry, root of sumach . . .* did you see from behind Rachel's black skirt the woman whose Sioux name means split rock, a ghost dancer from the Dakota plains . . . *barbed wire, armed guards around the residential school, Sioux children held hostage, circles of ghost dancers grow wider, feet moving at the pace of the youngest, weakest, moving in a solar path, right to left, coming from their tipis carrying nothing, entwining fingers, believing the ghost shirts will protect them from the white man's guns. Ghost shirts the women have painted gleam white, medicine paint red, crow feathers black . . . hungry, starving, pressed to give up more land to whites, mourning their loss, they fall down in another place where the spirits are who will tell them what they must do to bring back the buffalo and all the ancestors . . . waiting for answers, how to make sense of it all, drawing together, circles within circles, moving as one, and beyond them, watching, other dancers of a different sort circling within time, biding it, waiting for winter snows of a hard Dakota winter, when the Sioux are at their weakest. . . .*

What would the Sioux woman and Rachel know of each other, what language between them in Rachel's kitchen, this great inland sea, wide plains, horizon never coming any closer, wind rising, sky heavy, a Dakota blizzard overtaking the Sioux, white soldiers encircling women, children, the old people, their tipis, their flag of truce. The men already disarmed, taken up a ravine, out of sight. Already taking the child from her back, binding her to her breast with hands shaking so she can barely press nipple into searching mouth. Her body sags, legs collapsing, body moving body out of time, not feeling, watching herself running with the other women away from tipis, the flag of truce. Grandmothers, children, pregnant women cry out, stumble, fall to another place, their infants sucking on milk from breasts of emptying bodies, tripping, struggling, nowhere to run, ghost shirts everywhere stained red and the snow, women wrapping babies tight in their shawls beside, underneath them, before they are gone.

The baby's mouth is not holding her nipple, red like medicine paint smeared over the tiny face and wrapping blanket, and on her breast. She cannot reach to wipe it off. Soldiers' voices hollow echoes, calling to those hiding in the bushes to come out and they will be safe. She cries a warning that will not come out of her, *little boys coming out of their hiding places all shot together; soldiers jam rifles up the noses of their ponies and fire;* river of ice moving through her. A boot turns her from side to back. She is somewhere else, doesn't feel the baby slide off her breasts into the snow. Gone on ahead, looking back at it all, then nothing. Until the baby comes to her dressed in white man's clothing. *Army details wait out the blizzard for three days before collecting frozen bodies of wounded and dying women and children, men, now buried in snow, throw them naked into a long trench, stripped of their ghost shirts which are taken for souvenirs.* A rumour of a baby in blood-matted frozen wrappings found alive.

With so many wounds, a miracle she is alive, they tell her. She does not feel alive. No one needs to tell her her baby is not with her. Out by Wounded Knee Creek a soldier hesitates before throwing a matted bundle into the trench with the rest, brings it instead to the refugee camp. Her own child, stronger than she is, now lying beside her fretting and crying for what she has no strength to give, must be taken from her and cared for while she sleeps.

She does not understand what the white man is saying. Shakes her head. There must be some mistake. She is very weak. Where is she? . . . where is my child? she keeps calling. There is an offer of money. She is told her child will be well cared for. A very important man, a General will give her child everything she could want. You can't look after her the way you are, you may not live, the Indian agent keeps telling her. The General, a puritan whose ancestors fought with George Washington, is taken with the idea of this Indian child's survival after three days out in a Dakota blizzard, of possessing such a wild and tenacious thing. The Indian agent has already promised her to him, although the mother is refusing. The agent, anxious not to embarrass the General or himself, suggests the General come to see her. They stand above her, the General in his dress uniform, smooth dark hair, closed flat eyes that stare without seeing her. You would not want to offend this important person who is doing such a good thing for you . . . will you take the money? She says nothing, turns her eyes away from them. Keeping the child will go hard for you and the child. Think of her, what a good thing you are doing for her . . . you'll take the money? It is not a dream.

Various records will state the child is found, having been abandoned by her mother, thinking her child killed in the Wounded Knee Creek massacre, and that the child is adopted by the General, after the mother first refused and then agreed and was paid a sum of money. The child, given the name Daisy, after the General's mother, becomes a celebrity. Upon his arrival back home, the General holds an open house and hundreds come to see his newly acquired daughter. *In another version the child's mother is killed at Wounded Knee Creek.*

The archives contain a reply from Ottawa, five years after receipt of the letter regarding the matter of the Sioux woman who hanged herself. It asks *if she had any children and if so, that since the Sioux neither take nor get Treaty, any children of hers be taken into an industrial school where they will be properly trained and cared for.* Two months after Riel is hanged, Daisy is growing up in Washington; Rachel becomes wife of Robert . . . to become noted for his prizewinning strains of wheat, his ten sons, their war service. The birth of a daughter, you.

Rachel dies alone, in poverty, the birth date on her gravestone by a muddy winding prairie river out by six years. Is the story

Rachel's? Must Lily who came out of you read what is written in, on her cells to know? What does this mean to know, to fall into a story and not be able to get out? Sun directly above, horizon circling, has it always been there, this panic? In her rented metallic grey Sunbird, Lily follows the dust of Muriel's white Chrysler racing a grid of dirt concession roads to here, wary that at any moment Muriel could abandon her with no sense of direction. She checks a field of sunflowers, their attentive heads all turned, east, she thinks, since it is 11:30 by her watch, sun overhead, Muriel's dust ahead, driving like she wants to get this over. The speed, dirt roads, dust, undefined space alarm Lily. Where is home, your question, hers. Is this it? these fields you run through? You and Rachel in the buggy, crossing winter, Rachel driving the buggy faster than she knows how, no bearings in the whiteness, looking for the end of it, or the beginning, does this land ever stop?

RACHEL LOOKS FOR THE BEND of light, eyes straining for it, the sign she is here, home. The horizon circles, moves with her, with the tireless haunches of the mare tracking space—sky, earth, stubble, dry grass, shades of light. Indians look away when she passes. Something about them bending her to look again. They are laughing. A field of crows fly up, blackening blue air. The mare lunges, her son wakens. Eyes of strangers looking at her, eyes that are, are not her mother and father; an alteration. Do we know the father? He's gone; she tells them it doesn't matter; feels the turning away in her, and from her.

Eyes of strangers the circling horizon, landfall, horse and cart come to rest. Rachel and her son arrive at a place that will be her home for the next fifty-three years. She will never leave it. Home, inhabiting the territory of, language of, silence written on the whole body, in the bloodline? She remembers him tall, with a straight back, can no longer remember his face, imagines one for him out of what is there in her son's. The gentler tongues there say the small quiet boy is not much like the tall, good-looking Scot

who came out three years earlier to homestead in 1882, when Big
Bear refuses to sign away Cree territorial rights and is told by the
white government that all rations will be withheld if they are not
onto their reserve by November of '93; and Poundmaker as well,
when he demands complete control of reserve affairs be given to
Band councillors.

RACHEL MUST GET HERSELF out of here, these eyes of strangers,
her mother, father staring tight-lipped at her big belly curving
unmistakably, staring back at them across the gap of their silence,
something moving between them that cannot be spoken or healed.
Jane feels her going, Rachel can tell, an infant's curved fist reaching
up from the silence between them to strike the blow they've both
been waiting for, Rachel as gone as the mother Jane never saw. And
if he won't have you, what will you do, the unspoken question
Rachel sees lying in her mother's eyes. I wasn't seduced, she says.
    Rachel glances sideways down the kirk pew to the hard outline
of Jane's face. That Rachel let this happen to her is a pain Jane
holds somewhere deep. She will not take it out again. The
Reverend is giving Rachel a head pain, original sin, the wages of it,
pain of it. Women get both, the pain and the work. Rachel feels
her mind playing tricks on her, telling her things about herself she
never knew, she's somebody else, alone, not connected to anyone or
anything except this narrow space; she doesn't know if she's Rachel
Forrester anymore, or who that is. Fallen, like they say, for the
pleasure of it? But what would they know about that in here, the
Templars' kirk. Do they hear, those Templar ghosts, what the
Reverend has to say about wages of sin?
    She glances again down the pew to Jane, has seen her standing,
stilled, above the Templars' kirk, by the stone mill, looking out
over the land quilted with blue flax falling into a distant line of
hills, to Crahill, the sight of her mother standing there raising fear,
hunger; herself swooping now, beyond moss and lichen feeding on
kirkyard gravestones beyond the thickness of these kirk walls

holding Templar bones, following the land until there, in shades of moor and fen, bogs and gorse of Crahill, searching, resisting she doesn't know what, something, someone that draws, then drives her away.

When did sameness become other, a hole opening up between them full of work, exhaustion, fear in her mother and father of losing it all? A still deeper nameless thing in Jane that reaches out to claim Rachel, that Rachel resists, knowing it has already seeped into her. It is from the very coldness of her being Rachel conceives connection, follows a curve of light beyond this place, images of herself crossing water to a distant landfall, and the life in her belly beats on her swelling flesh like a drum.

Outside the kirk, field labourers are uniting with trade unions, rioting for better pay, better hours, women demanding an end to female bondaging, no more women hiring themselves out in the market to strangers, living and sleeping in the same room with them to pay the rent on a shack for their own families, while their husbands, if they have one, hire themselves out where they can in the fields, quarries, the mines. Inside the kirk is original sin, the wages of it, the price women pay.

Going to the fields harder now, her son asleep when she leaves and returns, more Jane's than hers. It suits her the men leave her alone. How she got the child, her own class not good enough for her the men use against her when she tries to organize the women field workers, the lowest paid, who have to house their families in whatever the tenant farmers provide, under whatever conditions, and try to keep themselves and theirs alive and able to work. Conditions better here because this is an experimental farm, and her father now a Steward, but her wages, her mother's and sister's and the rest of the women's are not enough. Without you, she tells the women, your families wouldn't survive, your husbands and sons, fathers and brothers couldn't buy land for themselves. What part do you have in that land? The land cannot be worked without your labour; where would farming be if you stopped? We'd all starve, the women's answer.

Anna Parnell burned in effigy, along with the Pope, on Guy Fawkes Day. Unruly women, they are called, members in the Women's Land League from Ireland, travelling through Ireland, Scotland, England, agitating for rent strikes, supporting those evicted, providing shelters and essential needs for the landless who, after four years of blight on their potato crops are being evicted for non-payment of rents. The women preach total restructuring of society and separation of Ireland from Britain. They go too far for the more prosperous farmers who want reduction in rents but not eviction, not loss of their land. The British government has already produced a law to allow for arbitrary and preventative arrest without trial by jury. The women have taken over from the men, who are either arrested or lying low, and who in a state of general alarm are withdrawing from the kitchen's heat. Police break up the women's meetings, held in large industrial centres of England and Scotland and in rural areas. Children parade in the streets in protest. It is only a matter of time before the women are arrested as well. Unlike the men, the women are not held as political prisoners but under statutes related to the control of prostitution, as vagrants. Separated, kept solitary, without conversation, some for several months, denied the right to speak, *hold your tongue*, even while walking in the exercise yard. Only the poor and landless remain in support of the League and the women who are left cannot support their actions except to provide assistance to those evicted from their homes.

Anna Parnell, betrayed by political parties in Britain and Ireland, which continue to refuse membership to women or the peasantry, will grow silent, a recluse in self-imposed exile, and drown swimming in dangerous seas three years before Archduke Ferdinand is shot at Sarajevo and Rachel's son goes to war.

Rachel does not ask how money arrives, sent to her father care of the experimental farm, from an address of grain merchants in Glasgow, sent on behalf of a brother, who, the letter notes, recently emigrated to Canada . . .

Is THIS IT? Leaving cars, following Muriel down this path in an
overgrown set of tracks between yellowing fields of ripening canola,
uneven ground, abandoned farm the map calls it, homestead,
Indian land he, your father, bought from the colonial government?
to where yellow converges with a dark green thickness of trees
surrounded in barbed wire. Muriel lifts a sagging top wire, stands
on the bottom strand. Lily slides her backside through carefully,
barbs loom immense in the corner of her eye, places her foot on
the bottom strand, takes the top strand cautiously in hand, holds
for Muriel. Watch, Muriel says lightly. Lily follows her glance down
to her shoe and sun-dried cow shit soft in the middle below it,
shifts her weight and steps down beyond into weeds and grasses she
has no names for.

UP TO THEIR KNEES NOW in shepherd's purse, lady's mantle,
burdock, Queen Anne's lace, nettle. Lily looks for what she's
brought with her, the song broken loose, what you tell her up on
Jericho Hill under a night heron's beating wings, turning over in
your hands again, again, seeing, feeling random throb, heart
flinging blood into space, seeing the garden where you went with
Rachel, flowers up against the house, encircling trees your father
plants, dead snakes your brothers hang along the fence, the crow
whose feathers you try to pull to make it stay.

The garden now disappeared into wild herbs of the field and the
trees, dense, twisting back on themselves thicker, darker than an
olive grove. Abandoned house falling in on its foundation, coming
loose from its root cellar, insides slipping away into the hole,
burying itself. Faint warm nausea keeps Lily from looking inside
through a window's glassless upper sash, eyelashed with rotting
curtain remnants the colour of tea stains; the bottom half glassed,
milky with dust, mould, dark images, reflection of trees, the ones
your father plants.

Muriel tells Lily she should take a picture, camera hanging
forgotten at her side. Muriel is quiet otherwise, Lily glad she is

here, feels a child watching from behind every tree, limping and
sliding between them, a point of light Lily's eye follows, feels your
silenced breath along edges of her skin. Sun hot on Lily's head,
pressing down, light womb greening her into your spaces, Rachel's;
breathing silence, silent, Lily is you, her.

Yes, Lily says, pointing camera at window.

THE THING IS, the librarian at the National Library of Scotland
tells Lily, those old streets were often renamed at some point in the
intervening years, in this case, a hundred and thirty-four, but we
don't know when, so you can see it's pretty much luck, a very long
shot, to find the new name. He looks at Lily sympathetically. How
long are you here? Just to the weekend. Lily wants to look at old
newspapers, 1880 to start with. He brings her 1880 on a roll of
film, asks if she's familiar with reading microfilm, demonstrates
anyway, saying, you'd be surprised what people do with these—but
I'm sure you'd be fine. What did you do to that hand? Lily puts it
back in her pocket. Just a bit of a burn, she says. His face wrinkles,
whether in sympathy, or that anyone could be so careless, Lily isn't
sure. He disappears, not promising anything, he'll see what he can
find out about Wallace Rd.

Lily rolls the microfilm through January 1880, headlines in *THE
SCOTSMAN . . . arrival of Zulu warriors at Waverley Station, an
opportunity to see our friends in their War Dances, Songs, Marriage
Rituals and Great Military Fete of the Krall . . . war in Afghan,
Parnell in America, the Pope sending aid for the relief of the distress in
Ireland, starving peasants, demonstration for the need for relief in
outlying areas of Edinburgh . . . REAL SEAL JACKETS . . . Tay River
Disaster, Night train goes into River, Sunday Travel the Cause? Expert
Witnesses State New Bridge Structurally Sound, no mechanical, no
human error, fierceness of the wind that blows the train from its tracks,
impacting bridge, river, river bottom . . .* Lily looks up into a shining
face above her, watery smile. He points to something in his hand,
holding it out to her. Lily looks down at her watch, two hours

gone. It is only February 1880. We're in luck, he is saying, lays an old city directory in front of her, points to a footnote, *Wallace Rd changed to Dewar St.*

You should be able to find Dewar on a city map, he tells her. Lily doesn't need to look. There in her eye, a row of abandoned flats plastered over with Rolling Stones posters, corner of Dewar and Torphichen Rd. She's passed it every day, a quick two blocks from the hostel, Haymarket Station close by. Fierce flurry of gulls, hearing the sight of them, tumbling through her, altering course. Jane and her infant Rachel lying together at this corner. Rachel's infant eyes stare at Jane's, looking for the end of it, or the beginning, middle, whichever it is. Memory of absence at her own birth hidden in Jane, in Jane's bones and blood, stares back at Rachel. Jane and Rachel lie together on a bed in a flat in Edinburgh. Gulls snap the air with their wings just beyond a dusty skylight, below it stone stairs spiralling down dusty light past an open door. Rachel's eyes follow light from the open door to her fist curled below the curved shadow of Jane's breast, where they both wait, exhausted by the blow that splits them, binds them. Waiting for the afterbirth, Jane weeps for the emptiness, hollow sore-tooth pain in her belly. How could they know Lily would come promising you pictures of *No. 1 Wallace Rd.*, clicking the shutter from across the street, between buses and lorries taking the corner, until the roll is done, know she would lose the film? Natal, maternal, of, like, or from a mother, birth, death, you push me out the door of your other heart, your other heart, the force of the blow splits us my open pores sucking on air and others' fear to know my own, name.

DOES LILY WANT TO GO and see her cousin? Muriel wanting to know, move on from here. Alright, Lily says, not sure. She did not expect there would be anyone left here, your brother's son. A bit of a recluse, Cam mentions. Lily has a feeling, vague and unsettling as she once more follows Muriel's dust to a horizon circling a rise of land, littoral of abandoned cars, a shack, miniature horses thrusting their heads beyond their fence, curious, shyly alert. She follows in a kind of trance, an overload she can't identify.

Her cousin holds out his grease-stained hand. Beyond coveralls and John Deere cap thick with more grease, Lily is aware of a grizzled alert face and eye; the other eye doesn't work, she remembers this now. Him there beyond Neal's shoulder, Neal's hands around her neck, squeezing hard. Lily can't speak, swallow, breathe. Don't be a tease, you're a big girl now Neal says in Lily's ear, head disconnected from heart, lungs, other heart, the force of the blow splits, her pores sucking on air, others' fear, learning her own. You send Lily here, summer in the country on your brother's farm, Lily ten, Neal sixteen, the one-eyed cousin who tinkers with old cars and farm machinery, the silent watcher, nineteen.

He is charming, talkative about his visits to Winnipeg, to his aunt, you. Lily says she doesn't remember them. She doesn't. It is a complete blank. You were out with all your boyfriends. Something in his tone catching Muriel, too, silent to now, watching Lily. She would be too young then for boyfriends, Muriel says quickly, quietly, letting her recover. Yes, Lily's voice empty. The smile drops from his face.

Your letters to Lily infrequent, brief, half a page. You sign them Mother, nothing else, never mention the word love. This one longer, comes to Lily in Toronto a humid day in June, lilacs below the window cloy, her shorts, T-shirt stick to skin that won't peel from her. Jan, Stephanie oblivious, curled into naps, soft napes glistening. Hot tea, Lily remembers you say, opens pores, cools the blood. Your letter, brown rings, tea stains, she reads it again . . . you remember Neal, your cousin, you say . . . flew his plane into the side of a mountain . . . a sigh somewhere in Lily, is it relief? Lily watching all of them, her aunt and little cousin Ellie standing by the hen house, this silent cousin there somewhere in the background, still figures transfixed by the cry of the horse, Neal's, as he runs it against the barbed-wire fence to break its too wild spirit, horse rearing, Neal forcing it into the barbs. No wind, no sound, until the horse's cry in Lily's spine, horseflesh glowing red in hot dry sun, she turns away.

Her cousin telling Lily now, Neal's widow and children live in Edmonton and Blair's family are in Winnipeg. Blair took in Ellie's two kids when she left them and headed off to Montana. Lily remembers Blair, another cousin, at the time a younger softer version of Neal. And Ellie, small, rag doll child hanging on her mother's leg.

Muriel reminds Lily to take pictures, takes one or two of Lily and her cousin, with the little horses peering out from behind them. Lily asks herself if the lies pictures tell are true. Send me a picture of your mother, her cousin says. Lily says yes she will, smiles, shakes his hand. Knows she won't, can't.

I'll take you back to town, Muriel tells Lily, there's things I need to do. You should talk to Hannah McFarlane. She'd be about the same age as your mother. You'll have to go up to the hospital north of here though. Muriel's Chrysler turns off just before town. What is not being said? What hasn't been asked?

Lily looks into Cam's impassive face. Why was the farm abandoned? He grew prizewinning wheat, all those sons . . . Cam wordless. A high-school student there now, working afternoons for the summer. Cam pulls out a file drawer. Hannah Mcfarlane organized these, he says. Filed by family name. The student, red hair hanging down around her face, pulls cards, Lily looks at a display of early photos of the town. Cam points out Robert Jr., the oldest, a short, slight man in the town's band, playing a french horn, tells her Robert Jr. played lots of instruments, violin, piano . . . the red-haired girl calls him over to the files. Lily stares hard at the deteriorating photo. Have you lost what strangers know, or just the words, the telling?

A small file card slides down the counter toward Lily, the student and Cam talking between themselves and Lily suspended somewhere, unable to hear them, in her mind's eye the file card

moving like a cat, beyond speech, far enough away for her to
wonder if Cam leaves it for her to read, or perhaps not, so that it
may slip away unread, unknown. Perhaps it has nothing to do with
her. Lily picks up the card, pencilled in so lightly it is difficult to
read. Her grandfather's name, the same list of his activities and
associations, his prizes, she follows down the list with her finger,
ending with an item from the town paper, February 1901,
... *brought before Magistrate's court on a charge of assaulting his wife,
fined twenty dollars and bound over to keep the peace for a year* ... It
does not say who brought the charges.

1901, Rachel now has ten sons. You will be born three years
later. The shape of your silence alters in Lily. *What did I do wrong,
I must be crazy. I want to go home.* Your words, the weight of them
heavy in Lily's heart. Cam inscrutable. Who else would know
anything, Lily asks him. There's Hannah McFarlane, Robert Jr.
worked for her family all his adult life. There's Hazel White over at
the Seniors' Lodge, she's in her early nineties, you could try her. He
gives Lily a brief history of Hazel. Cam gives no sign when Lily
thanks him, of what he knows, isn't saying, or if he's just doing his
job. Maybe he doesn't like what she's doing, poking about in lives,
but she wouldn't know, can't tell. No signal, sign, marker; you gave
Lily only your silence.

SHE HASN'T TURNED the Sunbird's air conditioning on until today,
heading towards thunderheads rearing up along a northern lip of
sky so hot they turn haze to a pall of smoke hung over burning
fields as she follows the river, past the cemetery, on her right,
between highway and river, crosses the river twice. Asphalt in the
hospital parking lot sticks to her sandals. Hannah does not look
happy to see her. Propped in her bed, white hair, sharp face,
piercing eyes, an eagle stares out at Lily. Eagles sitting motionless in
cottonwoods, crows restless, flying from tree to tree, the river,
highway, aloneness in the bush, trees, Lily losing shape, happening
again, old woman with timeless eyes here to tell her she's on her

deathwalk. Lily doesn't know what that is. Sit down—Hannah's
eyes hold Lily's—I'm going to tell you the truth. Her radio is on.
You can turn that down, and you probably won't like what I tell
you so you might be better to leave now . . . Hannah's voice, her
eyes ask, *why have you waited so long?* Lily doesn't move.

Your mother made me very angry. Hannah's story of you she
calls truth. You left, never came back, Hannah's very blue eyes on
Lily and looking somewhere else, Lily feeling anger stored for years
smack up against her, coming from Hannah and setting Lily in
motion like a tuning fork, her own vibrations long, slow, waves
with nowhere to go. I may be wrong on that, Hannah says, she did
come back, once, but never again, not even for her mother's
funeral, none of them did, except Robert Jr. and John who stayed
in town and Wallace had a farm south of here. Two died before she
did, that leaves the rest of them and your mother. Why didn't they
come? They weren't that far away they couldn't afford it. Hannah
waits for Lily to say something, an acknowledgement, or maybe
permission to go on. Lily nods.

You know the two oldest brothers, Robert Jr. and John, put
your mother through school? Lily shakes her head. Tells Hannah
she knows nothing, except you had several brothers. Neal's father
one. Between Hannah's words a face peers in at Lily in the back of
an old model car, hot Saturday night, parked along the dirt main
street of a small town, lights on in stores and cafes along the street,
where Neal's father and Lily's aunt go while Lily waits that summer
in the country, ten years old, and this face peers in at her,
whiskered, eyes unclear in dusky light. She feels their curiosity,
does not like being stared at. So this is Jean's girl, he says, and is
gone, leaving his breath a stale alcohol *vapour on soft summer air.*
You sing it often, fond of that Stephen Foster song, *I dream of
Jeannie with the light brown hair, born like a vapour on the soft
summer air,* or is it *borne?*

Not so much as a thank you from her. No gratitude at all.
Hannah shakes her head. When Robert Jr. retired he'd put money
into that veterans' home in Winnipeg all those years and thought it

would be a home for him to go to then, but it didn't turn out that way. There he was, all alone, away from here and miserable. Your mother didn't go to see him there, not once. How do you account for something like that?

IS THAT YOU? you say. It's me, Lily. No, no, you frown, impatient, he was here. Who? You start to sing, wave your hands in time, a waltz and you are dancing, turning and turning out of your room the size of an interval and down the hall, your feet your tuneless hum leading the way for Lily from centre to edge, until centre is edge, edge and centre one. Did he like music? Lily asks you. Oh yes . . . he was like her. You begin singing again, wisps of something Lily can't catch.

Lily is thirteen, you a widow, a relict of my father, in the dictionary, *left behind, a species surviving from an earlier period.* In your new apartment by the river. You buy a hifi from Eaton's, on their time-payment plan, combination radio and record player and records, The Weavers, Scottish folk songs, Dvorak's *New World Symphony.* Marion Anderson, the first black woman to sing at the Met, a sorceress in her Met debut, Saturday afternoon at the opera; an exile on your record, singing Largo from the New World . . . *Going home, Going home, I'm just going home* . . . You do not carry a tune very well. Lily feels something trapped when you sing.

Lily's singing lessons over, piano gone, in its place a dining-room table that folds against the wall but can be opened to seat a dozen, its leaves stored away, never used. Lily does not know the secret of this table's expansion until disposing of your things. Elizabeth Place will only let Lily bring your clothes, dresser to put them in, lamps, a wicker chair to sit in, they provide the bed, and the pictures . . . moor, river, Indian summer at West Hawk Lake. No valuables, they say, and everything must be labelled, underwear, pantyhose, eyeglasses, pencils, pens, hankies, for keeping track of laundry, theft, loss. An unfamiliar diamond engagement ring, fire opal her father gave you gone, accumulation of increasingly delicate necklaces Jan and Stephanie give you over the years, which you can no longer see to put on, lie in a tangled skein. Lily wraps them in tissue, puts them in a soft evening bag she finds in your drawer, also never seen, no idea if it comes from near or distant past. Then she doesn't know what to do with them. Puts down her head and cries.

SHE WAS LIKE HER FATHER, selfish and bad-tempered, Hannah says, measuring Lily's expression to see if she's said too much, waits for a moment. The boys all left as soon as they could get out. Robert Jr. and John had a little house in town together. They brought Rachel and your mother in to live with them, to get them away from him. The farm was foreclosed, everything auctioned off. Your grandfather boarded in town with someone else. They had to keep him away from her. Hannah pauses, he mistreated her, abused her, you know . . . a prominent drunk. . . . Too much happening inside Lily. Hannah's pause acknowledges Lily's presence, a listener. Yes, Lily says, I was at the museum and found the note.

I don't know about your mother, out there on that farm, Hannah's glare wavers momentarily. Later, after your grandfather died, Robert Jr. and John bought a little house for their mother over on the other side of the tracks. She was totally dependent on them, I mean she had nothing. I'm sorry to have to tell you this, Hannah says, but it's what happened. What I don't understand is why they all left her, except for Robert Jr. and John, after all she did for them, particularly your mother.

RUNNING FOR YOUR LIFE, why you weep for Rachel now, living in your ever-present past? They didn't get their lives, you say, speaking of your brothers. She worked so hard and never for herself, meaning the child, you, the same as never for herself, the child, her—the first time Lily has ever seen you weep and every time after this when you speak of her the river flows. January 1938 when she

dies, fifty-two years to the day she marries your father; you a
mother yourself, Lily your daughter, two years old, dirty thirties,
another war coming. Hannah says you go back to Rachel one more
time; is this after Lily is born, have Rachel and Lily laid eyes on
each other? Lily falls into the whole of your absence, the immense
and silent space of you that resists her fathoming, place where a
child curls up between garden rows, waits, checking sky above her
for signs of the coming of what is lost, unable to let it go. Can we
lose what we never had, or do we come with everything intact and
have it taken from us by degrees, or all at once, calling the
innocence wholeness, illusion, fantasy, dreaming our lives? I can see
why she left, Lily tells Hannah, offering it to her.

You bring another point of view, Hannah says, lying back
against the pillow waiting, willing for the gap to be filled, Hannah
hungry for something, what is it she needs to know? Your
mastectomy, irregular heart, rain of small strokes flinging you out
of time and space, or it is others who cannot locate you, floating
free, coming to rest wherever you are.

IT PLEASES YOU to go for ice cream warm afternoons, soft evenings.
Helen, you call Lily. You and Helen go for mail and ice cream after
school, watch baseball in the field, you indicate with your hand,
over there, you say, the words right, left, have dropped away. Helen
smart, quick, but you do better in school because you work harder
than everyone. Sick in high school, you make it up at summer
school in Winnipeg, wanting university. You tell Lily you don't
know why Helen spent time with you, because her family had
money. Maybe she liked you, wanted you to be her friend, Lily tells
you. Yes, you say, agreeable, finishing your ice cream, somewhere
else now . . . your father's death, no money, coming back from
university, your brothers tell you there's no money to go on; back
to Rachel, penniless. Your tears for Rachel for you, *she didn't get her*
life, lost melody come again. You take Lily to the garden where you
went with Rachel, in the buggy . . . she was good, the best person I

ever knew . . . she could tell a good joke, we never wanted for
anything . . . you getting out of here, leaving shame, humiliation,
leaving her, missing undersong.

Has Lily ever heard you laugh? she can't remember. When you
take her, yourself, away from those rooms on Osborne Street you
are ecstatic, an unfamiliar intensity Lily cannot share. Lily has
never seen you this way, overjoyed, a kind of betrayal. The frozen
river breaks up, floods its banks, Assiniboine and Red inundate the
city, ice-age melt, glacial sea make islands, Lily fifteen, almost
sixteen, going south on a bus, Fargo, Minneapolis, St. Louis,
Kansas City . . . Lily lost, heading south into the heart of it, muscle
pumping, fist clenching, heart's blood, Commie Reds, North
Korea, hydrogen bombs. Something broken up there booming
down the sky. Supersonic jets *two times faster than the bullet from a
colt 45* shatter windows of hot Kansas afternoons. Her uncle
thrusts up his barbecue fork, that's gonna get us to the moon, he
says. Her cousin Rosella, nineteen and just home from art school in
Kansas city, doesn't say anything.

Honey, Aunt Helen says to Lily, keep your ear to the ground,
you're at the heart of things now, right smack in the middle of
America. The next president of the United States is going to come
out of little ol' Abilene, Kansas, just down the line. Aunt Helen is a
delegate to the Convention in Chicago. Aunt Helen not Lily's aunt,
your high school friend who left for school in Minneapolis, and
ended up in Kansas married to a doctor. An American citizen now,
more southwest than her Texan husband. Lily does not know why
suddenly she has an invitation to spend the summer in Kansas. She
suspects you ask them to take her. Lily has never heard of these
people before their letter arrives with its hearty invitation. *Your
uncle Lawrence, cousin Rosella, cousin Deedee*, Helen persists.

MIDNIGHT. FULL MOON. Earlier, black geese cross a window of green sky, cutting back and forth across the moon, their many restless voices moving over waves of your breathing. Dolores gone off shift, present in her absence reminding Lily to go, not stay. Replacing her a silent phalanx of white-uniformed, soft-shoed nurses arrive and wordlessly turn on the overhead light, remove your pillows, lower your bed and turn you over, replace your pillows and leave without acknowledging Lily's presence.

RETURNING TO HANNAH, her anger a place to call home, this journey a swallow's flight as swift as your breathing taking her toward morning.

Robert Jr. and John can no longer leave you, Rachel, out there with him, alone, all the others gone. Lily angry your silence is suddenly so full, tells Hannah she cannot imagine what it must have been like for you, for Rachel. Hannah unimpressed, holds her anger as truth, her version of you, tightly to her. Did you know Rachel? Oh yes, Hannah says. Worn out. She kept to herself. Hannah's eyes sharpen. This is just gossip, I can't say it's the truth, that she followed him out here from Scotland, tracked him down, with a child. A town's censure in Hannah's voice, not of the tall good-looking Scot who grew prizewinning wheat, but Rachel, the woman.

Lily can't find a record of their marriage in Scotland. Back in
Canada she checks the archives, ships' passenger lists for 1885
arrivals to the port of Montreal, *needle in a haystack*, one of the
many archivists tells her, impassive. Already late in the day. Lily,
eyes fatigued, microfilm blurring past, knows to search for a fall
arrival, Indian summer, does not know why she knows, or even
that she does until the needle simply falls out of the haystack,
under her own name, Rachel Forrester, with her son Robert, on a
ship out from Liverpool, the *Carthaginian*.

Found out when I wrote away to Scotland for Robert Jr.'s birth
certificate so he could get his pension, Hannah says abruptly. Lily
wonders why he couldn't do this for himself, doesn't ask. I didn't
tell him, Hannah says, he never knew. Is it merciful, unmerciful,
this knowing unknowing silence? He worked for my family for,
well, all his life until he was on the pension. He was loyal, would
get up winter nights and come over to the store to be sure the
furnace was working, that we were alright. And musical. John
helped, too, did odd jobs, carpentry and the like. A hesitation in
Hannah's voice here Lily notices, a slowing, eyes still fierce. You've
seen the grandson? Lives alone out in that shack, no phone, I don't
even think there's a proper floor in there. We've tried to get him to
move into town, but he won't come.

He would have to part with his horses, Lily says. He should at
least have a phone, Hannah looks hard at Lily when she says this.
Another drinker like his grandfather, but okay when he's sober. One
of the other sons drank too, died before Rachel did, lungs damaged
by the gassing in the war. She couldn't do anything about that.
Hannah looks uncomfortable. Lily apologizes for tiring her, staying
so long. You're not, Hannah says. I don't know where I'll go after
they get through with me here. I'll have to go some place, the
hospital can't keep me on. Wherever I can get in, I guess. A Seniors'
Residence, long building hugging ground, gaudy prairie turbulence
of flowers crowding around it, zinnias, marigolds, cosmos, salvia,
snapdragons Lily recalls passing, a couple of blocks from the turn
down Main Street to the museum, following Muriel's Chrysler.

Wait lists, Hannah says, answering Lily's thought, I put it off too long, never thought I'd get to this. The eagle looks out at her, cottonwoods move in wind, crows rising, river flowing, logging trucks accelerate down the opening road, heading for a collision in Lily, too much coming together unfinished. She leaves Hannah when the nurse comes. Stops at a farm along the highway to buy flowers, daisies, tiger lilies, and something close to the colour of Hannah's eyes, returns with them to the nursing station, stands there for a moment, then rips a page out of a notebook, folds it over, writes *thank you*, tucks it into the flowers and leaves them with a nurse.

Cemetery left, between Lily and the river. Under sheltering elms, across from railway tracks some overgrown bushes, very green, hide the remains of Rachel's little white clapboard house they built for her in town. Lily mistakes it for someone's tool shed. She lingers here. Deep green relief, tree canopy, tall, stately, unexpected, opening out onto sweet hot golden fields and purple that sweep Lily's sight, her, beyond what she accepts as knowing, the surprise of you, Rachel, feeling you both here, all of you breathing, the rhythm of you under her skin, that you cannot escape each other. Rachel, they are trying to disappear your daughter, write her out of her story, and yours, calling it psychosis. A fall from, or into grace . . . did you tell her to go, leave here and never come back? Rachel, is that what you tell your daughter?

MURIEL PATS FOUR ROUND BLOBS of dough with oil, slides them on to a baking sheet. Hannah never married, Robert Jr. never married, or John. Lily thinks, Robert going over in the middle of winter nights to be sure the furnace hasn't gone out, making sure Hannah and her family are alright. Hannah twenty, Robert forty. Another story? I have another stove in the basement, cooler down there, Muriel tells Lily, heading down the stairs. When they've risen, just put these in to bake and leave them on top to cool when they're done and they'll be all set to go with you tomorrow. You should try to see Hazel White over at the seniors' home before you go. She's about the same age as Hannah. Lily unwilling to follow Muriel down into root-cellar smells, shadows, to collapse into them. I did, she says, hovering near the bottom of the stairs. Hazel doesn't remember you. Men had their way, women had too many babies, too little sleep, and no help, Hazel sums it all up, darting about her room full of sheet music, knitting, an easel; many paintings stacked behind her furniture, a painting in progress on the easel of the flowers outside her window rioting against the wall.

Muriel muses . . . it must have been serious for charges to be laid, back then, 1901 . . . it doesn't say who laid them against your grandfather? I'll have to go to the archives again, Lily says, edging back up the stairs, wanting out of the cellar. Perhaps there are court records, perhaps it doesn't matter . . . it happened. Lily feels she knows everything and nothing of what you carry inside you. Is that where you're headed, back to Winnipeg? Muriel's voice rising up from behind as they climb the stairs. North first, Lily says, where I was born. Eating herself, feeding on silence, will she dissolve, drowning in her own fluids learning to swim this sea? She took me from there to Winnipeg when I was small. How old? Five, Lily thinks. April train, the war, leaving him behind, April when you marry. What is it you run to, or from? Is it Rachel, calling you away? Do you want to come to the bonfire tonight? Muriel asks, you're welcome to . . . it will be quite late. No . . . thanks, I'll be leaving early tomorrow. Trying to thank Muriel for her help, meaning it, in spite of the first night. Muriel feeling guilty too? attempting to restore Lily's good opinion of her hospitality, maybe in spite of Lily's irritability, but Lily feels something more. Fumbles with this communality, extended family, its weight, weight-bearing as sun draws down, her bags packed, Lily's last evening here. Deer have come and gone. Lily on Muriel's verandah goes with them, between river and willows their glowing shapes walk delicately on water, curl into their bent-grass hollows hidden under aspens shivering in a breath of dusk and the passing of a fox whose yellow eyes fade into an evening train's long slow wail; click clack along the track, tracking north. A restless urge to move on. Lily plugs in her earphones, Bach's *Brandenburg Concertos*, Nina Simone, Billie Holliday, Ella. . . .

WARM JULY NIGHTS, DRIVES FOR ICE CREAM, up to Jericho Hill, lugged freighters at bay, heron lifting, rising breath beat from water to lavender sky into present past, breaking silence, two children, you and Lily in the garden . . . *Tell me what you see* does not take Lily here, this backroad, Muriel no longer leading the way, Lily's Sunbird on its own, heading north now, to where you give her birth, your child, Lily, her childhood. This the part where you lose her, your marriage, husband.

Lily and you sit on the bed at Elizabeth Place. She tells you a story about who you married, when, where, about a daughter who doesn't know why you named her Lily. You begin to weep. I don't know, you say, your forehead wrinkling, perplexed. Lily must go to Vital Statistics to find out when, where you marry him, her father. Why doesn't Lily know? Why was it never spoken about, why is it your everpresent past stops here, stops when you leave Rachel? Or does Lily wait too long to ask? A Xeroxed copy of your marriage certificate tells Lily you marry as the Great Depression takes hold, school principal and teacher, both your fathers deceased, that the wedding takes place in Winnipeg, near where Lily goes dark winter evenings to practise piano, take her singing lessons.

Grass up to the horses' bellies when Rachel came, Lily's Sunbird kicking up gravel between ditches of wildflowers hood-high on either side, white yellow pink lavender, relic grasses disappearing into yellow, blue of ripening flax, canola, wheat, sky; native seed lying in the soil for years germinating in old gardens, graveyards, ditches . . .

sleek Greyhound taking her south inside a circling door of memory, bus window open to the night, slipstream taking her into the wild sweet clover, water-cool smell of it, descent of the swing, where summer screen doors squeak open, bang shut, over there, where they sell bait, rent rowboats. An oar scrapes, boat gliding over the open throat of waterlilies, light minnows pale freckled skin, your hand, bends it under water like a broken wing, angles down, turning stones to glowing flesh, you, the child lying on the dock beside you.

Under the bridge mute, mud-eyed catfish stare up, whiskers radar wands probing the space above, gridded sky. Ashes and smoke in the morning, cold iron stove, frost in the cracks at the backs of cupboards, shapes ice-cold burning hot, of no substance rock dense stone weight, dragonflies and beams of light colliding in electric blue streaks, comet tails, synapses, this hollow stone of silence where all sound comes from, resonating her, a drum, this sighing throb from deep inside, looking down the river, staring it down.

Lily standing on the roof of the Seven Sisters power plant, water so far below, boiling soapsuds, dammed, damming. Lace curtains moving at the window and bird sibilance from honeysuckle by the wall do not drown the hot noon headache, disappointment a roar of turbines is all there is to a place called *Seven Sisters.*

Is this where you live? she asks her father, wondering why he has brought her here. No, he says, his car shrouded in dust the link between this place and that. Rusted signs, Kikola, Sunkist Orange necklace singing knee-high weeds, his voice not on the road when he tells her *Camp Shilo*, the army camp. This where her father comes from? *They went every year to offer sacrifices to the Lord in Shiloh . . .* her Sunday School teacher, Mrs. Carmicheal, reads from the Bible. Today, she says, we don't sacrifice like they did in Old

Testament times, not since Jesus came and paid the price. Now we follow Him. She smiles, a beautiful lady with soft peachy skin and fair hair all rolled up in combs. She wears dresses only in shades of delicate grey or blue with a single strand of pearls and no children. Lily doesn't ask about the army camp, the price or where Jesus is going. Mrs. Carmicheal takes them out for ice cream.

Midnight in Winnipeg when the bus pulls out, heading south, neither you nor Lily looking at each other as Lily's friends and friends of theirs wave her off. Nor does she look at Gary, knowing his smiling grey eyes search for hers. She is sixteen, he, twenty-two, almost finished university. I'll take care of him while you're gone, someone tells her as the bus doors close. One delicate, sweet kiss still remembered, seemed a beginning, was an ending; his letter to her unanswered, she doesn't know why, nor why on her return and he does not seek her out there is pain of loss in her as though the world has closed its doors—nor when he marries quickly, leaves for Pittsburgh in the spring, she is relieved. And when, of Lily, he says, she put me back on the rails, she wonders if he means this is what she's good at. Still wonders. Do you and Lily share a disposition to mistake friends for enemies and those who are not for friends, or does Lily simply fear she may be like you?

Two a.m. in the Fargo bus station when she waits on a bench while they clean the bus, chill prairie night wind moving in through a broken depot door someone keeps trying to close, Johnny Ray wails his crying song from the juke box, imploring her to cry like a baby because someone, a lover, said goodbye. Who cries like that? would she want to? Lily doesn't know. Where would she start?

Behind her father's car crows, stumpy trees, water hurtling down flat worn rock disappear in dust. Dirt field beyond the gas pumps where Lily and her father watch Indians dance. Why are they crying? Singing, her father says. Canada's birthday, July the first, he reminds her. Dust, sweat, hot sun pouring down, one of them swings out, leans over a small dry bush. I want to do that, Lily tells her father, presses the cold bottle of Orange Crush against her forehead. Dance? her father says, his smile a little wan. Lily shakes her head, doesn't like to say *puke*. He is angry when she is sick in his car.

A small book full of his spidery pencilled words in your drawer, withheld somewhere Lily is not supposed to go. Something in her cries out at this faint evidence of his existence, disappeared into a drawer, then gone. You mention him once, when her grades are failing and she is skipping school, stealing money to go downtown to the Rio and Rialto movie houses on Notre Dame and Portage Avenue, or buying cigarettes; drinking your rye and gin comes later. Your father would be very disappointed, you say. It works. Lily from then on is at the top of her class, good. Good girls don't cry, she believes she hears her father's voice tell her.

Buses shine in the high noon heat of Minneapolis, buses going east, west, north, this one going south Lily stays on, watches the bleached still-life out on the platforms, eyelids half-drawn, suitcases at their feet. Soldiers, smooth-skinned, neat cotton chinos, matching shirts and duffle bags pile onto the bus like a basketball team fresh out of the showers. On the bus everyone can talk now, are family . . . the war . . . where you been? where you headed? where's home? Lily's never heard of Pusson, Inchon, the Yalu river . . . *Ike's gonna give 'em hell, like Harry did with Little Boy and The Fat Man* . . . little boy and the fat man? What does this mean?

The bald, grandfatherly man with a sunflower smile lifts an oversize summer fedora to the crowds waiting on the platform below the train taking him on through Kansas, Iowa, Illinois, on to Chicago, to beyond the Yalu river . . . *we like Ike, we like Ike, we like Ike*, they chant; he smiles, they chant, bombs falling one thousand yards away from the soil of Manchuria. Ike, World War 2 hero, will bring the boys back home from Korea. Daily papers full of guided missile ads: *ramparts of peace, engineering that aims at maximum power to the Nth degree . . . EVA PERON DIES; FABULOUS LIFE IS ENDED AT 30 . . . Argentine Vice-Presidency within her grasp: did cancer intervene?* Sunday's New York papers run the headlines. Who

is Eva Peron, Lily wonders, reading down the newspaper columns .
. . *her face once photogenic now shrunken . . . youngest of five
illegitimate children . . . well-endowed figure . . . artificially honey-
coloured hair . . . a favourite with various members of the military* . . .
does not tell Lily that Petra's mother Elena, now ten, in Buenos
Aires, will remember Eva, the President's dying wife, larger than a
woman's life is supposed to be admonishing the workers and
peasants to *want, you must learn to desire.* The army didn't like it, or
the families who owned Argentina. Eva it seems does not forget
where she comes from, nor is she allowed to.

You must learn to want, Eva tells Argentina's industrial workers,
the unions, the women, children, homeless poor, sick and
unemployed crowding the city. *You must learn to desire,* this the life
force, their birthright and hers. Her desire, it seems, to fill them
with her own. *My two daughters, love and hate,* childless Eva tells
them. The body of a union leader found in a ditch after a strike by
workers from the cane fields is whose betrayal? Does even Eva
know? Collapsing into her mission, making her place in history,
not one of those millions who are born and die, she will be
returned from death as *Evita the Revolutionary* when Montonera
guerillas waging a war of national liberation make her their patron
saint, of *love and hate,* of the *birthright of desire.* They gather an
unlikely family of followers. Disaffected sons and daughters from
all classes fall into a war in which all, anyone, their words, music,
dance will become vulnerable to death squads sent out from the
military junta's Ministry of Social Services in the Plaza de Mayo,
when senior police and military become warlords hiring assassins
for their own protection, and Petra's mother Elena has become a
medical student and pregnant.

Not sure if the father is alive or dead, not certain who the father
is, from among youthful faces appearing in dreams that waken her
with sharp bursts of automatic gunfire, collapsing her heart onto
this other heart in her. She does not abort her fetus, but gives the
infant girl she births to a French couple, older, childless, who will
take her daughter away from here, to Paris, light, life. They are

willing to let the child have her mother's picture and the name her
mother gives her, Petra; make no attempt to change it.

AT SUPPER THE PROS AND CONS of dropping the hydrogen bomb
are discussed by Helen and Lawrence, as she calls him, introduced
to Lily as *your Uncle Lawrence*, and Deedee, their eldest daughter,
and sometimes Rose, Lawrence's sister. Who decides whether to
drop the H-Bomb? America, Lawrence says. Is America the
grandfather with the sunflower smile and the big hat? Lily
wonders. Rosella, at nineteen, younger than Deedee by four years,
does not contribute anything to these conversations, or leaves the
table.

Rosella and Lily drive these flint hills now lost in grass, corn as
high as a house, this old sea bottom littered with bleached rocks
glaciers leave behind. Heat hammers their heads, even under the
oak trees along the shallow river cut. Lily watches for
cottonmouths along the river's banks, dust devils skip-topping into
whirling twisters spiralling her into Oz and the black widow spider,
dangerous female with the red hourglass on her belly. In the
moonlight Rosella's eyes have a peeled look. She sings softly, slowly
out into the heat, voice like the plucked slack strings of her
ukulele, what's that, Lily always asks, the words, threaded, frayed,
Rosella's voice moving them along Lily's spine . . . *Bessie, Billie,
Lena, oh Ella, what you have to put down to be so up* . . . the Blues,
what else? Rosella says.

The nude hanging on Rosella's wall sits with her tidy delicate
back to Lily, fragile paper-thin connection between them. Rosella
doesn't answer Lily's gauche question, is it a self-portrait? soft
glow of her cigarette, nude and shadows, coloured lights, jazz
dancing on the patio. Rosella becomes precise steel uncoiling,
coiling to *Slaughter on 10th*. Shadows embrace in puddles of
yellow light, cross the puddles toward Lily, Rosella between,
lowers her voice, *just a kid*, Lily hears her say, and the men leave
her alone.

Helen goes to Chicago to elect Ike. Lily and the family heat frozen dinners, eat them and watch for her on television. Rose comes to take care of her brother Lawrence while Helen is away. Lily wonders why he needs to be taken care of, because he is a doctor, too busy taking care of other people? Rose a willow whose branches sway out and around her brother, smoothing, absorbing, veiling. Only Rose calls him Larry. Deedee and Rosella not like Helen, Deedee big-boned and dark, like her father. Rosella is Rosella. What can you do? Lily goes blank at the first thing Lawrence has said directly to her since she's been here. That Helen's absence leaves long tracts of silence more apparent today, when Rose makes a late dinner for everyone to eat around the table. Lily feels the willowy Rose sway and flutter in the currents between them all every time her brother speaks. Can you ride? he says, again to Lily. She looks to Rosella. Horses, Rosella drawls. Take her tomorrow, he says to Deedee, ignoring Lily. Rosella's eyes question hers, is that what you want to do? Lily feels mocked. Deedee doesn't look her way.

Okay? Deedee shouts above the jeep's noise, rush of wind past Lily's ears, Lily's teeth clenched. She nods. Deedee takes this to mean go faster through the tall green forest of cornstalk tassels swinging against the sky, hurtle up, down, around sandy backroads between dunes covered in scrubby brush, already a sage blur. Lily tries not to grip at the seat with her hands but then she has to. Deedee doesn't say anything, presses her foot on the accelerator.

The palomino's name, Lightning. Deedee tells her to rein him in, call him by name and let him know Lily is sure of herself. Wrapped around his spine, belly, how does she lie to a horse? She wants to touch his neck, stroke the flow of his mane; will this confuse the issue of who is in control? Already moving to a rhythm not hers, flex, reflex, heart pumping, rib cage moving beneath her thighs, her eyes on his head and the reins lying against the grain of that flowing. Go with him, Deedee says from somewhere behind. Hill rims sky, horse and Lily already there, too quick for fear,

heading she doesn't know where, until Deedee's hand grabs the
reins, leads them back down, her voice tight—keep him on the
road. Lily smiles inside herself, reaches her hand out to touch the
horse's neck.

Deedee gets hell from the family for putting Lily on the
palomino. Summer hurtling through her mind, things collide, blur.
Helen returns from the convention, disappears without perceptible
flinch into someone in a frilly apron, fussing, flattering stroking,
scurrying along her route between built-in fridge-freezer, oven,
table, trash compactor, laundry room. Rosella, Deedee come, go;
here, not here. Helen chops, dices, in gadgets Lily has never seen
before, flick of switches mobilizes the doctor's dinner, the leavings
puréed down the sink with the flip of another. Gawd, what did we
do before garburators, Helen snorts. Time you were heading home,
honey, your momma'll be fretting about you. Lily doesn't know if
this means she's overstayed. No one said how long she was
supposed to be here. For the summer, you tell her. Your idea, she's
sure, the widow parcelling out her needy child to strangers. You
may never get this chance again, you tell Lily. Helen pats her on
the arm. But what about Bea? That's what I want to talk to you
about, Helen tells her, looking away, have you told your momma
yet? No. Well, don't. It's best you go home. Her voice leaves no
doubt about it. It has nothing to do with you, hon . . . it's just Bea
is a little unstable right now. She gets too involved, you get my
meaning? She doesn't, is wondering what she'll tell Bea, since she's
already said she'll go. Helen says she'll tell Bea. Lily says no, she
wants to tell her herself. Helen frowns. Well, I'll come with you
then, hon.

BEA AND ROSE COME for dinner while Lawrence is away. If Daddy
was here, he wouldn't let Momma have her in the house, Deedee
says, meaning Bea. Shut up, Rosella's voice, sharp, like Lily has
never heard. A Texan woman, which is not what bugs Daddy about
her, Deedee says. Says she left her old man because he beat her up

and went to the police and they said what did she do to make him so mad? Daddy says she shouldn't have left and it's unnatural for her and Rose to live in the same house and Bea's daughter to grow up without a father. Bea's ample breasts rest against the table's edge as she leans towards Lily and describes the journey she and Rose will take through the Colorado mountains to Oklahoma, New Mexico, all the way to the Texas Gulf salt marshes, to pick up her daughter, who is with her grandparents. Bea smiles a lot. Lily notices her teeth, very even and white against olive skin, her hair, black, spreads back from her face like wings folded against her head. Rose's hands flutter around the straws in her iced tea. Wait 'til you smell those salt marshes, mm-mm, Bea says, looking at Lily with eyes that say, quick, jump in, all things are possible. Lily looks uncertainly from Bea to Rose. Bea ... Rose is saying softly, maybe her momma wants her home ... Lily watches Rose's hands crimp the straws between her fingers. Well? Bea looks at Lily, are you ready for an adventure? You mean it? Why not? she laughs, oh, we'll all have a great time together.

ROSE AND BEA live in a different part of town, their house small, darkened by furniture aged with varnish and tacky with humidity. Bea laughs her powerful laugh, rich, warm, scary, brings down from the attic the cardboard suitcase she has found for Lily. Sits down hard when Lily lies to her that you say no to a trip you know nothing about. Helen says this way it won't hurt Bea the way the truth will. Is it the money? Bea says quickly, it doesn't have to cost you anything—oh, I bet she's worried about her baby going all that way with strangers, I should have talked to her. Bea ... Rose says protectively, weeping river willows, silent currents sighing through Lily.

Let her be, you're right, her momma doesn't want her going all that way, Helen says and Lily sees something move in Bea's eyes, a smile that is not hers attach itself to her face. Lily queasy when they leave in Helen's station wagon and Bea reaches in the open

window, takes Lily's hand, runs along beside the car. In the
fierceness of Bea's goodbye Lily feels something left behind, relief
when Bea finally lets go her hand. Bea's face receding, Lily on the
Trans-Canada highway, west out of Winnipeg, Ruby there on the
steps of a rundown garage and convenience store and Lily doesn't
see what she sees. Why this return of Ruby from disappearance?

Lily can't remember when she first started not speaking to, not
seeing Ruby, grade nine, ten, when appearance suddenly becomes
critical, life threatening, and Ruby heavy like her mother, who
smokes, drinks coffee and reads the papers in her housecoat, the
spaniel reeking of old age asleep under her feet. Their house dark
cool in summer, hanging on between a taxi company and a White
Rose Gas station, big trees and rank caragana hedges separating
them on either side. Ruby's father home from the war, thin,
chain-smoking, restless. Their boarding house is where Lily hears
important news like President Roosevelt dying, atom bombs
being dropped on Hiroshima, Nagasaki—did not know it was
Little Boy and the Fat Man, and VJ day when World War II is
finally over.

You angry when you know Lily goes there, because they take in
boarders? Lily wonders then. At what point does she know they are
Jewish? Does this matter to you? Lily never knows. In the drift to
unfamiliarity, she does not remember when their house disappears,
along with the taxi company and the White Rose Gas station, into
a supermarket and parking lot that seems to have always been
there, remembers now hearing they move to the city's fringes to
run a garage and store, as she gets on her bicycle to ride away as
though she doesn't know it's Ruby, doesn't see her there, or the look
on Ruby's face that could be about anything, all sorts of things that
have nothing to do with Lily, or even that she imagines it, Ruby
going swimming at the YWCA pool. Lily doesn't have any money,
can't swim, has to wait for Ruby by the front desk and the Coke
machine. Lily has never seen a Coke machine before. She is
holding Ruby's money for her until after swimming, for a Coke
Ruby will get from the machine and says she could share with Lily.

It is very hot and Lily is afraid Ruby has left already, or will never come, or perhaps did not mean what she said about sharing. Lily so hot and thirsty she must put the money in the machine, hold the cold wet bottle curving her hands, press her forehead to it, her cheek, stare into it. She means to leave most, some, a little; betrayal by degrees, Lily feels it, nameless then in Ruby's look of wounded disbelief, the empty Coke bottle, Ruby sitting on the steps of a convenience store waiting to pump gas for the next car in off the Trans-Canada heading west, east, frowning down into the dirt when Lily doesn't stop, telling herself it may not even be Ruby. Not wanting to see what Ruby sees.

HER UNCLE THRUSTS HIS FORK into steak, lifts it off the barbecue, charred on the outside, bleeding in the middle. Lily says it's just fine. He laughs. Smiles at her. Looks pleased.

Rosella leaves tomorrow on a bus for the Texas Gulf for a holiday before going back to art school in Kansas City and an hour later Lily leaves on another bus heading back north. Tonight, Lawrence is taking them all to a movie, the Greatest Show on Earth.

Lucky you, Rosella says to Lily, don't think I'll make it. Rosella and her father stare at each other. Helen bounces up between them, a warning look at Rosella. Let's go, she says, there'll be a line-up, I don't know when we last got your uncle to a show, hon, you should feel honoured, she says to Lily. I'll just clear away these dishes.

Lily can't find space that belongs to her. She must give an accounting of why she is here. She doesn't know why. She must explain that too. She doesn't like to be seen. Lawrence wants to know what she thinks of the movie. He bought the tickets. Fine, is what she says, fine seems appropriate for the moment, but the moment caves in. A circus movie, the dangerous high-flyer, woman aerialist coming between brothers, circus blood; sequined clown hanging by her teeth, slow-turning strobe. Lily watches her pull herself back up by her own body onto the bar again; swung now by a man, wider and wider, beyond the limits of the safety net, she will have to let go in mid-air, reach for the next man's hands, tossed between them. Lily knows it's camera work, scans the high-flyer, Amelia E. tipping her wings, heading for the sun, red hourglass on her belly, into empty full, silent sound. More becomes less when she tells him she thought it was fine. Thought you would, Lawrence says.

ROSELLA'S BUS PULLS AWAY. She does not look at Lily or wave goodbye. Don't mind her, hon, Helen tells Lily, she does that when she gets upset. We've still got to wait for your bus so let's go get us a milkshake or something. She takes Lily's arm, leads her to the lunch counter. Ten a.m. by the big electric clock on the wall. They both have iced tea the colour of pond water in glasses that sweat. Lily feels a weight of heat pressing down on her, the effort of moving through it, heading north.

A woman in a gold flowered dress and white high-heeled sandals strapped to neat ankles sits down from them, sipping Coke and drawing long on a cigarette, blowing smoke out her nose and thumbing a *Life* magazine with a picture of Ike on the cover. Beyond her a *Whites Only* sign on the door to the public toilet. Lily has seen these signs around, asks Helen now why the sign is there. Helen says, hon, if you sit on these stools with your legs together it's more ladylike, tapping Lily's bare knees. She glances down, surprised, her shorts wrinkled already and riding up. Didn't your momma ever tell you not to spread your legs like that? Helen sighs, your momma and I aren't really sisters, you knew that, didn't you? It was just something we kept up, her having all those brothers and all ... she looks at Lily in the mirror behind the counter, stops, waits ... well, hon, didn't she tell you anything? A nervous laugh, dubious look on Helen's face Lily carries with her.

They didn't have a lot of money, your momma's family. She's a very proud lady . . . maybe it was having all those brothers, but compete, she'd compete about everything, being the youngest, the only girl, I guess, I don't know. Helen's southwestern drawl disappears, her voice trails off, uncertain. I never met your daddy, she says, suddenly returning, familiar Helen. He was a lot older than your momma, played the saxophone in one of those jazz bands, if you can imagine it, somewhere up on that godamn prairie edge of nowhere . . . that's really all I know, hon . . . I was real sorry when she wrote and said he'd died, first time I'd heard from her since I left for Minneapolis, don't know how she got my address. Lily leaves the iced tea. Depression, hard times, you know. No, you wouldn't. Your daddy and momma taught school up there. I met your uncle in Minneapolis, he'd just finished medical school . . . well, shit, Helen snorts, air exploding up from her belly and out her nose, studies herself in the mirror. You ready to go, hon? She pats Lily when her bus comes. Come back anytime, hon, Lily hears her say at her back. An apology? for what?

Soldiers sit clustered around the woman in the gold flowered dress, one telling her his life story. The bus swings around behind the depot, past wild sweet peas and delphinium in morning glory vines tumbling through the weeds, out onto the highway east to St. Louis, north through Minneapolis, back the way she came.

It doesn't look the same. Shadow of the man standing alone among other still and moving shadows threading his cool blue jazz, footprints circling music, *Someone to Watch Over Me*, Lily singing her heart out, wakes up. Back of the bus smells of gasoline, remnants of conversations she can't quite catch, transparent wings of the electric blue dragonfly beating inside her head. Swift silent flight darting across the lake. Moonlight plays with her fingers, drifting where he takes her hand, says he doesn't know what's out there, milky way silently winding, unwinding her. Cars roar past, tearing open silence, headlights pulling at curves, rushing on until it is too late to fathom if it is for her he says this.

The St. Louis depot sweats. Glassed in, hypnotic ceiling fans turn with heavy movement, sluggish, something muffled. Black woman ahead on the escalator, shopping bag hanging from one arm, holding a small boy's hand with the other, fans herself in a drift of motion the child extends too far, pulling the woman forward, knees riding the drift into metal teeth. Everything moves, feels underwater until the woman is on her feet, bent over moaning softly at her torn stocking, cut knee, small boy, grandson perhaps, clutching her by the leg and holding himself to keep from peeing. Lily asks if there is anything she can do.

You could wet this for me, the woman says, holds out a clean pressed man's handkerchief she takes from her purse. Sure. Lily embarrassed by the *Whites Only* signs. They both look away. She brings the hanky, cold, wet and wrung, hesitates in front of the woman now sitting on a bench, grandson huddled up beside her where he can't see her knees. The woman takes the cloth from her quickly and dabs at her knee without speaking. Lily hovers. It'll be fine, the woman says. A bandage? she says it tentatively, the woman already shaking her head, boy curled up at her side staring into the hip spreading like sky over him, her face, neither friendly nor unfriendly, withdraws.

The woman in the gold flowered dress watching this says to Lily, not from around here I guess? When Lily tells her, no, she says, thought so, something cleared up for her. You meant to be kind, but you oughtn't to let them do that. Take advantage of you, make you feel bad, she says, when Lily doesn't respond. You got relatives coming for you? Lily shakes her head, doesn't bother to tell her she's heading north. Well, you take care honey, the woman says, be careful girl, don't go talking to strangers, if you get my meaning. Following the Mississippi north, to the Red, long look of the river in your wary eyes. A heart dividing, what sound does it make, what return?

RETURNING TO BIRTHPLACE a disappearing act of homecoming in this sea engulfing her, the Sunbird; criss-crossing roads and missing gestures of inhabitation; heart, hand, her hand, on the steering wheel, turning, turning away. What is it you don't want to see, Lily to see? Story lying deep in the gut, hidden in the muscle contracting on itself, something deeper still pitting itself against gravity, moving through gaps, up her spine, brushing her shoulder, atlas bone; an aftersense, loss and finding come together; goodbye, hello; yours, Lily's? An urgency to get on a plane back to you.

PSYCHIATRIST #3 INFORMS LILY your brain no longer exists, *destroyed* the word he uses. Otherwise you are fine, he reassures. Clean-looking, elegant and boyish. She estimates his age to be around thirty; not innocent, already an angel of destruction.

Lily's eyes have already told you the story, where she's been, what she knows; your eyes waiting too long swim out of silence into hers. This unfamiliar familiarity, Lily holding you some kind of homecoming. It was so hard for her . . . I was afraid of him, to go anywhere with him, your voice struggling at Lily's ear, struggling to get past the rigid jaw their drugs have given you, and the drooling, the inability to sit up on your own or walk, strapped into a wheelchair. You brush at your mouth with a clenched hand. Lily tucks Kleenex into it when it comes to rest a curled fist in your lap. What have they done to you? Why did she leave you, let them do this? You have slipped like water through Lily's hands, the way her father did, disappearing into a memory of water, shape of trees, line of light, folded edge; nothing, it seems, can be touched, let alone held, not even herself.

Nurses behind their desk hold a muted conversation with the psychiatrist when Lily asks for the names and dosages of the drugs they have given you. The doctor's smile fixed.

We had to change your mother's medications several times to find something, some combination that will eliminate her aggression. Whose, Lily wants to say, stares at the doctor's smile. With brain degeneration, the process of dementia your mother is undergoing, there can be hallucinations, paranoia and psychotic behaviour.

Can be? What actual aggression are you talking about?

I would have to check her charts, you could talk to the nurses.

I just have. The psychiatrist eyes Lily's pen poised over a notebook.

We have her on four medications, an anti-psychotic, anti-anxiety, chloral hydrate to sleep and digoxin of course to control the rhythm of her heart. And oh, yes, Dr. Franklin adds, your mother had a slight heart attack last night, we've cut back the anti-psychotic dose slightly and she will be wearing a nitroglycerin patch from now on.

She's ninety, that's too many drugs.

No, no, Dr. Franklin says quickly, as though speaking kindly to a child who is about to have a tantrum, who has got it all wrong. He reminds Lily you are an involuntary admission.

Excuse me?

It means that we are able to do whatever is necessary to control your mother without any legal action against us. We start by seeing how much she can tolerate to make her compliant.

Compliant with what?

Medications for one. She's uncooperative.

Not surprising. Is this what you mean by aggression . . . non-compliance? The doctor checks his watch, tells Lily you could provoke someone stronger than you to hit back.

We could be sued. They could be sued.

By whom?

The family.

I'm the family. Has it occurred to you that my mother may simply not be able to say what she feels, thinks, and nobody hears what she's trying to tell us? Don't you think that could be very frustrating? Dr. Franklin shaking his head as Lily says it.

I'm required to do this.

Based on an *if?* Lily says. He looks at her, says, if you want to put it that way, turning, turning on his heel. Smile gone. Lily wondering if this intense coldness is the beginning or the end of rage.

SURFING CHANNELS, unable to stay with any wave, breaking before it does, whatever carries her. Now watching the smileless man with a broken face and slow small flat words overcome with the impossibility of answers, reciting for the camera a story of a woman. This is her dog, he says, and the house she is forced to leave behind. Dog at the end of its rope, needle on a seismograph, running back and forth in mud in front of shell-shocked remains of a house now occupied by invaders driven there from their homes somewhere else. Not a photo, dog barking at an invading television camera, invader holding the camera.

Lily surfs, returns to the man now showing some of the many photos he has salvaged or taken himself, families, villages, houses, gardens, children, animals, to give to people like this woman, documents of her, their past, he says. It is all there is left for him to do, he says, voice frayed. Is he Serb, Croat, Muslim, what is the woman to him? he is asked. Does any of this matter, the man asks in return, says it never mattered.

Then who is responsible? What does the past tell? Whose story? The woman is never seen, this man with the broken face speaks for her, of houses, gardens, family, traditions, land. He does not mention the loss of herself, her body, the death of her by violation, body taken from her. The war crime that is never mentioned will be her shame, belongs to her, her wordless humiliation, she who will be punished if she appears before a television camera to speak of it. Rachel moves in Lily, Rachel, a town's shame, she who is punished, sin eater. And her daughter, silenced.

THE DOG STANDS looking out at Lily, not from among the trees as she used to, waiting to take Lily through to tide flats, a run on the estuary beneath Trans Oceanic's power lines, looking at her now from an openmouthed back end of a moving van, empty boxes waiting. Giving Lily one last long look she turns, steps into an empty waiting carton, van door sliding shut. Lily wants to cry out *no wait*, a cry separating skin from bone, how can it make no sound?

Mom? you okay? Yes, fine, Lily says, struggling up out of sleep. Where are you? she asks blindly, to locate herself, following Jan's voice. Back in town for now, I got a lung infection out on the site. I may get back in for a late planting, depends on the weather. So how was Scotland? Oh, by the way, I met someone up here who asked me to say hello to you . . . since when did you get involved in the river coalition? I didn't, haven't . . . who was it . . . what makes you think I wouldn't get involved? Lily still feeling her way around the dream, for a way out of it. Margot Ryan, she's a lawyer. Enthusiasm in her daughter's voice.

Oh. Yes I've met her. Lily surprised by an edge in hers. Jan silent, waits for more. We met just before I put the house up for sale, how did you come across her? I'm stuck in town here so I'm doing some work for the coalition . . . how's Gran? I took her for a picnic yesterday, Lily says, wanting more about Jan. Jan and Stephanie riding the fear away from the weight of us, you, Lily, Rachel. She has your face, Rachel, I mean the strength, the moving forward out of the picture.

Lily needs to get you, herself out of here, away from these drugged absent forms of abandoned bodies shuffling down halls until they reach wall, turn, shuffle back. And these anonymous psychiatrists who sit with their backs to them, in their bunker behind the nurses' desk, writing notes to themselves in their charts . . . *schizoid* . . . *paranoid* . . . which of course you will be if you are being injected with mind-disabling drugs, a normal reaction. Nurses at the desk look away when she tells them she wants to take you out for a picnic lunch. It requires Dr. Franklin's permission, which he eventually and reluctantly grants, his favour. As Lily and he gaze at each other over the abyss of you—in Lily's mind he has become the Red Queen shouting *off with her head*, or sometimes the Mad Hatter—the Queen steps back, Lily plunges forward, following a missing heartbeat, a fox's yellow eyes through the trees into the long slow wail of a train moving through too long a space, lost, or found.

Potato salad with hot dry mustard, devilled eggs with finely chopped fresh parsley, lots of green onion, fresh local tomato and roast beef sliced thin in sandwiches, ice cream, lemon pound cake, strawberries, strong tea. Your favourites. Lily collects them all, lays them out between Lost Lagoon and the ocean, sun-dappled under water-seeking willows swaying over you, moving stream finding its way from lagoon to ocean, speaking into the air around you.

What's that? Water, Lily suggests. You do not look convinced and Lily wonders what it is, who, you do hear. Lily rushing from car to you, bringing a small table, another folding chair, afraid you will think she's gone and left you there and not know where that is. Lily thinking like Lily, who requires location, this rushing anxiety, weight of you, believing the impossible possible. Breathless, table and chair in hand, Lily returns to find the geese have stopped their cropping, lie half circling you, your smile, for whom or at what Lily will never know.

Eating goes slowly. You throw roast beef, bread to the crows who join you. The geese sleep. You prefer cake, ice cream, tea. Lily doesn't know, now, how she thought you would eat all this. Your throat seems to have forgotten how to swallow since they began to drug you. Waiting for it to remember, ocean's breath stirring willows above, cedars beyond, you look around uneasily. The trees, moving in the wind, Lily tells you, seeing your look. Maybe we should go now, you tell her, shy fear, afraid to show itself in your eyes, in Lily's gut. You bare your teeth at her, scream when Lily tries to help you from the car. This pain, it must be bad, she's not a complainer, says the nurse with friendly eyes who tells Lily she grew up near where you did.

Maybe you need to get out of there for a while, Jan telling her, get your life back . . . have you heard from Steph? Lily wants to tell Jan, daughter of a daughter, that staying with you on this edge is *it*, getting her life back, or getting it, for the first time, this psychiatric miasma, both edge and centre, resist point, friction where it happens, the silencing . . . speak nothing, remember nothing, do nothing, freefall off the edge into the gap between sleeping and waking, seeing it as in watching the dream, how real is that? But Lily can say nothing about this to Jan. There was a letter from her when I got home, what Lily says. It must have come while I was in Scotland. She's talking about going to Guatemala next, with a woman she's met. Guatemala worries me.

Guide books Lily takes from the library describe colourful people and ancient traditions, spectacular scenery—a chain of volcanoes to the south that begins near Guatemala City and stretches northwest to Mexico, and mountain ranges to the north high above the rest of the country, where most highland villages are accessible only by foot or horseback, some easier to reach than others and well worth the effort, the guides suggest. They advise that the *more quaint and picturesque villages* are found along roads that end in mountains, requiring a lot of doubling back, that the best time to visit any highland village is on its market day when families come in from the surrounding areas, or at the time of the town's annual festival, usually several days of religious and carnival celebrations, music, traditional dancing in costumes that depict animals, gods and conquistadors.

One guide book suggests the wise traveller will apply common sense and be aware of the local political and security situations in any of the highland areas as well as any current army manoeuvres. *More disappeared than in all of Argentina's "dirty war"* does not appear even in small print, an absent footnote.

EARTH ONCE DISTURBED never lies the same way again. Petra doesn't remember when she first hears this, knowing it the way a child knows it, not knowing she knows until she hears it said in Argentina on the hunt for the *desaparecidos*.

The largest mass grave is within the city of Buenos Aires, surrounded by a brightly coloured wall, encircled by abandoned factories, apartment buildings whose oocupants would watch headlights sweep the curtains of their windows and wait for the shots, so they could go back to sleep, move out if they could, and say, remember nothing.

Now gravediggers fear coming here, fear the spirits who occupy this place. Students from the university, a new generation, who are willing to come to do the exhumations drink a lot when they are not working, play loud music while they do, joke nervously and worry silently about another coup.

Petra, working on her doctorate and part of the team identifying the disappeared, the desaparecidos, in mass graves within the city of Buenos Aires, lies across boards spread over open holes, reaches down into dark earth from which the overburden has been removed by wary and barely willing gravediggers, and begins spooning it up. It does not take long to brush against bone, expose a progress of skull, skull shards, bullets and bullet casings, arm and leg bones, nylons, a shoe, teeth, breastbones, another skull; the bodies stacked head to feet, just as they said. Sneakers, a sock, more bullets, bone fragments. The bones, grouped by rough indications of age and sex, are bagged in clear plastic and taken to an on-site morgue, a decade ago full of abandoned bodies—morgue workers write to their President complaining of overwork, no time off, standing in maggots . . . .

Petra locates her mother to the evening she is returning late from her clinic in a poor barrio of Buenos Aires, but cannot trace the line connecting this point of her mother's departure to Petra's own birth, to here. Does it describe an arc, a circle, ellipse, a spiral? Elena Marin. Petra's grandmother changes their family name to Marin when they arrive in Argentina. Has her mother never married? There are no other records, dental, medical, of other births, only her grandmother's death certificate with the cause of death inked out. From the location of her clinic, Petra's mother left from the same police station all these bones, named *No Name* and numbered, passed through. How can there be so many homeless indigents, as they are referred to in official records, so many transients, and all so young, with bullet holes in them and thumbs dipped in purple ink, telling of their singular existence.

Petra lifts in her hand a female skull, gently brushing the dirt away, or a shattered breastbone, a pubic bone, running her finger over the unmistakeable grooves birthing a child has left there. It rains for days, weeks, winter in Argentina. And then it is unbearably hot.

They go to the cafés in the evenings. Petra always leaves early to go back to her room to go over transcripts of interviews, with morgue workers, gravediggers, those who survived, witnesses, relatives still searching and what they have provided of antemortem x-rays, medical and dental records to match with postmortem bone and teeth radiation. Searching for names to go with bones, bones with names, and always for the young woman looking out from the photo. Elena, what was she like, walking down the street that night, tired from a day's work at her clinic, hungry perhaps, going home to make dinner? to eat alone? Was she still so slender, so intense, so dark?

Jorge comes over later, tells Petra she should stay with the others, with him, better than being here by herself. Jorge telling her what he thinks is best for her is something she has begun noticing. They drink more wine, hold on to each other as they drift into sleep and startle awake, on guard to keep themselves from falling into dreams, into what they've seen, smelled, handled. In Jorge's dreams every woman's flesh turns to dirt. Petra births her mother's bones.

Mad women, they say, in the Plaza de Mayo. The state threatened by women, mothers and grandmothers, children, by something deep in heart's blood greater than fear stalking the silence of the disappeared. *You cannot alter history, say our children never were, or hide their bones. Do not bury our children again,* they cry. But the burying has already begun. Military court finds the junta has done nothing wrong.

In civil court Petra listens to a prosecutor who may have been studying law when Elena was taking her medical degree and who didn't happen to be picked up in the wrong part of town, or a woman out alone at night, perhaps the son of someone too dangerous to touch. So here he is now, trying to prove members of the military junta are directly responsible for what those did who followed orders.

Two of the judges sit slightly forward to watch slides of an exhumation projected onto a screen. Between them another sits leaning away, his elbow on the massive carved bench hiding the lower half of their bodies, his hand on his forhead, shielding what? His eyes, forehead, has he a headache? The backs of the chairs these men sit in, raised above everyone else, are of similar heavily square, carved wood. The judges' bodies soft, vulnerable. All of them, prosecutor, defense attorneys for the absent defendants, everyone present in the court, herself, Jorge beside her, all soft, white bodies, larval, moving, wriggling through dirt and bones, curled along a curve of skull, dropping into her hand.

Petra looks down at her hands, clenched. Jorge puts his over hers, takes hold of one, holds on.

The course of the trial comes down to bone, a pelvic shape up on the screen, a groove there tells that the female whose bones these are has given birth to a full- or nearly full-term infant. A young woman in her twenties, bone measurements indicate. Next her skull appears, an oddity from birth in the shape of her upper jaw, holes where she has been shot at close range. Finally there appears a photo from a family album. The bones labelled *No Name* become someone's daughter walking home from work on an April day, several months pregnant at the time, and in the courtroom a mother cries out, where is my grandchild, my daughter's child? Petra is staring back at the young woman with long dark hair gazing down at Petra from the screen, from someone's, a mother's, family photo album. Feeling a deepness that is hollow, a void, she pulls her hand from Jorge's, hurries from the courtroom. It takes Jorge several minutes before deciding to follow her out. He does not find her again.

LILY IS TRYING to picture the other woman, if she's the same age as Stephanie, older, not younger she hopes, worrying about their safety, how careful they will be, how aware of the dangers. You mean Em. Em? so you've had a letter . . . a space here between words before Jan answers that Lily is aware of but has no means to read. Em and Steph left here together. I didn't know that. Didn't you? Why didn't she ever mention her, why didn't you? Lily says in blind surprise, rushing on. How would Lily have known? Stephanie eighteen, making her choice, leaving without warning, without telling Lily. Nothing more. Lily will not call her a runaway. She couldn't tell me? You had Gran to think about.

Blindsided again. Lily uses the word, speaks it out loud. I don't know what that means, Jan says, angry. Anger always there somewhere that seems to be about Lily, her voice tight now, an extension of her body, *tighter than a G-string*, how an ear specialist puts it to her, referred to him because her ears ring and she loses her balance. Late winter afternoon darkness, she is his last patient, receptionist gone now for the day. Right, Lily says, getting up, walking out, feeling his eyes. Must have been flu, she tells Bruce. Now her ears itch more than they ring and she finds herself pitching forward too fast.

HOW ARE THEY? You ask it suddenly.

Who?

The others. Lily hesitates . . .

Jan, Stephanie . . . your grandchildren? Lily says it uncertainly.
You smile.

How are they? You listen carefully, ask if they will come for
Christmas. Lily explains the distance, cost. Yes, you say . . . they're
fine, though?

Yes, they're fine.

The nurse from Manitoba, Aileen, draws Lily aside. Metastasis
from breast to lung to bone is not psychosis, it's likely great pain
she can't tell us about that makes her seem so angry when we touch
her. Her eyes, blue like Hannah's but softer, hold Lily's somewhere
deep, ancient, comforting. I don't think your mother should go
back to Elizabeth Place, she adds, it's not good for her there. She's
going to need a lot more care. Where then? Did I tell you I'm
leaving, Aileen answers, going back to Manitoba. She moves you to
a corner room, looking south and east, over trees and gently rising
land, until your discharge to, where? Let's go, you say, suddenly
grasping Lily's arm. Let's go. I don't belong here. Lily has no answer
for the urgency in your voice, except to hold your hand,
unfamiliar, becoming less so.

LILY LOOKS UP FROM HER BOOK of stories threaded with your deep cough, breathing work, your seldom voice. I took the morning flight down, Jan says, looking over at you from the door of this last room along the hall before the balcony on a medical ward. They want you out of here too. No heroic measures does not rate what they refer to here as acute care. The nurses overworked and angry, at you, Lily, the doctor with two bony stumps for fingers on one hand who admits you and resists their anger, does not drug you, other than morphine for your silent pain. She'll be glad to see you, Lily says. I thought you could use some company, Jan's voice turning Lily to water, river moving her, nowhere to stop, rest. Jan has never seen her cry. She would be appalled, Lily believes, not knowing why she does.

Hi Gran, Jan calls and you rise from your pillow against the weight of your lungs. Hello? Hello? who's there? you call, morphine already pulling you back. It's Jan, Lily says. You smile, open your eyes, rising up from wherever you've been, face lit with an expectation of life. How are you? you say. Lily sees someone tall, erect, striding to greet her granddaughter, Lily watching you both, from outside somewhere, looking in. Daughters of daughters. Jan picks up the book Lily is reading. *The Burning of Witches?* you need to get out of here, she says, as though speaking for you as well. Lily looks over at you, thinking of Crahill . . . *the women confessed to their sins and were burned,* one minister notes, in Crahill records from 1713 . . . women alone, different, not sufficiently well-behaved, too close to animals, who know too much, healers, midwives, women who see too clearly, dream too much, do not belong to men, do not hold their tongues, women who do burned as well, in and by their silence, women for being women. Jan, a great-great-granddaughter's great-great-granddaughter of one of them. Quite suddenly she is shaking. She can hear Jan telling her she'll stay with you, to get some rest. Lily has forgotten her life, waiting here for yours, for more, expecting it to come from you. This you give to Jan when Lily is not here. You return for Jan, up, walking, Jan's arm supporting you to the balcony, into October, sunlit treetops, land falling away to a distant blue pacific haze of water, mountains too blue too much sky you tell her you are falling. Jan takes you back to your chair where you are propped up with pillows. I'm going to a beautiful place. Your voice clear when you tell her. Lily a stranger, someone you don't know, waits.

I'm here, Lily says. Turn that off, you cry out. Lily flips off the tape. Listen to the words, Jan says. Lily hasn't, taking only time to buy what tapes she can find, Celtic music, something to fill the spaces between your ragged breaths, ghost cough, seldom voice which frighten, panic her with what she has mistaken for emptiness. Plays them softly, like elevator music, did not think to read, or listen . . . *where dips the rocky highland Of sleuth wood in the lake There lies a leafy island Where flapping herons wake The drowsy water rats There we've hid our fairy vats Full of berries And of reddest stolen cherries . . . Come away oh human child To the waters and the wild With a faery hand in hand for the world's more full of weeping Than you can understand* . . . checks the notes, "The Stolen Child," by Yeats, too late for Lily to tell you she did not know this is what slips over the lip of your ear . . . *I wish I was in Carrighfergus Only for nights in Ballygrant. I would swim over the deepest ocean, only for nights in Ballygrant. But the sea is wide, and I can't swim over Neither have I wings to fly. If I could find me a handsome boatsman To ferry me over to my love and die. Now in Kilkenny it is reported*

They've marble stone there, black as ink. With gold and silver I would transport her But I'll sing no more now, till I get a drink. I'm drunk today, but I'm seldom sober A handsome rover from town to town. Ah, but I am sick now, my days are over, Come all you young lads and lay me down. I wish I was in Carrighfergus, Only for nights in Ballygrant . . . now you think Lily is Rachel, call for her, listening for Bert's music, eyes staring for the light. You sing, hug the nurses, Jan, not Lily, open your arms, he's right here, you say, hand touching your breastbone; slip into another place between here and gone. In Lily's dream a grandmother dances, shows them how, in the shadow of trains riding the curve toward around beyond them, the double curve. They dance to the pulse of her heart's blood, then theirs, her hands sure wings beating on their chests, the cage, broken shell.

TORONTO? WHY? BLURTS OUT OF LILY, some child. Remnants between them of a late dinner in Lily's apartment, candles working their way down to smoky stubs. What about tree planting? hemlock, balsam, fir under Lily's hand, rough skin, tracks etched in sand between her fingers, until Lily notices her hands working the paper serviette, twisting. She lays them in her lap, waiting while Jan pinches out the candles.

It's late. What time are you going in to the hospital tomorrow? They don't like me going in before nine. I get in their way, but I go in for eight anyway, so she'll eat something and get her morphine. I'd like to stay up ... there hasn't been much time to talk. Won't they feed her if you're not there? Lily feeling the slippage, Jan, Stephanie, you, stranding her. If you can't, don't eat, shouldn't that tell Lily something? Waiting for your throat to remember, eyelids drawn, Lily and you caught in your throat worn out by drugs jamming word of you she needs; life not sustained without food, Lily surviving on what is left of you.

I've been accepted at the University of Toronto. I see. Seeing nothing. Where will you stay ... have you enough money? I took a loss on the house but I can manage rent on a place together. It was in my mind, if you'd wanted to stay here in Vancouver, and Stephie, if she wanted ... *but the sea is wide and I can't get over* ... Lily stranded at sea, with you, following river, river bed, glacial cut.

128

I can stay with Margot, she's got a house with extra rooms, Jan hesitates . . . I'll be working for her, and taking pre-law. Jan already up piling plates into the sink. Leave those, Lily insists, then washes them for something to do while Jan makes up her bed on the sofa and disappears into the bathroom. When Lily brushes her teeth, the lights in the living room are out. Has it always been this way?

She has taken Jan to the airport this morning for an early flight to Toronto. Fall classes already begun, Jan puts off saying goodbye to you until you do it for her, slip between sleeping and waking, no longer walking with her to the balcony, to the arc of blue and light falling on October trees, or sipping obediently at tiny spoonfuls of ice cream laced with morphine she eases into your mouth. You stare at Jan, I'm tired, I'm sick, I'm old, I'm young, you say, your last words to her. Lily not sure who it is you speak to now.

You and Margot would probably have lots to talk about, Jan says to Lily as they slip from Granville to Marine Drive, onto the bridge, rounding the curve onto delta, estuary flats, Lulu island, the airport, long arms of the Fraser River reaching around them and out into space. Lily waits for more. You're both from Winnipeg. Until now Jan has expressed no interest in Winnipeg. Lily listens to how Margot can speak French, lived all over Winnipeg in a lot of foster homes and ran away when she was fourteen. Well, you seem to have her life story. Lily doesn't want to hear more, to know if Jan knows more about this woman, a stranger, than she does about Lily, than Lily does about you, is this possible? Both of them silent then, until they are at the departure doors and there is only time for Jan to get her bags out of the car and rush off. She hugs Lily. Thanks Mom, look after yourself. I'll call you.

Better let me call you, Lily says, you don't want to be running up Margot's phone bill. She regrets this, the look on Jan's face. Raises her hand, bye, she says as her hand drops, Jan's face already closing. Lily's hand tightens by her side. It could have been you and Lily, the unwelcome thought that rides the curve with her, back across the bridge, through acidic air from the wood mill behind the Fraser Arms Hotel, sulphurous smell of the chip barges heading oceanward, to here, your room overlooking tops of glowing trees falling away down to sea level, distant fields, freefall into you. A nurse combing your hair when Lily arrives. We almost lost her last night, she murmurs pleasantly. Lost, mislaid, forgot? You are smiling, at Lily or someone else you think is here. I'm back, you say, your face awake, alert, shining, the way Lily has never seen it. They're all trying to help, you say, smiling to yourself. Who? Lily wants to ask, who do you mean?

Go home, she'll be fine, Dolores had insisted the night before and promised to ask the night shift to call her if anything changes. No one did. Lily afraid you will come when she's not here, find yourself alone at your going what she tells herself. They do not want you or Lily here, in this room they say is needed for someone they can save. So the surprise to find a nurse combing your hair, your shining face, the young girl there Lily has never met but knows she knows. Is it Rachel combing your hair? Some time after Jan says, goodbye Gran, you leave catheter and IV tubes behind. They find you at six a.m. sitting in the corner of a stairwell at the end of the hall from the nursing station. They who are frightened and want to disable you with an anti-psychotic drug. Lily refuses, feels collective anger, impatience and is bullied by a doctor, large and beefy, who tells her you are so demented it won't make any difference and will make the nurses' work easier. They want to tie you into your bed. For your own protection, they say. Not now, Lily says, it won't happen again; hardens her skin to their angry eyes. They insist on giving you laxatives, because of the morphine, force them down and must suction everything out of your throat in order for you to breathe. Lily chases one of them from your room, Maria of the banging furniture and doors, who threatens under her breath and from between her clenched teeth and calls you demented when you cry out while she makes up your bed.

Now you and Lily left alone together in the long afternoon of your breathing, not breathing. Lily going deeper with you, waiting in the space of silence for your breathing to begin again, Lily no longer able to breathe on her own, waiting for yours, her breathing difficult, out of sync with her own body, until her body comes in sync with you. Time for her morphine, a nurse says at Lily's shoulder, disappears, leaves it for Lily to slip into your ice cream, the tiny spoonfuls they say you spit out when they try. Your eyes, mouth close. Fluid gathering around your lungs, bleeding somewhere deep inside they won't find, you slip out to sea. Yearling gull calls from the balcony, peers in at you and Lily from around the door, edges away to hide itself when Lily looks. Hangs around, comes again, watching Lily feeding you sips of melted ice cream, sun a red ball sliding down behind you. Mama, you say to Lily, I'm still here.

You still here? Dolores's familiar greeting coming on afternoon shift; she looks in at Lily from the door. I'll get her up soon for supper, she says, disappearing, returns with fresh sheets, nightie, disposable diaper. Hello Jean, she says, you somewhere in between breaths. Hello Jean, she calls again, louder this time, in your ear, shaking your shoulder . . . Jean, are you there? *Yes*, your voice, suddenly clear and strong, annoyed. Dolores doesn't look at Lily. I'm going to get you up now Jean, for supper; her routine, not yours. You are propped with pillows into the recliner so you will not pitch forward or hang sideways, rag doll, morphine taking you down, but you struggle against the gravity of water gathering on your lungs, hot, restless; Lily takes your hand, slips into you, down your throat, swimming, swimming swimming her own natal sea in yours; will she drown, learn to breathe, grow bones, scales, wings? A vee of silent geese across your window, bellies soft, golden in evening light; their return in moonlight, voices restless.

Rachel holding her son against her on the bumping cart watches them rise from a sea of stubble and Louis, from his cell in Regina sees them go, as the cart takes her south across a land of disappearances to where you come out of her, her second heart, the blow that splits you, binds you to her, Lily to you. I don't know where to go, your voice whispers into Lily. Follow your heart, it's all any of us can do, the voice of a someone in Lily she doesn't know slipping off her tongue. Your eyes fly open wide, Lily's hand goes to your seamed chest, drum, heart space, clenched fist pounding, red muscle beating on her shore skin something deep and different. Lily runs for Dolores.

My mother's heart, she says, it's going wild. What is it you want me to do, Dolores does not ask, reminds, bringing Lily back to remembrance of papers signed. No heroic measures to keep you here. Palliative Care. It rings hollow. Hollow rings hollow.

I don't know. All Lily can think of to say. Her heart's working too hard, it's all ganging up on her, the doctor without his fingers tells her. It's all that water on her lungs, he says. Go home, get some sleep, Dolores tells her, going off shift, her voice coming to Lily from far away, an intrusion, you breathing too heavily now, moaning, sighing, struggling for breath. I'll be staying, Lily says it again, holds her breath when yours stops, waits, counting, until your next wave sighs down her ear, water beating on your lungs, hers. The count, seven, grows longer with the night. You and Lily alone again now and the night and the breath work, so much work, your hair, grown long, soft silver streaked red, wet, pillow soaked with it, your eyes an infant's staring into light. You cry, groan, is it pain, exhaustion, wanting it to be over, this work to go, or stay?

Lily counting, in the widening space between your breaths, ten, twelve, knowing this arrival of departure is out of time, too big to fit, yet she counts, with her unsure hands on your back, shoulders, neck, face, arms, hands, skin so soft startles her fingers, massaging, holding, joining, melting into the bones of you she can't let go. Nurses, the night crew, assault team, part her from you to turn you, from left to right and back again, through the night, through your breathing work, silent in their uniforms and padded feet, turning all the lights on, ignoring Lily, hauling you around on the bed, one more body to shift, they place pillows between your legs, around your back. Bedsores reveal your skin, disintegrating. You stare up at the light, moan and cry when they move you. Rattling congestion in your windpipe panics Lily wanting them to do something, anything. Too deep they say, suction won't reach it, turn out all but the night light, leave Lily there with your rattle.

IS YOUR MOTHER RELIGIOUS? The doctor asks Lily. No one knows, except you, and you aren't saying. Lily doesn't know. Agnostic what you tell her so many years ago. No, she tells him, the moulded brown plastic Christ nailed on a cross that hung on the wall facing your bed Lily has removed, relieved it is not nailed in place, slipping it underneath spare pillows on a closet shelf. The doctor asks if you would like one of the nuns to visit you. I don't think so, Lily says.

You call Bruce a Holy Roller, Lily a fanatic, when she tells you Bruce is a born-again Christian, Lily quoting Bruce because she knows nothing about Christians except what she carries from the United Church Sunday School, scraps of Bible verses suggesting we are sheep, or possibly goats, in need of a shepherd, children in need of a father. Bruce's religion insists we are sinners in need of a saviour, a sacrificial lamb of atonement, someone's death for our sin. Guilt and death the punishment for telling God he doesn't exist, trees do?

Your eyes open. Do you see Lily? Wordless. What is there to be said that would contain the life of silence, absence you've shared? Lily pats your face with a damp cool washcloth, the fleeting, self-conscious ghost smile there Lily wants to be more than involuntary, a recognition. Five a.m. A man in his pyjamas wanders into your room looking for the bathroom. Lily steers him out, hears the rapid padding of a nurse's rubber-soled shoes on the tiles, too late, the trickle of his pee outside the door.

They come again to turn you in your bed, dove grey the sky at your window, space between your breaths, the apnea shortening. Have you made it through another night, like the night before when they *almost lost you?* They turn you as they did before and leave. One of them comes back. Sometimes they need to know it's all right to go, need to be told that, she says, looking at Lily with a kind of neutrality that feels like rebuke. Back under the tall elms by Rachel's white clapboard house, looking up into trees that were here when you leave her, green darkness, hot sun, your breathing now long rolling swells against Lily's skin rocking her in them, drawing her deeper, deeper into you, taking her with you, rattling in your windpipe. This work, for the child who won't let go. I love you, Lily says suddenly. I know you love me. Not knowing if any of this is true, not knowing what love is at any or this particular moment, except that awkward inappropriate child with a grip that won't let go. It's all right to go, another lie, another story, sense of betrayal seeping through Lily as she lets the words past her teeth. No words from you, your breathing shallow, rapid, running out of breath, a sudden roaring rush of air from your mouth, surprise, is it embarrassment on your face, you close your mouth, eyes still surprised.

CROWS HANG LIKE BATS UPSIDE DOWN in trees, split the air with their voices, doubling their cawing. Hanging by a claw they look up and down, shoulders pressing that space not counted as sky, checking the gravity of their weight, setting the sky rocking . . . blue, black, the skin of her where it breathes . . . rocking, wrapped in a floating memory, water, lungs slipping under, swimming; you walking unburdened through halls of yellow lightness, easing the weight on Lily's chest. She opens her eyes and for a moment desk, computer, bookcase, chest of drawers, stationary bicycle, clothes from yesterday, days before, thrown over chair and bicycle, over the end of her bed are what is unreal, without substance, what her mind cannot reach out to touch, mind returning to your ashes on the dining room table, contained in a plastic bag, in a plastic canister. She doesn't know what to do with them.

Heavy, when he puts them into her hands, the weight of you, what has fallen through the grate along with remnants of someone else. He explains there will be pieces of your bones, teeth, no gold fillings or they would have been extracted. Your wedding band Lily takes from your finger as water gathers, swells under your skin and nothing fits. When did you do it, Lily asks. He checks his records. Last Wednesday afternoon, late afternoon.

Lily sleeps heavy while they do it, sleepwalks, seeing, feeling the bottom of her spine disintegrate, earth and ash, wet, after-fire smell of it taking her into greyness. Feeling them stir, scrape your ashes, she panics, feels your fear and displeasure, a wounding, you do not want to be burned, lose your body. Too late. Lily, always claustrophobic, did not want to put you in the ground, burning is freer. Remembering the other Jean's mother, father burning in fire, released spirits, do they mingle with yours? You never said what you wanted, would never speak of death, or your dying. How could you, who never got your life. Lily tells you this, can talk to you now. I'm sorry, she tells you, I didn't know what you wanted. No service. No one to come except Lily. She calls Jan. Leaves a message.

How do you plan to dispose of the ashes, he asks her. I don't know, Lily says, brings them home to here, some between world of multiple choice, drifting, unwilling to get out of bed, waiting your appearances, feel of your presence near the bed, waking her during the night, early morning with your hand like air brushing her cheek, gentleness brushing away time, new story with the old, sum greater than its parts. She talks to you, hesitantly at first, then as to an embryo she carries around inside her.

On her way to the bathroom, she slides her toe aimlessly around in the pile of mail fallen through the slot, bills, requests for donations. Out from under them faces of Mexican children look up at her. *In the marketplace*, printed on the bottom of the postcard. *Will be in Guatemala tonight, Steph*, written on the back. *Say hi to Gran for me*, scrawled as an after-thought along the bottom. She ran away, Lily tells you, without finishing high school . . . with her friend Emma, needs to tell you, say it out loud, hear herself say it, no longer sure what real or goneness is. What's left of Lily sinks, floored, wailing, tearing at her hair, pulling it out by its roots if she could. Pain that feels ancient she can no longer carry, has to get out of, it out of her, coming up through her body, undoing her. Medea and Hecate, queens of anger, darkness, arrive without ceremony.

FEELING THE NECESSITY of ceremony, Lily searches for a basket in galleries and stores selling Indian art. The ones she can afford are too small. Lily doesn't know why she wants to bury your ashes in a basket woven from grass. In one store when she tells the purpose of the basket, the women behind the counter grow silent. Masks on the wall behind them, jewellery worked in silver, argillite carvings enclosed in glass, expensive works of art. My grandmother weaves them, one of the women tells her. She's out on the coast. I don't know if she's doing any right now. Do you want to leave your name and phone number? She can tell by their eyes they will not call her. Is it her unsureness they feel, something inappropriate, are they telling her to find her own way? She thought they would see what it was she needed to do.

In a small studio two women weave rainforest tapestries. Light among trees greets Lily's startled, flattened eyes hiding behind dark glasses. Sharing the studio with them, she discovers, is a basket weaver, Ulle, Icelandic as they are, who explains to Lily the reeds she uses are from natural sources, but imported, most likely from the Philippines. But I can weave local grasses into them, if you like, she adds. I get them from the river, tidal marshes, where the forest opens. I have a cabin up there. Where? Up along the coast, Ulle vague, as though Lily will follow her there. I'll be picking over the weekend . . . bentgrass, sweetgrass, seashore bluegrass, golden sedge, foxtail . . . ? Those, Lily says, just what you said, can you weave all of them into the reeds? Whatever I can find. Ulle says it carefully.

She is with Rhian again, up in the trap hills, what would she gather there, fringed gentian, maidenhair, heart's ease? Would the ash and beech, the poplar still stand among stone ruins and the crows thick among them? What roots there for healing? And to colour her cloth. But Lily has no loom, and only broken threads taking her to where a faint blue haze of Crahill lies across a long remove of rolling fields, no landfall, not yet, land falling away. A candle flickers. Scent of balsam. Ulle's basket, its spiralling reeds and woven grasses glow burnt earth and sage, your ashes in their plastic cylinder inside. The feel of an altar. But no religion, except for loss. A ceremony of loss, marker of where you fell, and Lily. Where is the story now? Loss a death with many faces . . . love, desire, hope, words Lily cannot accommodate. Rain, misty light penetrating driftcloud, hitting water then her eyes with scattered brilliance. Communities of wintering ducks whistling, calling, back and forth across the water, moving as one away from shore when she passes. It's alright, don't go, she hears herself say; solstice low, the afternoon already dark by four, bringing her home for Christmas Eve; knife in one hand, tomato in the other, over green lettuce in a blue pottery bowl, feeling you and Rachel moving together across the fields towards Crahill, dry blowing snow, night sky, Lily still waiting. Let me go, your voice winding Lily's inner ear, shifting her weight. Heaviness in Lily says, too soon, not yet. They take her in a gentle dance, delicate figures swirling, gentleness turning wild, wilder and wilder Lily lighter and lighter spins, dancing with herself until giddy and disoriented she drops the knife with a clank on the salad bowl. Waits for Jan, Stephanie to call.

Almost midnight, almost Boxing Day when Jan wakes her. Three a.m. Jan's time, Lily expecting some kind of emergency. Sorry, didn't think you'd be in bed already. Just got home from a party. She's been drinking, the giggle, she hasn't heard that since Jan was little. Margot says to wish you a Merry Christmas . . .

Merry Christmas . . . to her too, and you.

Guess you haven't heard anything from Steph? No, should I? sharper than Lily means it to be. Well, just thought I'd call and say hello . . . what'd you do today?

Went for a walk.

That sounds exciting.

You know, I'm really tired, so maybe I'll just say goodnight.

Okay, bye. A click in Lily's ear, loaded revolver, she has seen it there before, in her head at her head. Furious with Jan, for being drunk, for being in Toronto. Lily would have paid for her ticket back here. She avoids the word home.

I want to take Gran's ashes to Winnipeg in the spring, when the ground's open. Maybe I'll come then, what she tells Jan back in November, Lily's birthday, Jan inviting her to come for Christmas.

Suit yourself, Jan tells her, you can stay here any time.

What about Margot?

She suggested it.

Oh, Lily murmurs, well, then thank her for me.

Heard from Steph? Lily wishes she wouldn't ask, then, and now, expects Jan to be the one to hear from her.

No, nothing . . . why didn't you tell me?

She didn't want you to know.

She's too young, Lily's voice disappears into her throat. A couple of women on their own in a country like Guatemala? choking it down, the rawness in her throat. She must be getting the flu. Dark brown mouth of the river running under, through a moment when the child doesn't know if she will or can stop it taking her, do you know about the river, your child Lily, walking back the way she came, unaware how long she's been away, nothing the same now she's felt the call to leave you leaving her. Back to you, scrubbing floors, your *where have you been?* Feeling your fright, wanting it, some sign, nothing more said. Later the child will pretend to slip off a dock into the river, knowing she can't swim, surprised when her feet sink into river mud with no bottom and she goes under, bobs up, someone grabs her hand, nothing happens. Do you see what Lily sees? Faceless, slipping between the trees in the garden the child walks the darklight down the gravel road, through tall grass, voices coming from the grass, from firelight in the field by railway tracks. Her heart pounds her ribs. The horse pounds the open field, nothing ahead but more field and a meeting with sky, or earth. Bareback, she has nothing to hold onto but the horse's hairy mane, *Mother Mary meek and mild, look upon a little child, Ave Maria, consider the lil*—laughing cousins beyond the curve of her ear filled with hooves beating on hardpan July pasture, feeling the slide, the jarring of her head hitting ground. She has migraines only narcotics relieve, which she doesn't take, fearing them more than the migraines. She simply goes to bed until they are over.

WINGS DIP AND RISE TOO CLOSE TO GROUND, too much for everyone on board, a collective cry startled out of them, Lily holding hers until it slides back down from her throat when the plane's wheels hit runway, bounce, hit and bounce again and the landing finally comes to a halt in front of the domestic arrivals terminal. *Arrivals Terminal* a collision of meanings, multiple choice again in a drift of words, arrival's end, arrival past hope, consummation, finis, curtains; or borderline, languishing in margins along anxious boundaries, juggling possibilities, more arrivals of departure. Lily picks up her backpack, remembering something Bruce once said about afternoon flights being the roughest, but that was prairie flying in Harvard trainers and Mitchell bombers from the Second World War, when Bruce spent his summers between university sessions on the prairies training as a reserve air force pilot, graduating to jet fighters up from Gimli in sky over Winnipeg, and Selkirk, the glacial remains, and Lily looking up sees his very distant vapour trail unravel across the sky long before she meets him.

Late west-coast spring already early summer in Toronto, the falling away of years disorienting her as she stares out the bus window, tries to make sense of altered patterns of familiarity, of what she sees, remembers, can't remember, of where she ran to, clickety clack down the track, North Superior shore, mostly

140

through darkness, to where you weren't, or so she thinks. Calls you from here to tell you she's marrying Bruce, words rattling into your silence, which splits, parts like the Red Sea. You tell Lily she's crazy. Is it the religion, or something else you see Lily doesn't? *Love, mercy, trust,* when does she first hear of such words, know of their existence? Not from you. When is silence a lie and when is it truth? or is it both? Truth when Bruce's religion says there is love in this world, but it comes at an awful price? To whom?

Beyond Lakeshore Boulevard water and sky are humid grey, hospital where Jan and Stephanie are born sweating beside it. She's forgotten this humidity. Euphoria with Jan's birth, Lily's first. The anaesthetist is singing when he clamps the mask over her face. It's too much, Lily yells at him, her voice far away and his from long distance laughing *go to sleep little mother, don't worry* . . . Lily returns on a wave of nausea, mask still over her face, this time oxygen . . . you aspirated, someone says at her ear, Jan still inside her. A specialist introduces himself, far, far away, telling her something, giving it a name. Lily doesn't know what he's talking about. She doesn't ask. Leaves it to him to birth Jan, remove her from this inert body called Lily. In a twilight sleep she can't feel anything except the need to have this over. And then a nurse apologising for punching her in the stomach. Blood gushing out of her hits the wall. We have to do this, get it out of you. Something about the placenta Lily is not able to deliver, either. But Jan is soon weighting her thighs with the drum of her heart and Lily so high on her sits upright without drinking or eating for a day and a night as she must because of the aspiration pneumonia, sits without noticing time and cannot stop smiling. Indian summer. Lake Ontario emerging from fog intensely blue, white sails folded butterfly wings a line in Lily's eye between water, sky.

When Steph is born Lily is on the other side of the hospital, away from the lake, overlooking a power plant, staff parking, a street of joined brick houses with porches, verandahs, windows that look out onto the hospital's behind. This is all she remembers, it happens so fast, and that the doctor, a different one this time, tells her he doesn't want to be late for his wife's dinner party. Is it a joke? Six hours ago when she starts to bleed he tells her on the phone to save what comes out for him. He forgets that something he orders for her after the birth will stop her breast milk, apologises, becomes annoyed when she is upset, and yells, I apologised didn't I? Where was Bruce? Flowers, flowers, and the house trim painted. Where were you? Bruce calls you, Lily does not, does not know why, now, leaving the bus at the Royal York, searching for some memory of bringing Jan and Stephanie to their first cry breathing out of water. That first breath cry out of each gone missing somewhere only her body knows and isn't telling, not out here on Front Street. She calls a cab to the Annex, Huron Street, the address Jan gives her.

She wants the driver to go up University Avenue. Big mess at Queen's Park, he says, looking at her in his mirror. Oh? Big protest today . . . a riot, he adds. Best to go another way. Riot? here, Ontario? Lily laughs. Lots of people, police, he says firmly.

But not a riot.

Where I come from it's a riot . . . police the same everywhere . . . following orders, he says, when Lily doesn't answer. His eyes smile at her from the rear-view mirror, apologetic. You are here for a nice holiday? Tomorrow will be fine.

She knocks, waits, eyeing a couple of thick black mountain bikes locked onto the porch railing, blue recycling boxes mostly empty except for newspapers, the patch of weedy grass gone to seed. They agree Jan will not come to the airport to meet her. She knocks again, feeling a stranger who doesn't belong. Margot bounds up the stairs behind her in sweats, pulls out her key. She's forgotten Margot's irritating energy. It smacks up against her, Margot already taking hold of one of her suitcases. I'll get those, Lily says quickly. Margot sets it down again. Jan mustn't be back yet, she says. Lily thinks of a bird chirping, a rather loud bird. Inside the foyer is a door into an office Margot tells her she shares with a community legal advocacy group. So don't be alarmed if you hear the front door opening, people wandering around, faxes coming through. Margot heads up the stairs. I'll just bring my other bag inside, Lily murmurs. Margot doesn't wait for her.

The second floor opens out into a southern facing living room, a bedroom, Margot's, and bathroom on the east and large kitchen at the back. An old house with high ceilings and bay windows. Not a lot of furniture. Lily's eyes roam unpacked boxes stored in various corners, supporting lamps, a cd player, plants. Wood floors in the living room gleam in light from a bay window, an orange cat with large paws curled on it, sleeping with a smile on its face. It jumps across from the house next door and comes in the window, Margot says from behind her, points up the stairs to a third floor. Guest room's up there on the front, Jan's is next to it. Bathroom's down here, I'm afraid. I have to go out, a dinner appointment. Just make yourself at home. Jan must have been held up. The kettle's there and there's coffee, tea . . . ? I'm fine. I've got some tea in my bag. We must have some somewhere. Margot rummages in a closet kind of pantry off the kitchen, which Lily notices is short on cupboards. From the kitchen window another seedy patch of yard, backyards, fences, garages, a lane, trees. I know Jan planned to be here, Margot says, emerging from the pantry with a tin of coffee and a package of no-name tea bags. She should be here soon. The pause is awkward. Lily moves toward the stairs. I'll do a bit of unpacking.

She can hear Margot in the shower downstairs; wants to, but does not look into Jan's room. The window in Lily's room looks south over Huron and west to the stone turrets of Casa Loma. She has forgotten how many trees there are in Toronto, how the land climbs up from the lake and rolls north to boreal forests and under the land or cutting through it, water, flowing back down to the lake, effortless as gravity. In her eye evening light turning Casa Loma weightless, colour of sand, floating up from a sea of darkening trees; evening train floating by on the wake of its horn in her ear. Where is she, why isn't she here? Lily asks you. In the back of the guest-room closet upstairs, in the carry-on bag, your

ashes in their basket of woven reeds and grasses that seems more
suitable to Lily than under the earth or scattered by the wind across
it. A ringing phone jangles her nerves, strained already listening for
Jan's arrival, identifying unfamiliar noises. Margot, wondering if
Jan is here yet. The traffic downtown is still a mess. They've likely
been held up. A mess, the second time she's heard that word today.
Mess, disorder, chaos, disaster . . . they? She's with a friend, Margot
chats on edgily, don't worry, they should be back soon. I'm on my
way home now. Irritation, resentment, anxiety stewing when Lily
puts down the phone, when Margot arrives and still no Jan.

Did you get something to eat?

I had something on the plane and a sandwich I brought with
me—allergies, I carry food with me.

What kind of allergies . . . cats, dust, that sort of thing? Jan is
crazy about the neighbour's cat. It spends most of its time over
here, and vacuuming doesn't happen very often. I'm glad you've
come, Margot says abruptly, you should have come sooner. I was
sorry about your mother. Lily silent, losing words, losing, always
losing wells up in her. Margot who arrives at the stairs first when
there is a key in the front door.

From over Margot's shoulder Lily's eyes collide with her
daughter's swollen, bruised face, stitched lip, ear and nose rings,
close-cropped hair, the friend behind her, stitched cuts on his head,
whites of one eye red, the other already swollen shut with bruising,
nose and earrings gleaming. I'm all right, Jan says, moving away
from Lily to sit on the couch beside him. His hair cropped like hers,
Lily notices a wisp of dyed orange hair left growing down the back
of each of their necks, holes in their jeans. They could be twins. Lily
stares at this stranger her daughter, these strangers, wonders where
she is. Margot, in the middle, telling them she'd heard downtown
the police were in riot gear and she thought maybe they'd been
arrested, turns to Lily—I couldn't find out anything and I didn't
want to worry you—as though this is a reasonable explanation for
withholding, Lily watching the curve of Jan's body against his,
remembering with anguish the small child body's curl into hers,

listening to her daughter say they had to wait in Emergency and then go get a prescription filled for some kind of painkillers, that they punched out her tooth.

They? Lily's voice breaking in, loud in her ears. They all turn to look at her as though surprised to see her there attached to a voice, dismissing her from the conversation. Have they? or has she? Lily sees the black uniforms, helmets gleaming, gladiators, armoured, long black batons banging on clear plastic shields, jamming into bellies and crotches, across heads, shoulders, breasts, taking her daughter down, kicking her when she falls. But why, what was Jan doing, why was she there, for that matter why is she here, living in this house? Margot asking if anyone wants tea, something to eat, soup? Think I'll just go to bed, Jan says, her look pulling the boy beside her away from his glances toward Lily, to follow her up to her room, leaving Margot and Lily in uncomfortable silence. She's in shock, Margot offers.

I can see that.

I would have said something sooner, but there was no point in worrying you for no reason. At least they weren't arrested. Jan has a good head. She can take care of herself. In Margot's voice Lily hears approval, satisfaction, something proprietary.

Today her head took a beating.

It *was* their decision. Margot's thin smile when she says this recalls by absence the bright energetic smile Lily remembers from the museum, the café, another lifetime ago. A different impression now, brittle, hard, tense. I'll show you where the towels are. Margot opens a door inside the bathroom, hands Lily a large bath sheet. Just take what you need. You must be feeling jet-lagged. We all need some sleep.

Lily treads softly up to her room, undresses in light from a street lamp, sinks into bed without rummaging in suitcases for a nightgown. Should she have come? What did she expect? Jan and a boy whose name Lily doesn't know sleeping together in the next room, Stephanie ghosting in and out on a postcard. Where to look if they go missing?

Stephanie her fearful child, of bridges, ladders, night, forest
shadows, her own, ghosts; whatever caused such an unexpected
flight, to Guatemala, country of shadows, fear, danger? Whatever it
is her daughter imagines, creates, runs from, must be stronger. Lily
afraid that might be her. Stephanie gets to Mexico through Em, Jan
tells her. Lily wonders why she never met Em, Emma, or knew of
her, did she ever come to the house? Em's my age, Jan tells her,
travelling with a group down the west coast in an old school bus,
heading for Central America with tools and school supplies.
Wherever the bus stopped along the way, if there was room, anyone
could get on, as long as they were willing to contribute work, find
food, help raise money and camp out, they could get to California,
or Mexico, or wherever the bus went . . . between sleeping and
waking Lily reaches for the child reaching and drawing life back
into her without a thought, tomorrow too far away to be felt in this
light containing it, all tomorrows, this light her face, the child's . . .
fragments, debris of first love, the journey out from centre, hungry
whole, hole at gravity point, zero, weighted waiting for whose
return? for return from this waiting. Can each exist without other?
With whose stripes is she healed; a door opening to new death?
Something missing in her, lost, taken, *you, I, we* . . . resist her.

The dream a sphere of very bright light becoming smaller
spheres attached to one another by strips of the same bright
material as the spheres they join. She can see into the centre; the
void of the spheres and beyond to the other side is very blue before
it flattens, becomes a kind of grid, flesh and earth tones. She keeps
looking for someone, waiting, the grid a map, the further she
moves across it, the further it goes. Edge falls away to where she is,
a dot in a pointillist painting, fragments of light points on the
map, locations, someone died here, someone gave life here, made a
promise here, was murdered here, a sickness was healed here, a
garden planted, someone went missing here, unexplored land here .
. . something soft, very soft, made from the material of the grid,
part of it or caught and held by it. She can see this soft brown
shape, like a bat, stretched across grids, a face looking at her from a

great distance. She is standing in another dream, someone has come or gone, and she is wondering if they will come again in another dream, dream of a dream dreaming the memory of the dream of the memory of the dream, freefall into the rhythm of an irregular heart. Lily awake in shadows of an unfamiliar room, off the map. Shadows familiar, presence, Lily watching Rachel watch Jane searching play of light on mist, of cloud-shadow across fields unfolding to distant trap hills of Crahill. Or is it Rhian, Brunis, Gertrede, released spirits roaming free? Rhian's Lia, who escaped burning, holds out to her the little bag of finely woven silk, inside it, beside the stone that curls around itself, the fine red thread, is Jan's broken tooth.

Do you need money to get your tooth fixed? Morning light in the kitchen is not kind to either of them. There's no tooth to fix, Jan's voice flat—it hurts to talk. They can't have knocked it out by the roots, it's broken off, you'll need to have it seen to. Do you have a dentist? Jan looks over Lily's shoulder, away from the window.

I should go downstairs for a couple of hours.

Where's . . . ?

He had to go to work.

I thought you were taking this week off?

A couple of hours isn't the whole week.

No, Lily says, cautiously, fumbling over this continuing departure. Jan joins the women in the back office downstairs.

Lily finishes unpacking, feeling aimless, shifting the basket with your ashes to an empty suitcase, sliding it into a corner between a table and the wall. The furniture in the room is new pine, the kind one buys and puts together with screws that match prearranged holes and keys that match screws, turn them, lock them into place; the wood smooth to her fingers, like polished stone, fingers swimming over the surface of things, feeling for light, lightness. The plan to go to Winnipeg on the way back to Vancouver, leave your ashes there, have them buried in your husband's, Lily's father's grave is tentative, Lily waiting on word from you.

The fridge more or less empty when Lily looks in, rummaging around for an egg to boil for breakfast. She shops at the supermarket next to the railway tracks, below the castle, stocks the fridge with food she can eat. Margot, Jan tells her, is hardly ever there. Lily watching her diet very closely when travelling, or she will be sick with migraines, low blood sugar. It is embarrassing, but nothing she can do anything about, except be careful. Lily's body may be telling her something, but she's not getting it, not yet, whatever it is. These debilitating episodes have never been spoken about, by either Jan or Stephanie. Bruce, who was never ill, thought the source of the trouble lay in Lily's head, a weakness women inherited from one another. Going and coming again with her bag of groceries Lily can hear women's voices, laughter from the back office, clack of a fax machine, high-pitched phone beeps. She closes her eyes, flashing lights, nausea, the pain inside her eyes as she climbs the stairs; she's missed the signs.

You okay? Jan standing uncertainly in her doorway, Lily on the bed, stifling whimpers, unable to bear the sound of Jan's, anyone's voice . . . the curtains, close them please, she mumbles, wanting to throw up again. I'll leave the window open so you can get some air. No, close it. Lily's tongue thick, voice slurring out of her. It'll be hot up here, Jan reminds her of the humid day ahead. Lily's teeth chattering. She doesn't answer, doesn't remember falling out of consciousness; house resonating an empty quiet when she returns, light beyond curtains, clammy wet in her clothes under the quilt. Making her way downstairs to the bathroom Lily staggers a little, weak, her balance off, lights still flashing behind and in her eyes, the awful pain in her head gone though; bones of her neck, face remembering it. She pees for a long time, showers with water as hot as she can stand, washes her hair, rolls and pins it up on her head. Then she has to sit down. Summer evening out the kitchen window. Almost eight. She looks for a note from Jan. There isn't one. Makes herself a boiled egg and toast. The surprising thing is the migraine is over so soon, usually eighteen hours, most of it without sleep. The house empty, Lily restless, euphoric in this release from pain. She dresses, decides not to leave a note.

The Annex not an area Lily remembers of Toronto. No one on the streets. Bloor when she comes to it still vaguely familiar, construction everywhere. She turns west, sun behind haze, sky greyish, sluggish wet air sweating onto her skin, stops to look at a poster in a bus shelter. AIDS. An unusual image that draws, then shocks. She walks on quickly when she notices the man watching her, tall, thin, grey. Cut from the herd and stalked, no longer free to wander, gaze in windows, she must keep going up Bloor Street without looking behind to see how close he may be. She turns suddenly, gratefully in to an open door, gingered smells of a health food deli, bulk foods, vitamins, herbal teas; biblical name over the door. She has her packsack with her, which she takes most places, emptied of everything but her notebook, pen, her glasses, scoops some bulk bulghur wheat for pilaf, oats for porridge and brown rice into plastic bags. She didn't see any of these on Margot's kitchen shelves. She reaches across the bins for twist ties. Her eyes collide with his. Fifteen, on her way home from choir practice at the United church no longer just around the corner from Osborne Street. Lily must take the bus home to where you are sleeping. His *hello, Jean* stops her, thinking he is a friend of yours, until she sees his eyes. How does a stranger know your name? She hurries down Osborne Street into the Margaret Rose Tea Room, a rabbit frozen silent, those eyes filling street, tea room, her. Lily no longer sings in the choir. Decides she is an atheist.

Lily takes the gun from her head, turns it onto his eyes, between his eyes, pulls the trigger, carefully twists wire ties around her bags, pays for them, checks the window, enters the street again, looks behind, watches ahead, walks on past Spadina, past Bathurst and Honest Ed's and up and down a few of the side streets here where people are out on their porches, old and middle-aged women in black, and old men. As though she's invaded their privacy they stare at her without smiling, across the peppers, tomatoes, broad beans, the grape vines and flowers crowding small hedged or fenced patches lining the street of joined houses on either side.

Back at Bloor orange patio lights have come on under the awnings of sidewalk cafés. She's tired, hungry, buys a newspaper, sits down at a patio table, orders tea, juice, a roll and salad. A large family gathering a few tables away, the patriarch who orders for all, his wife, daughters, sons, in-laws, grandchildren, a little boy off his chair, wandering about, two little girls in white dresses, wriggling in their mothers' laps and whining to get down too.

Lily eats, sips her tea, reads, notices the patriarch staring at her, thinks perhaps she's been watching them too much, settles down to read the rest of her paper. A kind of bliss settling, air gone from heavy to soft, no matter it is getting late. When her eyes lift from reading they encounter a hostile stare, the patriarch reminding her she is alone at night, no rings, in shorts and t-shirt, with a backpack. Would it be acceptable if she was twenty? Probably not. Hardening the skin of her eyes to keep out his burden, she thinks of turning the gun on him too, that spot right between those eyes. But the gun is gone. Instead she orders another tea, finishes her paper.

IN A SMALL RESTAURANT UP FROM THE LAKE, the cook holds open the swinging door into the kitchen and eyes Lily suspiciously after she asks the server to have her chicken washed under the tap to rinse off the marinade before they cook it. Jan's silence Lily takes for sympathy with the cook. They walk off the meal, have hardly spoken. The swelling is down in Jan's face. She says it doesn't hurt to eat, annoyed, almost belligerent when Lily says they needn't have come out for dinner. I wanted to. Lily losing the thread of Jan does not know who this is, an unfamiliar in a familiar body becoming less so. Pangs in Lily, a fragment cut off from the whole struggling to be whole again, birth work shadowing Lily.

Why were riot police there?

Haven't got a clue, why don't you ask me why I was there?

Yes, all right.

It didn't just happen to me. A dancer had her toe broken. She doesn't belong to any political group, just wanted to support single mothers. We went to support the anti-poverty coalition.

How long have you known Ted?

A while.

You've never mentioned him. Is that why you didn't come back for Christmas?

I couldn't afford to.

I was going to pay for your ticket.

Why didn't you come here? I didn't even know Margot . . . you
were living in her house.

Margot wanted you to come. She suggested it. I told you that.

So what did you do?

I don't know what Margot did. We went to a party.

You and Ted?

If you'd come, we were going to have Christmas dinner at
Margot's.

Haven't seen her since that day I arrived.

She's hardly ever around except when she works downstairs. She
travels a lot.

How long since she moved in? Lily wanting more, not these
perfunctory questions and answers.

I don't know, something like nine or ten years. Jan's voice
irritated—this demand of Lily's for information, bearings—she
rents the house, shares rent with the women in the office
downstairs. It's a mess, I know. That word again. There's a woman
who comes in to clean when it gets too bad. Margot hasn't got
time. Apology and approval for Margot; protecting her, from Lily?
What they do downstairs Lily has yet to figure out, it slips into
long crowded spaces between words as they turn back the way they
came along the boardwalk, toward cooler air now, haze thickening,
flaring lamplight up into the trees. A small boy, just beginning to
walk, lets go his parents' hands and stares up at the light, reaches
for moon rain, lucent leaves. The moon out there aureoled in mist.
Lighted lamps haloed along the boardwalk trail, between Beaches
property and the dark-moon-sheened lake wordlessly touching
what it can reach. Further down a dark, curving shadow of bench
beside the darker shadow of a man standing alone with his
saxophone. The blue jazz a wail moving like water, a wake in the
air, through this silence between Lily and Jan so familiar it could be
you walking beside her; Lily the child, Jan unreachable.

Lily frowns out at the fog in front of her, wanting to be out of
it, somewhere dryer, clearer, somewhere warmer. They never speak
of their father, Jan and Steph, not to her, perhaps to each other,

have never grieved in her presence. Already divorced when he disappears, is this why? But his absence comes much sooner. Lily casting back trying to locate when it was Jan first told her they both knew a divorce was coming, but couldn't or wouldn't say how they knew . . . *we just knew, Steph mentioned it first. Little Steph?* Lily shocked, asks what she said. Again Jan can't or won't remember. *This isn't about Stephie and me, is it? I thought it was . . . about losing your father. That's not who we've lost . . .*

Jan's voice low, her face turning lakeward. Pardon? Lily says. I said, when are you going to stop mourning who Gran wasn't? *Go back*, your words in Lily? To where? Lily's version, her story of you, you are not what you seemed, neither is love, nor silence; is this where she is? They've come to where the boardwalk ends, climb stone stairs back up to the street. Fog thins the further away from the water they walk, flares all the lights along Queen Street, shadows and edges fraying, falling away, Lily sitting beside Jan, unable to stop the streetcar, get off, out of a silence that knows what's too much to bear letting out, another kind of resistance, wisdom?

SATURDAY, AND THE DAY of the dragon boat races, she didn't know that. Has come early, taking the Bay bus down to the waterfront, pushed at, shoved, as though she isn't there, doesn't exist, surrounded and carried along by everyone moving onto the bus, their eyes unseeing her, finds herself standing beside a large woman seated in one of the single seats by the window, the last one before the row seating at the back of the bus. The woman does not make eye-contact, talks to herself, no one, someone. Beware of the Ides of March, you know March is when you die my husband was killed by a bus, March, is when you die . . . three or four men behind her grin at each other, wait for what will come next. She pulls the cord, looks at Lily. Here's a V.I.P. seat.

Take care, Lily says, something protective flaring up in her. Take care, the woman repeats the words, carries her weight past Lily.

Bleached hair pulled back off her face with a child's headband, a lot of makeup. The men start to laugh. *Jerks*, tumbles out of her mouth as she sits in the seat vacated by the woman, feels their sudden silence, and some vulnerability to risk brought on by her voice. It persists even out here on the water. Fresher here, looking back on that line between city and sky blurred in humidity; harbour, black blue gold tinted glass of King and Bay receding from her eye. Centre Island where the crowds are, the megaphoned voices.

Hanlan's Point quiet, mostly cyclists. Lily startled by clear water lapping shore, her, a sudden rush of audible sights, small birds on long legs running along the sand in front of her, crows moving the air with their wings, mourning dove somewhere behind, ahead. Haze over the water, sailboat appearing and fading into it, her eye on it, following the disappearance, appearance, Lily gone, her body beach, somewhere without edges she knows is not fog. Divided, wanting to stay here letting her body become water, sand, light, a bird, at least stay and eat her lunch, rest her sore feet. But she must remember where she is and not get careless. Perhaps it would be better to go where there are more people. Aware now there isn't anyone around except for a couple of young men who've come up the beach behind her and are fooling around on a fallen tree; there, in the corner of her eye. Conscious of her pack, her wallet and camera, she decides to walk back out to the asphalt road, across the grass toward the megaphone voices. Wanting to stay, but if something happens the question will be asked, what was she doing out there by herself anyway? the question thrown open by her willingness to be here, explorer. And she will be dismissed. Lily not able to believe it wouldn't happen is determined not to go that way, for Jan and Stephanie's sakes. Her feet more painful now, happy to see a woman playing with her child by a water fountain, asks her which way to Centre Island. The woman doesn't speak a lot of English, tries to be helpful, far, she says, pointing with her left hand, searching for another word. Bridge? Lily asks and the woman's face lights up. Yes! she says, bridge, motioning, go. She points again with her left hand. And go left? The woman nods, relieved, repeats Lily's words, go left. They both smile, nod, say thank you.

Lily wanders past dragon boat races to formal gardens, stone fountains, benches where she can rest aching hips, thighs, legs, feet, knows she'll get no further today. Unable to walk where she wants to go. What look to be swans in the channel turn out to be painted wood pedal-boats when she crosses the bridge. Her disappointment child-like and the channel idyllic winding between mossy green banks, fluffy trees beckoning, but the ferry is coming, bringing more people, and she has a need to get away from this density, enclosure.

Ferry Passengers Are To Remain Seated Until The Ferry Docks ... they stand shoulders pressing, a relief to see the ferry make it to the dock, compressed humanity expand, stream off. It takes a while, she needn't have rushed. Few returning downtown this early in the day; she has the almost empty ferry to herself going back to the crowds still waiting to come across. She limps away to catch a bus back up to Bloor, to a matinee where she can rest her feet, disappointed they are too sore to catch some of the outdoor jazz, that she feels old. Air conditioning in the theatre far too cold after being in the sun, she shivers through a film about a middle-aged woman with an academic career and occasional lovers, recently divorced or married male colleagues usually; a young woman has fallen in love with her, a circus performer, high-wire aerialist, her own youth calling her back to what, whoever has gone missing? rescuing the amnesiac whose feet know the way, who falls lightly into grace? You hated it, being old—is this what it comes to, falling in love with your youth too late, feet too sore for the highwire? *They* were old, not you. You avoid park benches.

Lily sits on one under a cool green canopy of trees at Queen's Park, surrounded by still mangled flowers and shrubbery, remains of Jan's tooth here somewhere, *beat them into silence and say it is for God and country* a strange untranquil point at which to rest her feet and watch Saturday afternoon slide by, her eye following traffic

north around the curve to yesterday's museum escalators taking her
up and up, back and back into remains of antiquity, the imposed
chronology, timeline putting so much distance, space between her
eye and whoever shaped and fired what was once someone's water
pot. She doesn't want to go back to the house, not just yet. If her
feet didn't hurt so she'd return to the art gallery and Barbara
Hepworth's sculptures playing along edges of dark and light, shape
taking Lily within shape, edge within edge becoming centre, light
completing spirals catching it, taking it somewhere else, taking
Lily's eye along the curve of light and shadow to where it bends,
images appear on the eye's horizon, the bird, high and alone. Too
large for a pigeon, a gull perhaps in from the lake, turns, alters
course down, Lily's eye following not the bird which she can't see
but its reflection in the glass curve of the Hydro Tower—sky,
clouds, trees, the gull's wings vertical, underbelly navigating the arc
in unison with its own reflection, then gone, slipped off the edge
into its solitary flight. What does the gull know of collision with its
own reflection, of taking itself for an other?

SHE IS COOKING CHICKEN WHEN MARGOT arrives, disappointment
on both their faces, Lily hoping it would be Jan turning her key in
the lock, Margot surprised to find her here. I thought you and Jan
would be out? Lily apologises. No, no, not at all Margot says,
recovering, I cancelled my dinner plans, just thought I'd come
home, have a bath and go to bed. Jan upstairs?

Off with Ted somewhere for the night, I was just cooking some
dinner for myself, Lily walking through to the living room to turn
down the jazz tape one of Margot's she's put on—I've been
enjoying your tapes.

Hardly ever listen to them any more, forget I have them. The
cd's are better . . . you should play them.

I don't know anything about cd's.

Get Jan to show you. This heat, I need to change. Smells good.
What is it? Margot heads for her bedroom, peeling clothing as she
goes.

Chicken, some garlic, lemon . . . sorry, not a night to be
cooking. I'll finish as soon as I can, Lily checking her watch,
hesitates before asking Margot if she's eaten yet.

Umm, well, that's okay.

There's plenty. I thought Jan and Ted might appear, but I don't
really expect them. She lies, is cooking extra to leave in the fridge
for Jan to have after she leaves, babbles on to cover begrudging

Margot the chicken meant for Jan; feeling less intimidated by her.
Perhaps it is the drowned look of Margot's face, just for a moment,
when she first comes in. I'm cooking some rice I found in your
cupboard, there's makings for salad, part of a baguette.

Can it wait till I've had my bath? Oh sure, Lily says, turning
down the heat, rummaging for a lid to cover the chicken so it
won't dry out, pushes it down onto the pan with a sharp bang
obliterated by squealing pipes as Margot runs her bath.

Ah, Margot says, sinking down into a kitchen chair. I'd suggest
paying Jan to cook and clean for me but I think she'd leave if I did.
I could use a good wife.

Pardon?

Just an expression, couldn't we all—thank you, this looks good.
Beats takeout. How did you cook the chicken?

The usual way, I think.

Have you and Jan had a good visit? Pointed politeness tinged
with sarcasm? Lily not sure, regretting having suggested dinner
and Margot obviously exhausted and expecting to have the
evening to herself does not bode well. Jan downstairs most of the
time or with Ted, except for their foggy day at the Beaches and a
couple of visits with her downstairs at the office, a few breakfasts,
when she isn't at Ted's. I'm not sure, she tells Margot, this at least
closer to the truth.

She works well with the women, does some of my research,
some for them. It's been good having her here. She's very capable.
You must be proud of her. Each sentence punctuated by Margot
with a pause for Lily to fill, say something, anything. When she
doesn't, Margot moves on, filling the gaps with short sharp
sentences between mouthfuls. I know she's been looking forward to
seeing you. It's unfortunate the episode with the police happened
just when you arrived. A big shock for her, depressing.

She didn't talk much about it.

She didn't talk to me about it either, I'm just surmising this
wouldn't have been a good week for her. More silence. Lily eats,
swallows down something along with her food. Margot does not

normally seem at a loss for words, at least not with Jan. Well, Jan plays her cards close to her chest, she offers Lily. Lily doesn't respond, feeling alien. Even when Jan was little, Lily never knew what was going on, inside that is, what was bothering her, until she'd worked it out, and then she might let Lily know. Stephie spills everything to her, until the shock of Stephie gone without warning, nothing to prepare Lily, how can that be? Lily did the same thing with you, but different, surely; you both knew. What is it Lily can't see?

Well, what do children and parents really know about each other anyway? Margot's eyes as she says it meet Lily's with a tired gaze. Lily looks down at her plate.

I think Jan said you were from Winnipeg?

Right, I moved around, so where did you live in Winnipeg, Lily? Lily does not wish to go there. Fort Rouge, she says, leaving it vague, hoping Margot will let it go. But Margot at one point lives with a family just off Osborne Street close to the river and just south of the railway yards, Lily and you just north, Margot saying she used to fall into that river on purpose and Lily caught back at the river's mouth in a sharp moment opening between them . . . if you're trouble they can send you back . . . Margot's bland voice giving no sign. They? Foster homes, didn't Jan tell you?

Just north of the railways yards, you and Lily, when you take her south on the April train to Winnipeg and Osborne Street. And a war later, you now a widow, Lily fatherless, April again, you find new rooms on the banks of a frozen river called the Assiniboine. Spring breakup, exploding ice, broken dikes, the piano you did not sell, too heavy to move, taken by water. I bailed out of pre-med courses and left for Toronto all she says to Margot, words slipping away into Margot's Oh? and movement of cutlery on plates, into awkward silence and the scrape of Margot's chair across hardwood, squeal of water pipes, kitchen tap running water into her glass, Margot telling her the best thing she ever did was run away, fifteen, on the streets of Toronto shouldn't have been okay but she guesses she got lucky, who knows how these things happen, guardian angel? Someone took her in, then took her on. A woman old enough to be her grandmother.

There are two postcards from Guatemala since Christmas, one for Lily, one for Jan care of Lily. *We're fine. Seeing the country. Meeting people. Visiting the Maya in their villages. They give us a place to stay in their homes, their food, they hardly have anything, even their land to grow their food is being taken away from them. Don't worry. Love Stephie...* have they any idea what's going on down there? Has she thought about Security Police reading this card? *Runaway* slips off Margot's tongue too close to the anguish of this detachment Lily feels.

Jan and I hardly ever see each other, but it is nice to know she's here, that I've been able to give her a hand with a place to stay, some work, which isn't easy to find these days . . . aren't you happy for her? Margot's voice trails off as she sits back down across from Lily and reaches for a chunk of baguette. Does she expect Lily to say something? What? An expression of appreciation?

She could have stayed with me, taken courses in BC . . . she seems to have been somewhat overwhelmed by you.

Me . . . ? I don't think so.

Perhaps you aren't aware of your influence, Lily persists, she hasn't even wanted to come home. She's not a runaway needing to be taken in. Margot up taking her plate to the sink before the words, painful as pissing stones, are out of Lily's mouth.

Uh, let's leave these dishes, coffee?

Tea is fine, empty, automatic words, Lily clearing the table, scraping dishes, stacking them in the sink, filling the sink with hot water. Might as well finish these.

When do you go back to Vancouver? Margot leans against the window frame, looking out, Lily closes her eyes.

Tomorrow. Winnipeg, not Vancouver, to bury my mother's ashes.

Jan said you had them with you. Lily wonders how it is said, spreads the dishcloth across the draining dishes. The boiling kettle whistles. Margot offers Lily water for her herbal teabag. Don't you want the teapot?

A mug's fine. Coffee drips; Lily dunks her teabag up and down.

I should drink that instead, Margot says, finally, watching Lily, I'd probably sleep better, not have such wild dreams when I do sleep. What about you? ... you do dream?

Sometimes ... I don't remember most of them, all Lily wants to say.

Fraying evening light out on the front steps and soft sounds of small birds flitting unseen among the trees above them, the spicy fragrance of a late dinner cooking somewhere mingling with fragments of conversation across lawns further up the street; parts of her alert and watching but not feeling. They sit quietly slapping at occasional needling whines of mosquitoes, turrets of Casa Loma glowing above the all-night supermarket lighting up the end of the street with a frayed neon glare from around the corner. A trolley bus sets wires humming along Dupont, streetlights on, neighbours across the street moving what's left of their lawn sale back into the house. They have one every Saturday, Margot says. No business permit ... silence, and then, are you happy, content, Lily? Margot's words seem to float past her. What would that be, a story that keeps changing to another version? Who is she, sitting on these steps, familiar unease in this need to explain herself, justify her need for a role. Good at it, she discovers, when Mrs. Carmichael takes her under her wing, Lily playing the lead in a Sunday School play, playing a man, playing it to the hilt, surprising everyone, including herself, something coming loose in her, she can impersonate, hide herself in someone she is not.

You've had a husband, Margot is saying, have a couple of great children, if Stephanie is anything like Jan, and a nice home I assume, haven't had to be self-supporting, can do what you want, don't have to answer to anyone. Why not contentment? Lily feeling cannibalised, collapsed into before, miniaturised and contained. Act of revenge, survival, can it be that simple, marrying the hope of love's existence in this world Bruce's religion held out to Lily for the price of her guilt and your truth? Could she have foreseen Bruce pleading with her for help when his god can't, the one who can take away the sins of the world but not Bruce's shame for being in Lily, for wanting her body, not her, Lily discovers; shame he keeps giving her, a gift bestowed, until it is hers. Leaving the only thing she can do for either of them, and now sitting here it comes to her as a small contentment to have chosen to do so long before Bruce and his plane go missing in bad weather over the mountain passes, wings shearing tops of cedar, fir, hemlock, the resinous scent flying up her nose, hitting against the roof of her skull, collision with stone, torn wings pitching downwards, slicing between trees toward a stillness of floating eagles, spiralling down, then surging along waves of sky. Animals shadow through trees, circling. The lingering presence of lostness, not being found, an accusation waiting for her to take it in, Lily feels leave her in a sigh, a long breath. Bruce, unlike Margot, is orphaned at twelve and taken in by an aunt and uncle to be the oldest child in their family. Lily does not mention this, any of it, says only that things are not always what they seem.

She learns Margot has no idea who her parents were, knows only what she was told from her file—bloodlines, she says, whatever that's all about . . . what's the point of digging up bones you have to bury again? I picked my own name . . . we invent ourselves, or someone else will do it for us, in Margot's voice a growing hardness, impatience, Lily wondering if this is where Jan's is coming from, taking it on. *To not know history is to remain a child*, someone said that, I can't remember who, Margot says, more to the air than Lily. Which version, Lily is wondering, back in Kansas now, dust-devils skipping over the fields and Bea's eyes smiling jump in, all things possible. Amelia E. tips her wings and a child runs, arms widespread and Lily feels the flutter, an arrythmia, her heart. Is the child less knowing of life, if less experienced at rationalising it?

What caused your mother's death? Do you mind my asking?

I don't think they knew. Dementia what they write on your death certificate, making you responsible, doctor evasive. The morphine? metastasis from breast to bone, to lungs? your heart too

long in the birth canal, born still, or just in time? Secret stories
carried in the blood and bones of the women we come from,
women unrecorded and absent from history and their own stories?
Mothers who were daughters, daughters who were grandmothers, a
line under the skin of poets, weavers, warriors and priests, healers,
witches working the land, labouring in fields, healing out of
themselves and their gardens. This how we lost our way, in secrets;
the violation, resistance of silence, so much fear, shame. Lily holds
your hand, tells you, follow your heart, it's all any of us can do.
Your heart goes wild. Is Lily responsible, singing to the tree with an
unfamiliar voice in a language she doesn't know? Wanting to know
what she'd never asked of the silence of you. *Dementia*, released to
climb trees and look for their coming, to your mother's garden
where you went with her, become unexpectedly Lily's garden too,
shattering Lily's illusion of Lily free, not free. She brushes away
something from her face, a whirring.

Moths, Margot says, spreading her hand, moving it as though
straining the dusk around them. They get in through the holes in
the screens. I should get some work done around this place, but
there's never time. Lily remembering Jan's cries there were moths in
her room, having to clear them out before she would go back to
sleep. They sit for a time without speaking.

Family is where you find them, Margot says. Even when they're
someones else's? stays inside Lily. I thought about children for a
long time, but I'm past it now. It would probably have been a
disaster. I prefer being on my own. Better aunt than mother. I'd
like to think of myself as a kind of an aunt to Jan. An adopted
aunt, since she doesn't have any, since you and I don't have sisters?
a kind of extended family?

You and Jan seem to have adopted each other . . . I think I
should pay you something for her living expenses. She feels it come
out quick and hard, Margot flinch.

She does work for me, good work, and I don't pay her enough
for what she does well. It will all be quite valuable experience if she
does go on to take law. She has a natural sense of what the law's

about and how to use it. She may change her mind and if she does she'll be more than capable at whatever she decides to do. Does Margot think Lily doesn't know this? The work is basically advocacy, Margot tells her, helping other women know what their basic human rights and their legal rights are. Violence has been a reality in most of their lives, or their children's, in one way or another. Jan wouldn't be here if she didn't want to. You know that about her too. She did tell me she wanted to live away from Vancouver. I didn't ask why.

There had to be a reason why she was the way she was, Jan says when Lily tells her Hannah's story of you, Rachel, just before Jan leaves for Toronto. The way she was? The way she treated you, the way she took her hate out on you. The way you let her and can't even see what it's done to you. And Lily sits wordless while Jan tells her she is leaving to come here, go to university and live in Margot's house.

She stands on the soreness in her feet. I think it must be quite late, her voice stiff, perhaps we should call it a night. Almost one— I have a plane to catch at seven tomorrow morning, Margot says, but remains sitting. It hasn't cooled off much, would have been hard to sleep anyway . . . can't see the moon from here . . . guess you'll see it tomorrow night in Winnipeg, hanging out there like a big hole in the sky. Galileo's moon, Lily thinks, what you see, feel, can you call it truth? Well, I'd better go up and put a call in for a cab for tomorrow while I'm thinking about it or I'll forget and go to bed. I'll need some work from Jan when I'm back at the end of the week. Would you mind letting her know I've left a note about it on her desk? Lily feels dismissed. Glad I decided to come home tonight, thanks for the dinner, Margot adds.

I'll let you know when I'm coming out to Vancouver, she calls up the stairs, Lily already fallen into bed, hears it as a question she doesn't answer. Out somewhere in the streets a cry broken loose, ghosting through street shadows, a wail, Lily awake, listening; closer now, an anguish of shock, pain, terror, betrayal calling out to a sleeping, absent street. She creeps downstairs, dials 911, hands trembling, an unsteady voice. The woman's voice crisp, clear, calm—Where are you calling from? Can you tell from which direction? I'm visiting, Lily says, I'm not sure, I'm facing south. She can't remember the street number. We'll send a car to check out the area, the woman tells her. Thank you, Lily says, surely others have called. The whole neighbourhood must be awake . . . No sound from Margot's room, Jan's room empty, no lights on anywhere. Silence. One fifty a.m., her travelling alarm, not digital, still has hands. Jan with Ted. Lily frozen knowing she wanted Jan to come home tonight, knows she cannot keep Jan where she has held her, and Stephanie, somewhere inside her, strong and safe and keeping Lily so. What is out on the street is in her, stealing her body, her children from her; locating her nowhere.

She's somewhere else now where light bends, follows the curve, reflects off hard terrazzo floors where two women walk surrounded in darkness, their feet making no sound. Neither do those of the figures following from either side whispering at them they have no shoes, watch where they walk; into a market, blue sky, yellow light on heaps of maize, tomatoes, beans, peppers, vendors call out to them, plants hidden in their baskets to ease pains of birth, for joy to go on when the body is exhausted, but they can't hear, hurry on towards a church white as alabaster at the centre of the square with matching Blessed Virgin hung with flowers guarding the door, her eyes cast down to endless votive candles around her feet, turning her to flaming tallow, her eyes the last to slip to shapeless wax . . . vendors, old women, young women, girls, children keep calling out from the marketplace a language the women don't know until they feel the warning, alter course, night roads, derelict house, root cellar, grave, cry broken loose a bird arrested in its flight, turns to stone, drops into a child's hand.

Lily sits up in bed, blood pounding her skin. Stephanie, Em, what has happened to them . . . birds, she can hear them outside, beyond the drumming, other sounds of life, a car starting up, Margot's taxi, Margot going down the stairs, unlocking the front door, shutting it behind her, locking it again, her steps across the porch, down the stairs they sat on last night, taxi door opening, shutting, taxi pulling away. Breathe, she tells herself, hands going for her breasts, feeling for lumps she's sure must be there, pads of her fingers rabbits circling the clock, against the clock, smaller and smaller circles, midnight, noon, midnight noon until she is at the centre. Breathe and walk. She paces around the bedroom, downstairs, the bathroom, kitchen, living room. The orange cat raises its head from its curled sleep. They look at one another. Don't go, Lily says, breathing hard. The cat blinks at her, leaps lightly up onto the windowsill. Okay, Lily says, backs away into the kitchen to make herself tea.

The cat still here lying curled on the sofa when she brings her tea and toast through, doesn't stir when she sits beside it, other than to curl more tightly around itself and its enigmatic smile. It permits her hand to follow the curve of fur along its back, to rest there, to trace from spine along the path of tail to its tucked-up oversize paws. She touches each of them lightly with her fingertip. The cat turns, lies on its back. She strokes its creamy belly and the cat catches her fingers in its paws, bats at them, suddenly bites. Lily's tea overturns onto her toast, her lap, Margot's sofa. It all lands on the hardwood floor. The cat gone out the window, sitting there blinking its eyes at her. She shuts the window. Damn cat, sorry, cat, she mutters, and cleans up the mess, hoping the sofa and floor will dry without a stain, cat watching her from outside the window.

A hot shower does little for the coldness, this detachment, numbness, this inability to feel needles of hot water pricking her reddening skin, even where the tea burned the insides of her thighs. A dull, distant rush of water that does nothing to wash away the dream telling her too many things and nothing at all. What is she to make of it? Leans to turn off the water, water's heat drumming on her skin a hand touching her shoulder, yours?

By the time Jan arrives Lily does not cry with relief when she sees her. This recurring despair in her that she's brought two women into this life for what waits for them here without their choosing, that she did it almost without thinking, without knowing, is this what Jan feels from her, runs from? I was just going to call a cab, Lily says. We had a late night. Friends came by Ted's this morning. I don't want you to apologise. I'm not, just telling you what happened. Margot left a note for you on her desk . . . how was the jazz concert? It was okay, nothing special. What about you, what did you do? A long day doing nothing in particular, Lily says, went to the islands, saw a film, got sore feet and came back here. I guess you saw Margot before she left. We had dinner here last night. Oh? Did I tell you Margot's a recovering alcoholic? No, you didn't. That's why there's no liquor in the house. I didn't notice. Right, I forgot. What will you do now? Go to Winnipeg with Gran's ashes. Lily notes the whites of Jan's eyes, bloodshot, rimmed with red. Should she say something? I'm going to have them buried with your grandfather. Can you do that? Apparently. Then what? Not enough sleep? Lily wondering. What can Lily tell her? Wait and see? She feels blurred, losing track of something, snared, she's someone else telling little tales to please, hide, escape the question. Does this mean letting you go, getting on with life? Lily tries to imagine what this means to let you go, how she would go about this. Could she do anything about this reunion with you after long absence . . . *how can I enter a second time into my mother's womb . . .*? many times, it seems. Maybe I should plant trees, Lily tells her, the infant lying between her thighs, Lily's curious feeling, this arrival of warm sweet flesh, the real mother come at last, not you. Maybe art school. I'll see, when I get back. What about all those courses you've taken? Can't you get a degree? teach? something? How will you support yourself, the insurance won't go on forever. Neither will I. Fine, Jan snaps. It'll be alright for a while yet, Lily says quickly, surprised by Jan's anger. She had meant to be lighthearted, looks at her daughter, trying to see where this has come from, says tentatively, hoping to lighten things, that she could do worse than end up a bag lady. Bruce's policy designed to get both his offspring through college. After that Lily is on her own. Great, so what are you going to do, go to funerals and visit graveyards for the rest of your life? She's still at it. Who? Gran . . . Jan already halfway down the stairs flings it back over her shoulder at Lily in the middle of the kitchen, listening, waiting for the door of the office below to open, then close.

She doesn't want your life, or mine, Lily tells you. Hard white light from a humid sky. She squints, leaves her bags on the porch to knock on the office door and tell Jan she's left the house keys on the kitchen table, then puts on her sunglasses and sits on the porch steps to wait for the cab. Is it because of Gran you do that work? Lily says, not looking at Jan when she comes out and sits beside her on the steps. The job was here when I came and I needed the money. What, Lily wonders, is she supposed to do now, doesn't know what to say to ease Jan's burden of her, this mother who imagines if she doesn't desire, seek her own, then her children's lives will be safe, this weight of you. What is it you want, she says finally, exasperated, besides for me to get on with my life, let you get on with yours, which I thought you were doing. Lily pushing out her voice to its edges where it simply frays, breaks; unable to make it hard, sharp, cutting. *Is it Gran, or me, is the anger love or hate, or both?* remains unspoken.

The forgotten cab turns the corner in the corner of her eye, an accident waiting. They are both standing, Jan taking one bag, Lily the other. She glances at Jan while the driver slings the bags into the trunk. Jan's face turned away. Lily moves to enter the cab, puts a hand out to touch her daughter's shoulder and stops when she sees Jan's face, the look, very old, very young. Did you notice that, Lily tells you, later in the taxi, after Jan's unexpected embrace, and hers back, becomes a less unsettling hello and goodbye.

SHE EXPECTS IT TO BE A ROUGH LANDING coming into Winnipeg.
Jesus Christ, the woman next to her murmurs, praying or swearing,
hand on her throat. *He's the Lily of the Valley, my Bright and
Morning Star,* Lily keeps her mouth closed in Sunday School when
the others sing, mouthing the words sometimes if she feels noticed,
pretending to know by heart, knowing her heart knows this is not
true. Her heart in her throat now as the big jet so low to ground
suddenly dips a wing as though it will alter course, follow its own
arcing horizon. Jesus Christ, the woman says again, out loud, when
the jet straightens, bounces onto the runway.

THE COFFEE SHOP past the hospital, past the bicycle shop, where
she waits with poached eggs on dry toast and a leftover *Free Press*
from yesterday until it is time to call the woman at the cemetery.
The shop where you buy the bicycle for her still here, Lily feels it
waiting for her, someone fell here; an unexpected turn when she
sees it. Not open yet. Hers not a normal CCM like everyone else's.
Smaller, narrower tires, faster, everything special, nothing regular,
parts difficult to find.
   You sure? you ask Lily. It's the one Lily wants. Spring, grade six.
Is it because Lily didn't fail, like she almost did the year before,
after her summer in the country so close to where you were born,

where they put her on a pony, bareback, slap its rear, laughing, sending it galloping out into a field as big as the world, its hairy mane clutched in Lily's hands, her legs too short. She feels the slide along a curve of galloping flesh, horizon between her and ground, feels herself falling off the edge, her head, shoulder colliding with a wall of hard, prairie floor.

The bike an extension of Lily, when walking becomes running and there's no place to go; Lily's other. She turns corners no hands, moves like wind in, around, through a city and beyond into space that takes her heart, breath; where she is centre, edge, circling horizon, emptiness. She can't remember how the wheel of the bicycle got bent, a car must have run over it on the shoulder of the highway, or how she got it home. Lily leaves it behind when she leaves you, a body to dispose of.

PARALLEL CURVES OF THE cemetery's stone wall and the river, the Red, silver under a humid sky, greenness of trees hanging over it almost black. She remembers a drier heat, more wind. The woman in the church office looks at Lily's empty hands. I've changed my mind. Can you show me where my father's buried? A Xerox copy is put into her hands of a larger map of the graveyard. *You are here/ Vous êtes ici*, the map indicates, with a circled X. I will make arrangements to have a small gravestone made. Lily doesn't say both your names will be on it. The woman, Lily discovers, is not the church secretary but the Anglican priest.

Lily does not know why her father is buried here. He's not there, you tell Lily, and never go near the grave, except when he is put into it. Refuse to go with Lily, go if you want, you tell her, and Lily when she is there caught in a gust of wind that tears zinnias, marigolds, last of the fall flowers from the child's hand, scatters them, seeds across gravestones and her out of there. Quarried limestone wall surrounding cathedral and graves, can it shut out the river? It is said the pipe organ mysteriously begins to sigh on its own, wind in grass, in cottonwoods and willows along the river, the river itself, another language, drowning the minister's Evensong sermon for a Christmas crowd. That spring the train takes Lily.

Following the river north, past St. Andrew's Rapids, Lockport, the quarries and their limestone remains of Red River settlements, to Selkirk. Her father left from here; came from somewhere else. From east, over that same northern Precambrian shore of Rachel's coming and Lily's going, returning from the first Great War, a sniper, you tell Lily, was it you? or did he, Lily can't remember now. His mother motherless, losing stepmother and father by the time she is twelve, Lily's age when Lily loses him; his grandmother losing her mother to consumption in a log cabin on the banks of the St. Lawrence River; his father adopted from England, a woman too poor to keep him.

LONDON BATHED in an evening's summer glow when Lily arrives from Edinburgh; the cab racing through almost deserted streets to Chelsea where she has a room for the night as big as a monastery cell she can barely afford in order to spend the next day at the General Register Office, mapping her father as far as these archival soundings will take her. She walks to the river in the rest of the evening's light, encounters the stone wall of the Physic Garden, follows it all the way round to the gate, which is locked. Apothecaries begin the garden over three hundred years ago, when witches were being burned, to explore the natural medicine of herbs and plants. Never open to the public until recently. Lily has come just after closing time. All morning in the archives Lily travels with her father back to Spanish Jews escaping the Inquisition. With no more days before the plane takes her on to Manitoba and you, she walks without map, heading north, perhaps, not knowing London, finds herself in narrow streets, a large square, a park of heavy dark trees surrounded by wrought iron and eventually standing in front of a small stone building. The plaque by the door says it is a Jewish Museum.

She enters on impulse. Finds herself in an airlock between two
steel doors and panicking. A male voice speaks through some kind
of intercom. She can barely understand his instructions she is so
claustrophobic. Finally inside, she has difficulty remembering, let
alone signing, her name and address which they tell her she must
do to receive an identity card to pin on her shirt before being
allowed to proceed upstairs. A dismaying warren of hallways. It
seems she is the only visitor. Still shaking, unable to stop thinking
about how to get out again. A woman upstairs at a little desk
checks her identity card, has her sign in again, and motions her
through. She can't just run down the stairs and out, must at least
show some pretence of wanting to be here. Lingers longer than she
wants, curious and childlike, wanting something, a story, feeling of
inhabitation. But then must get out as quickly as possible from
physical confinement, this learned and knowing fear, survival. The
guards take back her identity card, buzz her out the first door. She
freezes when the outer door does not open. An acrid taste in the
back of her throat, relief when her eyes light on a button she is to
push to let herself out, out in air, trees, sky, momentary euphoria,
still trembling.

LILY DRIVES WITH your ashes, can't put you into earth, cover you
over. Joined by a pair of pelicans. Yellow fields, red silo, blue sky
and the white pelicans leading her on through grassy narrows,
reeds, water, the Aggasiz basin, tideless Lake Winnipeg blue as the
sky the pelicans disappear into. Drawn north and north, Lily
follows the curve of water to more remains, Icelandic settlements
now, stony northern shores where they come with decorated trunks
carrying their lives. A worn smooth stone Lily picks up off the
beach fits the palm of her hand, her eye tracing, finger touching,
following a spiral line curving on itself, vanishing into stone it
came from.

The turn west through wetlands, then wild rice, land rising
from water a narrow neck between lakes fragmenting to vibrating

points of light behind her eyes. Beyond the neck a yellow sun on yellowing wheat with blue flax and crows. Between blossoming ditches Lily driving a child outstretched against a sun grown out of its sky, dark child disappearing into the picture; butterflies, dragonflies, red-winged blackbirds, meadowlarks, red-tailed hawks in the corner of her eye; Lily she can't find. The lost hamlet lying between two valleys, *good, mixed rolling land, once fairly bushy ... a forest fire,* late 1890s, *the land relatively clear when the first settlers came by ox-cart and horse and wagon.* The railway comes through in 1903, train #s 9 and 10 from Winnipeg to Saskatoon bringing twice-daily mail service from the east in the morning, west in the evening. By the time you and Lily's father arrive in the early days of the Great Depression there are two grain elevators, a livery barn, blacksmith, four stores, barbershop and pool hall, church, curling rink, an outdoor skating rink and a consolidated school to which children are brought by horse-driven school vans. She remembers the horses standing covered in hoarfrost, snorting and breathing hot steam into smoke, dry powdery crystals clustered around their nostrils and along their manes. By the end of the day red wooden vans are covered in hoarfrost too and the smoke from their chimneys joins with the breathing of the horses in fraying light of winter afternoons, waiting to take the children home again.

August 1940, a National Registration of Womenpower, for a country going to war. You have already taken Lily south to Winnipeg and Osborne Street. Was it on the #10 from Saskatoon, points west? full of young boys full of leaving high school and the farm to go to another war? Lily searching for the shadow of two grain elevators leaning against sky, finds herself in Saskatchewan, in the town named after the victorious admiral of a turn-of-the-century naval war of which Lily knows nothing. She doubles back, coming this time from the north, through trees, a forest she does not expect, spruce, pine, sandy gravel road, the child crying now, lost, wandering down the road and through the trees. Why doesn't she stay on the road, safer there, isn't it? A child who curls under a tree, watches an owl watching her. A red fox slips through the trees, yellow eyes, sharp face slipping into her. Past railway tracks and too far south now, the truck coming toward her, she'll be eating its dust. Follow me, he says, smiling, nameless, the truck old, rusting.

Where do you come from, the woman walking her dog asks Lily, the woman a pathologist from Winnipeg. Just visiting, she says, was never really here, sent away to school in the old country. The woman looks away. From Lily, her naked eyes, flesh? the pathologist has seen worse. I must be off, she says, pointing past a new bungalow on the corner, what's left is along there. An old man cutting grass in the yard stops, watches Lily walk the curve of overgrown road she barely remembers, past a community hall that by its shape was once a small wooden church. Above on a hill, a high and long pile of sawed green poplar logs. You loading the wood stove. Too much green wood, you say. Smoky, cold fires that soot up chimneys, set them to glowing like red iron in the blacksmith's magical cave that bends and, turning water to smoke, becomes a horse's shoe and Lily watches standing underneath the waiting horse; watches you fling green poplar logs into the washing and the soapy water rise out of the tubs into the air, fall back down, hit the floor and slide foaming over Lily's small feet. What sends you south against the clamour of ducks and geese returning, melting March air and a thickness of crows in poplars, taking Lily when April comes, on the train coming from Saskatoon all the way to Osborne Street? Away from here. Why? Voices calling over ice, swishing brooms, sharp crack of stone on stone colliding, air frozen silent shatters to slivers Lily feels before she sees hidden behind large spruce trees halfway down the road, the house, Lily's window looking down at her. Looking back the way she came, old man not mowing his lawn now, standing still watching her, staring. Lily staring back; still life, running figures.

IS THERE SOMETHING specific you're looking for? the archivist in Winnipeg asks Lily. Court and police records for the area incomplete. If we had a date, name, an incident, we might be able to find something for you. Lily doesn't know what she's looking for. Child, woman, her body the child, the fox with yellow eyes walks through the trees into the long grass, the poplars' thin white stems in moonlight. The grass swishes in her ears, dried-out weeds crack. Those around the fires look up, hungry, homeless, waiting. *A baby dead,* Anna says, *buried near the house, under it,* in it? Lily walks to the side of the house, can go no further, no nearer, yard full of large thick green malignant-looking plants. What might be underneath them, a sleeping snake? The crying from a small, flat, detritus-clouded window along the side of the house, partly hidden by the growth, wordless child smashing it with a hammer, pieces of glass falling around her into the weeds, small glints of light, dark, musty rot smell in her nose, nausea in Lily's belly, she backs away from this root-cellar smell of buried child.

Back in Winnipeg mercifully familiar trees still breathe here, along the Assiniboine's cut, greeting Lily with remembered shapes and soft green sunlit tears between the river and parking lot of a condo highrise that has taken the geography where you and Lily used to be, when Lily was you, running for you, becoming your absence, merciful lie. One last look at Osborne Street. Familiar, unfamiliar, Lily out of time, tune, streetcars gone, still here. She brings them with her. Lily takes your ashes with her back to the ocean.

CRIMSON SUNSET, HUMID HEAT WAVE, when the jet lands in Vancouver. A letter from Manitoba Vital Statistics waiting for Lily, in a pile of mail otherwise addressed to The Householder. She checks the answering machine. Stephanie's clear voice lifts her heart, then drops it like a stone. Lily never had this kind of power. You do. She replays her daughter's voice, strains to hear the unsaid in Stephie's too-bare message ... hi Mom ... are you there ...? I guess not, I'll try later ... don't worry, we're alright. Something not alright, she can hear in Stephanie's voice. Where are they? What's happened? Do they need money, are they hurt, sick? Did Stephanie call two weeks ago, or yesterday? She resists calling Jan, *resist, protective coat, dye cast, to refrain from accepting, yielding to.* Jan will tell her Stephanie is fine, not believing it herself, but that Lily needs protecting from her own anxiety, or guilt. Detachment, is this what's needed? to be unattached ... the letter from Vital Statistics tells her what she knows. A search of the records for five years before and after Lily's own birth turned up no siblings, no twin, no infant born dead.

Unable to sleep, Lily in the car with your ashes still beside her, no clear idea of what she is doing, except heading for the park, where you bring Jan and Stephanie to see parrots in the conservatory dome sitting like a moon rising out of the top of the hill, where they see Vancouver spread out before them, mountains disappearing into blue pacific haze and running east along the valley of the Fraser estuary, a circle of city, ocean, forest and fields.

In first light she parks the car by the road up to the dome, an image of a tree taking her with your ashes to the young linden near the bottom of the hill covering itself in delicate, creamy yellow blossoms, their fragrance travelling with Lily up the slope toward the brow of hill and trees there spread against sky, where the crows gather, flying up out of the trees as Lily climbs toward them, some high into the air calling, some swooping down over her, one so close its claws catch at her hair. She jerks her head and turns to see if the crow will come at her again, but this does not seem to be an attack.

Under trees on the brow of the hill, among the undergrowth Lily will plant you, in the scent of linden blossoms and salt air, under crows and wind. But she does not want to open the container, has never looked at what is left of your body, the ashes and bits of bone, some of which may not even be yours. Her heart may fail her now. What do you want her to do? The lid is off. So much plastic, a bag of ashes, grey, crumbly, fine, bone meal. What she is doing now against the law here. Lily's eyes draw, drawn away, meet those of an elderly Chinese woman doing tai chi at the edge of a garden on the other side of the trees. The gentle supple movement of the woman's body moves through an almost imperceptible acknowledgement passing between them, an unbroken wave lifting from the old woman's fingers to Lily's, your fingertips touching Lily's skin as she begins to pour your body out across the ground, working it into the soil with her hands in surprising waves of anger and relief slipping from one into the other with ease and out through her fingertips curled into you. On her knees weeping, not weeping, into the dirt, dirt floor, child in the root cellar, child under the bed, hands over her ears screaming mummy's hurt mummy's hurt mummy's hurt to how many generations, *root*, requiring affix suffix prefix, an elemental original source, headwaters, mainspring heart, derivation, stem, rock bottom germination sprouting verbs embedded; inscribed to settle, dig, delve burrow feel for her ground, indigenous body, her bone blood radical rooted graven frozen desire.

Given a stone for a fish, the child doesn't ask why, or for anything else. Collects stones. Her fingers curl deeper into ash, long wave moving through Lily, fighting the ashes taking her, your body her body from her, filling her mouth, nose, her lungs and belly, filling her hollow spaces, the gap Lily no longer looks into, is. Elusive fish belly gleam, wing glint bending light moving toward lost desire, the ghost that keeps returning; evidence of its existence staring out at her from the gap, the outsider within, her.

Brushing her knees, aware of what dust is on her hands, jeans, Lily resists scooping your ashes back into the emptied container, stuffs the plastic bag back into it instead, searches around for the lid, the woman doing tai chi turned away from her now. Lily turns and walks uncertainly down the slope carrying more weight than when she came, some wounded wing fluttering against her ribs a threatened shattering, child stretching arms widespread, running on ahead down towards the linden tree.

I didn't know you people started work so early, a man calls out to her, a man with a very large boxer dog on a leash. Say hello, Chum, the man says to the dog, intent it seems on conversation, intercepting Lily halfway down the slope to the linden tree. He asks her about some ornamental tree variety he's come across. Lily has to tell him she doesn't work here.

He's quite friendly, the man says, petting the dog's head. He was abused, doesn't like men, only women. The dog sits gazing off somewhere with his back to Lily. Lily unable to stifle a sudden spate of yawning, overwhelming fatigue. Well, goodbye Chum, she says. Shall we go home to Mother? the man says. His arms are around the dog's shoulders, hugging him. Lily hears him behind her telling Chum, I love you too, yes I do.

THE PHONE WAKES LILY FROM HEAVY SLEEP, a collect call, will she accept charges? Yes, yes, Lily pulling herself up to some kind of consciousness, Steph's voice now, not Steph's voice, another remove from Lily, something missing, absent. Alerted, she sits up, swings her feet down onto the floor, moves around cradling the phone to her neck, searching for paper, something to write down an address, some coordinates, listening hard from her belly. We decided to come back to Mexico. When? A couple of weeks ago. Why? Silence on the line. You still there? phone line throwing Lily's voice back at her, fear in it, sharp.

I'm fine, Mom. Don't worry. What's the matter Stephanie, what happened? Lily's heart constricts around the cries of the woman wandering alone in the night, crying for what she sees. Focusses on this, forgetting and remembering in her dream the women in the market stalls sell flowers with stems thick as trunks, leaves creamy calla unfolding erect golden tongues. That a wail is voice, silence broken. Actually we were kicked out of Guatemala, not really out of the country, just one part of it. We weren't involved in anything . . . just trying to visit the mountain villages can get you into trouble. What kind of trouble? We weren't arrested . . . just detained. They didn't charge us with anything. Did they do anything to you, harm you . . . soundbacks on the line mingle their words, lose some, voices, hers needing to know, not wanting to and

179

Stephanie's unable to tell her, protecting Lily from what she doesn't want to hear, what Stephanie doesn't want her to know. No, Stephanie says, something cool, detached, absent in it and Lily veers, sitting on Stephanie's bed, little Steph, afraid of the dark, moon shadows gathering in her room, along the walls and curtains, across the floor, tight little body curled beside her while Lily turns shadows into stories, giving them each names . . . the long, really long, lost slipper coming home, moon fairies hanging out the wash, sleeping butterflies, trees waving at her through the window, others Lily's forgotten now along this trajectory. Why would they detain you? Where were you? First they wanted us to leave the area, the Altiplano, so there'd be no witnesses. They raided one of the nearby villages while we were there. We didn't know where we were staying was near the village of an Indian woman who organised peasant resistance. Her father was murdered years ago for doing the same thing. They were after her. Then the soldiers wanted money. We didn't have any. They took us back down into one of the market towns. There was a man there from Canada, who comes down with school supplies who gave us a ride once before from the Mexican border and was on his way back. He paid them money and took us back to Mexico in his van. We could have stayed, but we decided to go back to the people we knew in Mexico, for a while.

Come home, Stephanie. Lily tries not to plead, or succumb to images of brutality. This is home . . . we want to stay, she hears her daughter say, a voice she can't or won't recognize, in six months there's a bus coming down from Canada going to Guatemala City with a load of tools and machinery. We can go back in with them. Why would you want to go back in? And do what? We'll see what comes up. It will be okay. We'll be safe. How safe can any of you be in that country?

The question never answered for Lily. Light on the balcony this morning washes over her writing out an application for art school. If she does get in, it won't be until next January. In the meantime there are courses in astronomy, oceanography, anthropology, with reduced tuition for those over fifty. Third Age, they call it. Very Aristotelian. Beginning. Middle. End. Marooned; the light this morning takes her eye, this other eye, to a crow's outspread wing, dropping a feather weighing heart's rage breathing out from myriad resistant threads, fireflowers floating in her eye, fish-eye lens seeing both ways, her balcony ferns and grasses, the tall thick geranium plants struggling to put out a few bits of colour in the shadow of highrises circling like so many concrete bunkers, a tangled green watery overgrowth living without flowering.

FORGET THE COLLEGE AND COME HERE and paint, Stephanie
writes, You'll love the light and won't want to leave. You could
meet Em. The people here are good to us, friendly, like family. You
and Jan could both come and we'll take you over to the Yucatán to
visit the ruins and along the coast to the butterfly forests where the
monarch butterflies come to spend the winter. Spirits of the
ancestors returning, they call them down here. We'll take you
hiking up the mountain to the smaller circle, no tourists there, no
logging. Think of it, Mom, all those butterflies hanging out in the
trees, opening their wings when the sun comes out. They can't fly
when it's cold, and they can freeze on open ground because it loses
heat so fast, so they climb trees as high as they can go while they
can still crawl, to catch the last of the sun before it's gone. If they
sense us breathing nearby they fall out of the trees like rain, like a
huge orange thing to scare us away; their version of safety in
numbers. We've held cold ones in our hands and revived them with
our breath.

I'D LIKE TO MEET EM . . . If you want Jan to come you should ask her yourself. I don't want her thinking it's my idea, Lily writes back. Do you remember the butterfly book, Stephie . . . ? I was thinking of taking some courses this fall . . . Come down here and meet these people, Stephanie's words, just beyond Lily's ear, the curve of it, inward. They're different, meaning same, someone's birth, anyone, everyone's responsibility. Everyone grandchild, sister, brother, mother, father, granny, grandpa, ancestor. Lily closes her eyes, there with Stephanie and Em in the garden, working for their food, cooking tortillas with salt, their beans. In the company of women they learn to survive, make their own cooking pots, sew, dye cloth and weave it on a backstrap loom. Two sticks, Stephanie describes, at opposite ends of the vertical threads of yarn, one stick attached by rope to a tree, the other to a strap around her lower back. Her body, the cloth in mutual tension. We want to make a home down here. Build it ourselves. The words rock Lily in you waiting for the second coming. Can a woman enter into her mother's womb a second time and be born again? Is the coming here, come already? Lily everyone's child. You'll think about it? Stephie asks.

I'll think about it . . . will you think about not going back into Guatemala?

STEPHANIE'S LETTER SAYS Em has gone back to the States.
Stephanie left down there, living with another family, many
families, in a Mayan refugee camp. Guatemalan refugees inside
Mexico waiting to go home again. Steph has joined a program to
go with them as a witness when they are repatriated, given land to
begin again. Stephanie the presence, eyes, a voice, against the
possibility of another violation. Whose? the thought sinks Lily's
heart. Lily angry, writes to Steph, you don't need to prove you're
not afraid. Come home, come home and go again later.

Most of them here are single mothers left with young families
and old people just trying to survive, whether they're afraid or not.
If I go back to Canada now, I'll never come back here. Stephie's
letter starkly brief.

Lily lies back on the bed, Stephanie's temporary address on a piece
of paper ripped from her journal lying on her chest. Late afternoon
sun reflects off windows of the apartment building across the street
into the bedroom, into her eyes. She closes them. Feels the
transcendent glow of dreams or hallucinations on her eyelids, moving
over the curve of lens, seeking focal point, virtual and real images.
Stephanie won't let her send money. Perhaps she will mention it to
Jan, about Mexico. Stephanie might not get around to it.

The butterflies arrive in early November, during the *Days of the
Dead, Las Días de los Muertos*, think about coming down then;

turning over Stephie's words, Lily turning on the curve of them curving, bending her ear taking her toward the play of another rhythm *da dada da da da dada da* ... a child's little room, behind an upstairs window covered in fronds, feathers of frost, layers and layers she melts an eyehole through to the world outside, within, with her breath and small hand, *da dada da da da dada da* ... *four little foxes went to the fair they saw some monkeys and elephants there they rode and rode on the merry go round four happier foxes couldn't be found* ... a lost memory found, you reading to her, is this her last sighting of you who pulled a crow's feathers to make it stay the winter, something black on white for you to get your bearings? the grip of an awkward child growing lighter, perhaps more tender?

PETRA, WITH A DOCTORATE IN FORENSIC anthropology, has become experienced in identifying victims in mass graves, is called on by human rights lawyers from many countries; these days away more than at home. Adjusts her life accordingly, lives alone, except for Noir, and he presumably has taken to the solitary state. She has tried giving him to Nicole, who would have him, but he yowls to get out until he is back home by himself, where he takes his distress out on her favourite chair. And truth be told, she likes to find him there when she returns.

When she is home, Petra teaches. In the field she trains teams of usually young students in the art of reading bones. The bones tell, Petra tells them.

Since Buenos Aires there have been many trips for Petra to diverse landscapes with elemental sameness—the ring of silent witnesses, the ones left behind, impossible to keep them away, but at least back far enough so vital evidence will not be destroyed as opened earth reveals bones caught in webs of rotted clothing. It is when she takes the bones into her hands those left behind begin to feel again, cry out, hands on their foreheads, across mouths, pressed against their cheeks as their lost ones appear to them bringing others who have suffered to these who see and feel the pain and rock with their hands against their faces. Children move closer to their mothers, or further away, feeling the blame in which the harmed are entrapped waiting for those who harmed them to bring acknowledgement of what they've done, which almost never comes. Those who harm appear as well, having lost a part of themselves to those they hurt. Petra never speaks of what she sees, feels around these open graves.

SHE DRAWS A LACY curtain to one side and gazes onto violet stones. Early morning a damp sheen from street cleaners washing away yesterday's detritus. Buses idling outside the Luxembourg Gardens where pear trees will soon blossom like snow. Still no taxi. Faucets, stove, lights, windows rechecked. Plenty of food and fresh litter for Noir. Nicole down the hall, as usual, will keep an eye on things, deal with her mail and Noir, now restlessly roaming the apartment, with intermittent leaps to a table by the window to butt her with his head. He knows the signs. Still for a moment, he stares with her down at the street while she absently strokes his glossy fur, which comforts neither of them. He jumps back down to the floor, prowls two green suitcases by the door, returns to rub against, not her, the furniture around her.

IN THE TAXI, PETRA'S HEART IS EXPERIENCING that peculiar heaviness that comes with each trip to another grave. Back to Guatemala, this time the peace process already signed, Mayan refugees guaranteed a safe return from Mexico where many of their children have already been born in the camps along the border; wanting to go home to their highlands where their ancestors are, their spirits whispering through the trees and into the marrow of their children's bones.

And now, another massacre at one of these relocated villages. Judicial investigations into this one plagued with death threats against human rights lawyers who initiated it and the witnesses, two children who are survivors, who were hidden in corn fields further up the mountain, where those doing the massacre were afraid to go. Also threatened are those who find the children and take them into protective care. Security forces insist the village was not massacred but the Indians abandoned it and the two children got left behind. When they are asked why the Maya would do that they shrug. Indians don't want to be Guatemalans, maybe they like it better in Mexico, maybe they fought among themselves, bandits are a serious problem in the area, that is why we patrol it. They smile as they say this, friendly smiles. They are mestizo, some appear more Indian than Spanish.

Now a grave has been located. A body dump off one of the web of trails accessible by foot. This high in the mountains the cold is damp. There is a river somewhere, speaking through the trees, where they catch *jutes*, little river snails.

PETRA FEELS SHE'S NEVER LEFT. Home this or any other opened grave she stands beside, this cave between thickness of trees, scent of pine on a rush of water moving down the mountain. Beyond and above, wings of hovering army helicopters thud a heavy regular beat, taking her senses, sending her heart into momentary and repeated arrythmic patterns of resistance. Who is it meant to intimidate? The international forensics team? the ring of silent watchers, the ones left behind? All of them climbing since early morning into heat of the day, to this open mouth.

Not here are the two children who survive, whose mothers managed to send them running to the far end of the corn fields where they crouched against the earth, covering their ears. They remain under protection elsewhere because of death threats they and the Canadian woman and a priest who find them have received. The woman from Canada who found them is here. She is very young, probably no more than nineteen or twenty. Tall, slender, dark. Watching her work, Petra notes her interest in the bones, learning, assisting in the preliminary exhumation, Petra reminded of herself, of someone.

The young woman had been living with these people of whom only two children are left, since they returned from refugee camps in Mexico, living there as a witness, an outside presence to protect them from further abuse it was hoped, now that a peace process is in place, signed by both government and guerillas. Once every ten days or so, she and others doing the same thing in several of the relocated villages in this Altiplano area meet together. It is a long hike down the trails she does not take alone, always in the company of an uncle or father who are elders from the village, or with the priest who travels through each week from village to village. The priest, a Jesuit, Fr. Rudolfo, she travels with this time, leaving the village very early in the morning as she always does, returning with him the next day. Which is when they find the emptied houses, corrugated metal roofs supplied by the government intact, broken corn, gardens as though crushed by great weight. Grannies and uncles and aunties who built her a house and took turns feeding her in their own homes each day, sharing ways with her, they and their children born in refugee camps, gone. She who calls and calls, feeling nearness, presence, a sighing and weeping through the corn fields and pine forests above, who finds two muted children, brother and sister, curled among corn stalks at the edge further up, a reserve plot.

SOME OF THE EXHUMATION team are from Argentina, also human rights activists Petra has worked with before. The young woman who found the children has asked to be part of the exhumation. Petra already aware of her interest and ability, is considering suggesting she come to Paris to study, but not sure how to approach it, with the young woman's mother here wanting her to go back with her to Canada.

The faces different. Bones of the mother's face flat, wider, looks a little Indian, although apparently not. Here because of the death threats against her daughter. A cautious woman. Petra can feel her fear. Here in spite of it, here with her daughter now at this mouth of bones, in this circle of witnesses encircled in turn by anonymous silencers. Petra drawn to the older woman as to her daughter, the daughter with that same skinless look staring out at Petra from Elena's photo. The mother not as tall as Elena, but dark like her and slender. Interesting face, open as much as it is closed, the eyes direct, look into Petra's. Quiet, retiring, the daughter not. An intriguing quality about the older woman which Petra has no name for, except, perhaps, presence, a double life, hidden, perhaps to the woman herself as well, a life living on anonymously in her, line below the skin, sinewed silence. A lot goes on in silence. Perhaps the mother would come to Paris with her daughter.

But Stephanie has no intention of going to Paris. She simply wants to hold these bones in her hands.

Ready now, Petra, as always, reminds them to keep back from the edge, the perimeter of the ring, so no vital evidence will be disturbed. Stephanie moves onto the boards across one end of the dig, Petra moves in beside her. Yes, brush here, a little more ... you can take it up now. Stephanie hesitates, then lifts a bone, holds it, and hands it to Petra. As she does, voices around the circle begin to cry out, Petra feels some of the weight leave her. Stephanie begins to see images, the others too, crying out with recognition, with seeing what they need to see but too much, more than they want.

Lily sees the butterflies fly up out of graves into the trees, out of her belly into sky, spiralling sun, strands of the river coming together in the long migration of the fourth-generation monarch butterflies born far to the north under a milkweed leaf; feeding on the milkweed's leaves filled with poisonous cardiac glycosides, they will be deadly to predators; too late in summer to mate before winter they move south. Petra sees them too. Light in their eyes a thousand suns and their wings the scales of fish, swimming, gliding, pulsing the currents, waves where none of them have been, searching the light, for nectar, water, warmth before the long journey back north to lay their egg under milkweed. Fragile wings a line of light, stories not yet told, river.

photo by Andy Mons

Fran Muir grew up in Manitoba and lived in Toronto and
Northern B.C. before settling in Vancouver. She received her MFA
in Creative Writing from the University of British Columbia. Her
work has been published in numerous Canadian journals and a
collection of short fiction, *Coming to Bone*, was published by Exile
Editions in 1997.

Muir returned to the birthplaces of her maternal grandmother
and grandfather in Scotland as well as her own birthplace in
Manitoba to uncover the voiceless voices in her family's past. *A
Line Below the Skin*, her first novel, reflects the "restored narrative"
of Muir's own family history and her exploration of silence,
memory and storytelling.